PENGUIN BOOKS

# IRONWEED

William Kennedy is a lifetime resident of Albany, New York. His Albany cycle of novels, which includes *Legs, Billy Phelan's Greatest Game*, *Ironweed* (which won the Pulitzer Prize and the National Book Critics Circle Award), *Quinn's Book*, *Very Old Bones*, and *The Flaming Corsage*. All are published by Penguin Books, as are Mr. Kennedy's first novel, *The Ink Truck*, his impressionistic history of his city, *O Albany!*, and a collection of nonfiction, *Riding the Yellow Trolley Car*. Mr. Kennedy's novels have been translated into two dozen languages.

# IRONWEED

□ □ □

*William Kennedy*

PENGUIN BOOKS

PENGUIN BOOKS
Published by the Penguin Group
Penguin Books USA Inc.,
375 Hudson Street, New York, New York 10014, U.S.A.
Penguin Books Ltd, 27 Wrights Lane, London W8 5TZ, England
Penguin Books Australia Ltd, Ringwood, Victoria, Australia
Penguin Books Canada Ltd, 10 Alcorn Avenue,
Toronto, Ontario, Canada M4V 3B2
Penguin Books (N.Z.) Ltd, 182–190 Wairau Road,
Auckland 10, New Zealand

Penguin Books Ltd, Registered Offices:
Harmondsworth, Middlesex, England

First published in the United States of America by
Viking Penguin Inc. 1983
Published in Penguin Books 1984

29 31 33 35 34 32 30



LIBRARY OF CONGRESS CATALOGING IN PUBLICATION DATA
Kennedy, William, 1928–
Ironweed.
I. Title.
PS 3561.E428I7 1984 813′.54 83-13470
ISBN 0 14 00.7020 6

Printed in the United States of America
Set in Times Roman and Helvetica Light

Portions of this book were originally published in *Epoch*.

Grateful acknowledgment is made to Warner Bros. Music for permission to reprint an excerpt from "Bye, Bye Blackbird," lyrics by Mort Dixon and music by Ray Henderson. Copyright 1926 by Warner Bros. Inc.; copyright © renewed. All rights reserved. Used by permission.

*This book is for four good men:*

Bill Segarra, Tom Smith,
Harry Staley, and Frank Trippett.

Tall Ironweed is a member of the Sunflower Family (Asteraceae). It has a tall erect stem and bears deep purple-blue flower heads in loose terminal clusters. Its leaves are long and thin and pointed, their lower surfaces downy. Its fruit is seed-like, with a double set of purplish bristles. It flowers from August to October in damp, rich soil from New York south to Georgia, west to Louisiana, north to Missouri, Illinois and Michigan. The name refers to the toughness of the stem.

– Adapted from The Audubon Society's
*Field Guide to North American Wildflowers*

To course o'er better waters now hoists sail the little bark of my wit, leaving behind her a sea so cruel.

—Dante, *Purgatorio*

# IRONWEED

# I. □

Riding up the winding road of Saint Agnes Cemetery in the back of the rattling old truck, Francis Phelan became aware that the dead, even more than the living, settled down in neighborhoods. The truck was suddenly surrounded by fields of monuments and cenotaphs of kindred design and striking size, all guarding the privileged dead. But the truck moved on and the limits of mere privilege became visible, for here now came the acres of truly prestigious death: illustrious men and women, captains of life without their diamonds, furs, carriages, and limousines, but buried in pomp and glory, vaulted in great tombs built like heavenly safe deposit boxes, or parts of the Acropolis. And ah yes, here too, inevitably, came the flowing masses, row upon row of them under simple headstones and simpler crosses. Here was the neighborhood of the Phelans.

Francis's mother twitched nervously in her grave as the truck carried him nearer to her; and Francis's father lit his pipe, smiled at his wife's discomfort, and looked out from his own bit of sod to catch a glimpse of how much his son had changed since the train accident.

Francis's father smoked roots of grass that died in the periodic droughts afflicting the cemetery. He stored the root essence in his pockets until it was brittle to the touch, then pulverized it between his fingers and packed his pipe. Francis's mother wove crosses from the dead dandelions and other deep-rooted weeds; careful to preserve their fullest length, she wove them while they were still in the green stage of death, then ate them with an insatiable revulsion.

"Look at that tomb," Francis said to his companion. "Ain't that somethin'? That's Arthur T. Grogan. I saw him around Albany when I was a kid. He owned all the electricity in town."

"He ain't got much of it now," Rudy said.

"Don't bet on it," Francis said. "Them kind of guys hang on to a good thing."

The advancing dust of Arthur T. Grogan, restless in its simulated Parthenon, grew luminous from Francis's memory of a vital day long gone. The truck rolled on up the hill.

FARRELL, said one roadside gravestone. KENNEDY, said another. DAUGHERTY, McILHENNY, BRUNELLE, McDONALD, MALONE, DWYER, and WALSH, said others. PHELAN, said two small ones.

Francis saw the pair of Phelan stones and turned his eyes elsewhere, fearful that his infant son, Gerald, might be under one of them. He had not confronted Gerald directly since the day he let the child slip out of its diaper. He would not confront him now. He avoided the Phelan headstones on the presumptive grounds that they belonged to another family entirely. And he was correct. These graves held two brawny young Phelan brothers, canalers both, and both skewered by the same whiskey bottle in 1884, dumped into the Erie Canal in front of The Black Rag Saloon in Watervliet, and then pushed under and drowned with a long stick. The brothers looked at Francis's clothes, his ragged brown twill suit jacket, black baggy pants, and filthy fireman's blue shirt, and felt a kinship with him that owed nothing to blood ties. His shoes were as worn as the brogans they both had been wearing on the last day of their lives. The brothers read also in Francis's face the familiar scars of alcoholic desolation, which both had developed in their graves. For both had been deeply drunk and vulnerable when the cutthroat Muggins killed them in tandem and took all their money: forty-eight cents. We died for pennies, the brothers said in their silent, dead-drunken way to Francis, who bounced past them in the back of the truck, staring at the emboldening white clouds that clotted the sky so richly at midmorning. From the heat of the sun Francis felt a flow of juices in his body, which he interpreted as a gift of strength from the sky.

"A little chilly," he said, "but it's gonna be a nice day."

"If it don't puke," said Rudy.

"You goddamn cuckoo bird, you don't talk about the weather that way. You got a nice day, take it. Why you wanna talk about the sky pukin' on us?"

"My mother was a full-blooded Cherokee," Rudy said.

"You're a liar. Your old lady was a Mex, that's why you got them high cheekbones. Indian I don't buy."

"She come off the reservation in Skokie, Illinois, went down to Chicago, and got a job sellin' peanuts at Wrigley Field."

"They ain't got any Indians in Illinois. I never seen one damn Indian all the time I was out there."

"They keep to themselves," Rudy said.

The truck passed the last inhabited section of the cemetery and moved toward a hill where raw earth was being loosened by five men with pickaxes and shovels. The driver parked and unhitched the tailgate, and Francis and Rudy leaped down. The two then joined the other five in loading the truck with the fresh dirt. Rudy mumbled aloud as he shoveled: "I'm workin' it out."

"What the hell you workin' out now?" Francis asked.

"The worms," Rudy said. "How many worms you get in a truckload of dirt."

"You countin' 'em?"

"Hundred and eight so far," said Rudy.

"Dizzy bedbug," said Francis.

When the truck was fully loaded Francis and Rudy climbed atop the dirt and the driver rode them to a slope where a score of graves of the freshly dead sent up the smell of sweet putrescence, the incense of unearned mortality and interrupted dreams. The driver, who seemed inured to such odors, parked as close to the new graves as possible and Rudy and Francis then carried shovelfuls of dirt to the dead while the driver dozed in the truck. Some of the dead had been buried two or three months, and yet their coffins were still burrowing deeper into the rain-softened earth. The gravid weight of the days they had lived was now seeking its equivalent level in firstborn death, creating a rectangular hollow on the surface of each grave. Some of the coffins seemed to be on their way to middle earth. None of the graves were yet marked with headstones, but a few were decorated with an American flag on a small stick, or bunches of faded cloth flowers in clay pots. Rudy and Francis filled in one hollow, then another. Dead gladiolas, still vaguely yellow in their brown stage of death, drooped in a basket at the head of the grave of Louis (Daddy Big) Dugan, the Albany pool hustler who had died only a week or so ago from inhaling his own vomit. Daddy Big, trying futilely to memorize anew the fading memories of how he used to apply topspin and reverse English to the cue ball, recognized Franny Phelan, even though he had not seen him in twenty years.

"I wonder who's under this one," Francis said.

"Probably some Catholic," Rudy said.

"Of course it's some Catholic, you birdbrain, it's a Catholic cemetery."

"They let Protestants in sometimes," Rudy said.

"They do like hell."

"Sometimes they let Jews in too. And Indians."

Daddy Big remembered the shape of Franny's mouth from the first day he saw him playing ball for Albany at Chadwick Park. Daddy Big sat down front in the bleachers behind the third-base line and watched Franny on the hot corner, watched him climb into the bleachers after a foul pop fly that would have hit Daddy Big right in the chest if Franny hadn't stood on his own ear to make the catch. Daddy Big saw Franny smile after making it, and even though his teeth were almost gone now, Franny smiled that same familiar way as he scattered fresh dirt on Daddy Big's grave.

Your son Billy saved my life, Daddy Big told Francis. Turned me upside down and kept me from chokin' to death on the street when I got sick. I died anyway, later. But it was nice of him, and I wish I could take back some of the lousy things I said to him. And let me personally give you a piece of advice. Never inhale your own vomit.

Francis did not need Daddy Big's advice. He did not get sick from alcohol the way Daddy Big had. Francis knew how to drink. He drank all the time and he did not vomit. He drank anything that contained alcohol, anything, and he could always walk, and he could talk as well as any man alive about what was on his mind. Alcohol did put Francis to sleep, finally, but on his own terms. When he'd had enough and everybody else was passed out, he'd just put his head down and curl up like an old dog, then put his hands between his legs to protect what was left of the jewels, and he'd cork off. After a little sleep he'd wake up and go out for more drink. That's how he did it when he was drinking. Now he wasn't drinking. He hadn't had a drink for two days and he felt a little bit of all right. Strong, even. He'd stopped drinking because he'd run out of money, and that coincided with Helen not feeling all that terrific and Francis wanting to take care of her. Also he had wanted to be sober when he went to court for registering twenty-one times to vote. He went to court but not to trial. His attorney, Marcus Gorman, a wizard, found a mistake in the date on the papers that detailed the charges against Francis, and the case was thrown out. Marcus charged people five hundred dollars usually, but he only charged Francis fifty because Martin Daugherty, the newspaper columnist, one of Francis's old neighbors, asked him to go easy. Francis didn't even have the fifty when it came time to pay. He'd drunk it all up. Yet Marcus demanded it.

"But I ain't got it," Francis said.

"Then go to work and get it," said Marcus. "I get paid for what I do."

"Nobody'll put me to work," Francis said. "I'm a bum."

"I'll get you some day work up at the cemetery," Marcus said.

And he did. Marcus played bridge with the bishop and knew all the Catholic hotshots. Some hotshot ran Saint Agnes Cemetery in Menands. Francis slept in the weeds on Dongan Avenue below the bridge and woke up about seven o'clock this morning, then went up to the mission on Madison Avenue to get coffee. Helen wasn't there. She was truly gone. He didn't know where she was and nobody had seen her. They said she'd been hanging around the mission last night, but then went away. Francis had fought with her earlier over money and she just walked off someplace, who the hell knows where?

Francis had coffee and bread with the bums who'd dried out, and other bums passin' through, and the preacher there watchin' everybody and playin' grabass with their souls. Never mind my soul, was Francis's line. Just pass the coffee. Then he stood out front killin' time and pickin' his teeth with a matchbook cover. And here came Rudy.

Rudy was sober too for a change and his gray hair was combed and trimmed. His mustache was clipped and he wore white suede shoes, even though it was October, what the hell, he's just a bum, and a white shirt, and a crease in his pants. Francis, no lace in one of his shoes, hair matted and uncut, smelling his own body stink and ashamed of it for the first time in memory, felt deprived.

"You lookin' good there, bum," Francis said.

"I been in the hospital."

"What for?"

"Cancer."

"No shit. Cancer?"

"He says to me you're gonna die in six months. I says I'm gonna wine myself to death. He says it don't make any difference if you wined or dined, you're goin'. Goin' out of this world with a cancer. The stomach, it's like pits, you know what I mean? I said I'd like to make it to fifty. The doc says you'll never make it. I said all right, what's the difference?"

"Too bad, grandma. You got a jug?"

"I got a dollar."

"Jesus, we're in business," Francis said.

But then he remembered his debt to Marcus Gorman.

"Listen, bum," he said, "you wanna go to work with me and make a few bucks? We can get a couple of jugs and a flop tonight. Gonna be cold. Look at that sky."

"Work where?"

"The cemetery. Shovelin' dirt."

"The cemetery. Why not? I oughta get used to it. What're they payin'?"

"Who the hell knows?"

"I mean they payin' money, or they give you a free grave when you croak?"

"If it ain't money, forget it," Francis said. "I ain't shovelin' out my own grave."

They walked from downtown Albany to the cemetery in Menands, six miles or more. Francis felt healthy and he liked it. It's too bad he didn't feel healthy when he drank. He felt good then but not healthy, especially not in the morning, or when he woke up in the middle of the night, say. Sometimes he felt dead. His head, his throat, his stomach: he needed to get them all straight with a drink, or maybe it'd take two, because if he didn't, his brain would overheat trying to fix things and his eyes would blow out. Jeez it's tough when you need that drink and your throat's like an open sore and it's four in the morning and the wine's gone and no place open and you got no money or nobody to bum from, even if there was a place open. That's tough, pal. Tough.

Rudy and Francis walked up Broadway and when they got to Colonie Street Francis felt a pull to turn up and take a look at the house where he was born, where his goddamned brothers and sisters still lived. He'd done that in 1935 when it looked possible, when his mother finally died. And what did it get him? A kick in the ass is what it got him. Let the joint fall down and bury them all before I look at it again, was his thought. Let it rot. Let the bugs eat it.

In the cemetery, Kathryn Phelan, sensing the militance in her son's mood, grew restless at the idea that death was about to change for her. With a furtive burst of energy she wove another cross from the shallow-rooted weeds above her and quickly swallowed it, but was disappointed by the taste. Weeds appealed to Kathryn Phelan in direct ratio to the length of their roots. The longer the weed, the more revulsive the cross.

Francis and Rudy kept walking north on Broadway, Francis's right shoe flapping, its counter rubbing wickedly against his heel. He favored the foot until he found a length of twine on the sidewalk in front of Frankie Leikheim's plumbing shop. Frankie Leikheim. A little kid when Francis was a big kid and now he's got his own plumbing shop and what have you got, Francis? You got a piece of twine for a shoelace. You don't need shoelaces for walking short distances, but on the bum without them you could ruin your feet for weeks. You figured you had all the calluses anybody'd ever need for the road, but then you come across a different pair of shoes and they start you out with a brand-new set of blisters. Then they make the blisters bleed and you have to stop walking almost till they scab over so's you can get to work on another callus.

The twine didn't fit into the eyelets of the shoe. Francis untwined it from itself and threaded half its thickness through enough of the eyelets to make it lace. He pulled up his sock, barely a sock anymore, holes in the heel, the toe, the sole, gotta get new ones. He cushioned his raw spot as best he could with the sock, then tightened the new lace, gently, so the shoe wouldn't flop. And he walked on toward the cemetery.

"There's seven deadly sins," Rudy said.

"Deadly? What do you mean deadly?" Francis said.

"I mean daily," Rudy said. "Every day."

"There's only one sin as far as I'm concerned," Francis said.

"There's prejudice."

"Oh yeah. Prejudice. Yes."

"There's envy."

"Envy. Yeah, yup. That's one."

"There's lust."

"Lust, right. Always liked that one."

"Cowardice."

"Who's a coward?"

"Cowardice."

"I don't know what you mean. That word I don't know."

"Cowardice," Rudy said.

"I don't like the coward word. What're you sayin' about coward?"

"A coward. He'll cower up. You know what a coward is? He'll run."

"No, that word I don't know. Francis is no coward. He'll fight anybody. Listen, you know what I like?"

"What do you like?"

"Honesty," Francis said.

"That's another one," Rudy said.

At Shaker Road they walked up to North Pearl Street and headed north on Pearl. Where they live now. They'd painted Sacred Heart Church since he last saw it, and across the street School 20 had new tennis courts. Whole lot of houses here he never saw, new since '16. This is the block they live in. What Billy said. When Francis last walked this street it wasn't much more than a cow pasture. Old man Rooney's cows would break the fence and roam loose, dirtyin' the streets and sidewalks. You got to put a stop to this, Judge Ronan told Rooney. What is it you want me to do, Rooney asked the judge, put diapers on 'em?

They walked on to the end of North Pearl Street, where it entered Menands, and turned down to where it linked with Broadway. They walked past the place where the old Bull's Head Tavern used to be. Francis was a kid when he saw Gus Ruhlan come out of the corner in bare knuckles. The bum he was fighting stuck out a hand to shake, Gus give him a shot and that was all she wrote. Katie bar the door. Too wet to plow. Honesty. They walked past Hawkins Stadium, hell of a big place now, about where Chadwick Park was when Francis played ball. He remembered when it was a pasture. Hit a ball right and it'd roll forever, right into the weeds. Bow-Wow Buckley'd be after it and he'd find it right away, a wizard. Bow-Wow kept half a dozen spare balls in the weeds for emergencies like that. Then he'd throw the runner out at third on a sure home run and he'd brag about his fielding. Honesty. Bow-Wow is dead. Worked on an ice wagon and punched his own horse and it stomped him, was that it? Nah. That's nuts. Who'd punch a horse?

"Hey," Rudy said, "wasn't you with a woman the other night I saw you?"

"What woman?"

"I don't know. Helen. Yeah, you called her Helen."

"Helen. You can't keep track of where she is."

"What'd she do, run off with a banker?"

"She didn't run off."

"Then where is she?"

"Who knows? She comes, she goes. I don't keep tabs."

"You got a million of 'em."

"More where she came from."

"They're all crazy to meet you."

"My socks is what gets 'em."

Francis lifted his trousers to reveal his socks, one green, one blue.

"A reg'lar man about town," Rudy said.

Francis dropped his pantlegs and walked on, and Rudy said, "Hey, what the hell was all that about the man from Mars last night? Everybody was talkin' about it at the hospital. You hear about that stuff on the radio?"

"Oh yeah. They landed."

"Who?"

"The Martians."

"Where'd they land?"

"Someplace in Jersey."

"What happened?"

"They didn't like it no more'n I did."

"No joke," Rudy said. "I heard people saw them Martians comin' and ran outa town, jumped outa windows, everything like that."

"Good," Francis said. "What they oughta do. Anybody sees a Martian oughta jump out two windows."

"You don't take things serious," Rudy said. "You have a whatayacallit, a frivolous way about you."

"A frivolous way? A frivolous way?"

"That's what I said. A frivolous way."

"What the hell's that mean? You been readin' again, you crazy kraut? I told you cuckoos like you shouldn't go around readin', callin' people frivolous."

"That ain't no insult. Frivolous is a good word. A nice word."

"Never mind words, there's the cemetery." And Francis pointed to the entrance-road gates. "I just thought of somethin'."

"What?"

"That cemetery's full of gravestones."

"Right."

"I never knew a bum yet had a gravestone."

They walked up the long entrance road from Broadway to the cemetery proper. Francis sweet-talked the woman at the gatehouse and mentioned Marcus Gorman and introduced Rudy as a good worker like himself, ready to work. She said the truck'd be along and to just wait easy. Then he and Rudy rode up in the back of the truck and got busy with the dirt.

They rested when they'd filled in all the hollows of the graves, and by then the truck driver was nowhere to be found. So they sat there and looked down the hill toward Broadway and over toward the hills of Rensselaer and Troy on the other side of the Hudson, the coke plant spewing palpable smoke from its great chimney at the far end of the Menands bridge. Francis decided this would be a fine place to be buried. The hill had a nice flow to it that carried you down the grass and out onto the river, and then across the water and up through the trees on the far shore to the top of the hills, all in one swoop. Being dead here would situate a man in place and time. It would give a man neighbors, even some of them really old folks, like those antique dead ones at the foot of the lawn: Tobias Banion, Elisha Skinner, Elsie Whipple, all crumbling under their limestone headstones from which the snows, sands, and acids of reduction were slowly removing their names. But what did the perpetuation of names matter? Ah well, there were those for whom death, like life, would always be a burden of eminence. The progeny of those growing nameless at the foot of the hill were ensured a more durable memory. Their new, and heavier, marble stones higher up on the slope had been cut doubly deep so their names would remain visible for an eternity, at least.

And then there was Arthur T. Grogan.

The Grogan Parthenon reminded Francis of something, but he could not say what. He stared at it and wondered, apart from its size, what it signified. He knew nothing of the Acropolis, and little more about Grogan except that he was a rich and powerful Albany Irishman whose name everybody used to know. Francis could not suppose that such massive marbling of old bones was a sweet conflation of ancient culture, modern coin, and self-apotheosizing. To him, the Grogan sepulcher was large enough to hold the bodies of dozens. And as this thought grazed his memory he envisioned the grave of Strawberry Bill Benson in Brooklyn. And that was it. Yes. Strawberry Bill had played left field for Toronto in ought eight when Francis played third, and when Francis hit the road in '16 after Gerald died, they bumped into each other at a crossroads near Newburgh and caught a freight south together.

Bill coughed and died a week after they reached the city, cursing his too-short life and swearing Francis to the task of following his body to the cemetery. "I don't want to go out there all by myself," Strawberry Bill said. He had no money, and so his coffin was a box of slapsided boards and a few dozen tenpenny nails, which Francis rode with to the burial plot. When the city driver and his helper left Bill's pile of wood sitting on top of some large planks and drove off, Francis stood by the box, letting Bill get used to the neighborhood. "Not a bad place, old buddy. Couple of trees over there." The sun then bloomed behind Francis, sending sunshine into an opening between two of the planks and lighting up a cavity below. The vision stunned Francis: a great empty chasm with a dozen other coffins of crude design, similar to Bill's, piled atop one another, some on their sides, one on its end. Enough earth had been dug away to accommodate thirty or forty more such crates of the dead. In a few weeks they'd all be stacked like cordwood, packaged cookies for the great maw. "You ain't got no worries now, Bill," Francis told his pal. "Plenty of company down there. You'll be lucky you get any sleep at all with them goin's on."

Francis did not want to be buried like Strawberry Bill, in a tenement grave. But he didn't want to rattle around in a marble temple the size of the public bath either.

"I wouldn't mind bein' buried right here," Francis told Rudy.

"You from around here?"

"Used to be. Born here."

"Your family here?"

"Some."

"Who's that?"

"You keep askin' questions about me, I'm gonna give you a handful of answers."

Francis recognized the hill where his family was buried, for it was just over from the sword-bearing guardian angel who stood on tiptoe atop three marble steps, guarding the grave of Toby, the dwarf who died heroically in the Delavan Hotel fire of '94. Old Ed Daugherty, the writer, bought that monument for Toby when it came out in the paper that Toby's grave had no marker. Toby's angel pointed down the hill toward Michael Phelan's grave and Francis found it with his gaze. His mother would be alongside the old man, probably with her back to him. Fishwife.

The sun that bloomed for Strawberry Bill had bloomed also on the day Michael Phelan was buried. Francis wept out of control that day, for he had been there when the train knocked Michael fifty feet in a fatal arc; and the memory tortured him. Francis was bringing him his hot lunch in the lunch pail, and when Michael saw Francis coming, he moved toward him. He safely passed the switch engine that was moving slowly on the far track, and then he turned his back, looked the way he'd just come, and walked backward, right into the path of the northbound train whose approach noise was being blocked out by the switch engine's clatter. He flew and then fell in a broken pile, and Francis ran to him, the first at his side. Francis looked for a way to straighten the angular body but feared any move, and so he pulled off his own sweater and pillowed his father's head with it. So many people go crooked when they die.

A few of the track gang followed Michael home in the back of Johnny Cody's wagon. He lingered two weeks and then won great obituaries as the most popular track foreman, boss gandy dancer, on the New York Central line. The railroad gave all track workers on the Albany division the morning off to go to the funeral, and hundreds came to say so long to old Mike when he rode up here to live. Queen Mama ruled the house alone then, until she joined him in the grave. What I should do, Francis thought, is shovel open the grave, crawl down in there, and strangle her bones. He remembered the tears he cried when he stood alongside the open grave of his father and he realized then that one of these days there would be nobody alive to remember that he cried that morning, just as there is no proof now that anyone ever cried for Tobias or Elisha or Elsie at the foot of the hill. No trace of grief is left, abstractions taken first by the snows of reduction.

"It's okay with me if I don't have no headstone," Francis said to Rudy, "just so's I don't die alone."

"You die before me I'll send out invites," Rudy said.

Kathryn Phelan, suddenly aware her worthless son was accepting his own death, provided it arrived on a gregarious note, humphed and fumed her disapproval to her husband. But Michael Phelan was already following the line of his son's walk toward the plot beneath the box elder tree where Gerald was buried. It always amazed Michael that the living could move instinctually toward dead kin without foreknowledge of their location. Francis had never seen Gerald's grave, had not attended Gerald's funeral. His absence that day was the scandal of the resident population of Saint Agnes's. But here he was now, walking purposefully, and with a slight limp Michael had not seen before, closing the gap between father and son, between sudden death and enduring guilt. Michael signaled to his neighbors that an act of regeneration seemed to be in process, and the eyes of the dead, witnesses all to their own historical omissions, their own unbridgeable chasms in life gone, silently rooted for Francis as he walked up the slope toward the box elder. Rudy followed his pal at a respectful distance, aware that some event of moment was taking place. Hangdog, he observed.

In his grave, a cruciformed circle, Gerald watched the advent of his father and considered what action might be appropriate to their meeting. Should he absolve the man of all guilt, not for the dropping, for that was accidental, but for the abandonment of the family, for craven flight when the steadfast virtues were called for? Gerald's grave trembled with superb possibility. Denied speech in life, having died with only monosyllabic goos and gaahs in his vocabulary, Gerald possessed the gift of tongues in death. His ability to communicate and to understand was at the genius level among the dead. He could speak with any resident adult in any language, but more notable was his ability to understand the chattery squirrels and chipmunks, the silent signals of the ants and beetles, and the slithy semaphores of the slugs and worms that moved above and through his earth. He could read the waning flow of energy in the leaves and berries as they fell from the box elder above him. And because his fate had been innocence and denial, Gerald had grown a protective web which deflected all moisture, all moles, rabbits, and other burrowing creatures. His web was woven of strands of vivid silver, an enveloping hammock of intricate, near-transparent weave. His body had not only been absolved of the need to decay, but in some respects–a full head of hair, for instance–it had grown to a completeness that was both natural and miraculous. Gerald rested in his infantile sublimity, exuding a high gloss induced by early death, his skin a radiant white-gold, his nails a silvery gray, his cluster of curls and large eyes perfectly matched in gleaming ebony. Swaddled in his grave, he was beyond capture by visual or verbal artistry. He was neither beautiful nor perfect to the beholder but rather an ineffably fabulous presence whose like was not to be found anywhere in the cemetery, and it abounded with dead innocents.

Francis found the grave without a search. He stood over it and reconstructed the moment when the child was slipping through his fingers into death. He prayed for a repeal of time so that he might hang himself in the coal bin before picking up the child to change his diaper. Denied that, he prayed for his son's eternal peace in the grave. It was true the boy had not suffered at all in his short life, and he had died too quickly of a cracked neckbone to have felt pain: a sudden twist and it was over. *Gerald Michael Phelan,* his gravestone said, *born April 13, 1916, died April 26, 1916. Born on the 13th, lived 13 days. An unlucky child who was much loved.*

Tears oozed from Francis's eyes, and when one of them fell onto his shoetop, he pitched forward onto the grave, clutching the grass, remembering the diaper in his grip. It had smelled of Gerald's pungent water, and when he squeezed it with his horrified right hand, a drop of the sacred fluid fell onto his shoetop. Twenty-two years gone, and Francis could now, in panoramic memory, see, hear, and feel every detail of that day, from the time he left the carbarns after work, to his talk about baseball with Bunt Dunn in King Brady's saloon, and even to the walk home with Cap Lawlor, who said Brady's beer was getting a heavy taste to it and Brady ought to clean his pipes, and that the Taylor kid next door to the Lawlors was passing green pinworms. His memory had begun returning forgotten images when it equated Arthur T. Grogan and Strawberry Bill, but now memory was as vivid as eyesight.

"I remember everything," Francis told Gerald in the grave. "It's the first time I tried to think of those things since you died. I had four beers after work that day. It wasn't because I was drunk that I dropped you. Four beers, and I didn't finish the fourth. Left it next to the pigs'-feet jar on Brady's bar so's I could walk home with Cap Lawlor. Billy was nine then. He knew you were gone before Peggy knew. She hadn't come home from choir practice yet. Your mother said two words, 'Sweet Jesus,' and then we both crouched down to snatch you up. But we both stopped in that crouch because of the looks of you. Billy come in then and saw you. 'Why is Gerald crooked?' he says. You know, I saw Billy a week or so ago and the kid looks good. He wanted to buy me new clothes. Bailed me outa jail and even give me a wad of cash. We talked about you. He says your mother never blamed me for dropping you. Never told a soul in twenty-two years it was me let you fall. Is that some woman or isn't it? I remember the linoleum you fell on was yellow with red squares. You suppose now that I can remember this stuff out in the open, I can finally start to forget it?"

Gerald, through an act of silent will, imposed on his father the pressing obligation to perform his final acts of expiation for abandoning the family. You will not know, the child silently said, what these acts are until you have performed them all. And after you have performed them you will not understand that they were expiatory any more than you have understood all the other expiation that has kept you in such prolonged humiliation. Then, when these final acts are complete, you will stop trying to die because of me.

Francis stopped crying and tried to suck a small piece of bread out from between the last two molars in his all but toothless mouth. He made a slurping sound with his tongue, and when he did, a squirrel scratching the earth for food to store up for the winter spiraled up the box elder in sudden fright. Francis took this as a signal to conclude his visit and he turned his gaze toward the sky. A vast stand of white fleece, brutally bright, moved south to north in the eastern vault of the heavens, a rush of splendid wool to warm the day. The breeze had grown temperate and the sun was rising to the noonday pitch. Francis was no longer chilly.

"Hey bum," he called to Rudy. "Let's find that truck driver."

"Whatayou been up to?" Rudy asked. "You know somebody buried up there?"

"A little kid I used to know."

"A kid? What'd he do, die young?"

"Pretty young."

"What happened to him?"

"He fell."

"He fell where?"

"He fell on the floor."

"Hell, I fall on the floor about twice a day and I ain't dead."

"That's what you think," Francis said.

# II.

They rode the Albany–Troy–via–Watervliet bus downtown from the cemetery. Francis told Rudy: "Spend a dime, ya bum," and they stepped up into the flat-faced, red-and-cream window box on wheels, streamline in design but without the spark of electric life, without the rocking-horse comfort, or the flair, or the verve, of the vanishing trolley. Francis remembered trolleys as intimately as he remembered the shape of his father's face, for he had seen them at loving closeness through all his early years. Trolleys dominated his life the way trains had dominated his father's. He had worked on them at the North Albany carbarns for years, could take them apart in the dark. He'd even killed a man over them in 1901 during the trolley strike. Terrific machines, but now they're goin'.

"Where we headed?" Rudy asked.

"What do you care where we're headed? You got an appointment? You got tickets for the opera?"

"No, I just like to know where I'm goin'."

"You ain't knowed where you was goin' for twenty years."

"You got somethin' there," Rudy said.

"We're goin' to the mission, see what's happenin', see if anybody knows where Helen is."

"What's Helen's name?"

"Helen."

"I mean her other name."

"Whatayou want to know for?"

"I like to know people's names."

"She ain't got only one name."

"Okay, you don't want to tell me, it's all right."

"You goddamn right it's all right."

"We gonna eat at the mission? I'm hungry."

"We could eat, why not? We're sober, so he'll let us in, the bastard. I ate there the other night, had a bowl of soup because I was starvin'. But god it was sour. Them dried-out bums that live there, they sit down and eat like fuckin' pigs, and everything that's left they throw in the pot and give it to you. Slop."

"He puts out a good meal, though."

"He does in a pig's ass."

"Wonderful."

"Pig's ass. And he won't feed you till you listen to him preach. I watch the old bums sittin' there and I wonder about them. What are you all doin', sittin' through his bullshit? But they's all tired and old, they's all drunks. They don't believe in nothin'. They's just hungry."

"I believe in somethin'," Rudy said. "I'm a Catholic."

"Well so am I. What the hell has that got to do with it?"

The bus rolled south on Broadway following the old trolley tracks, down through Menands and into North Albany, past Simmons Machine, the Albany Felt Mill, the Bond Bakery, the Eastern Tablet Company, the Albany Paper Works. And then the bus stopped at North Third

Street to pick up a passenger and Francis looked out the window at the old neighborhood he could not avoid seeing. He saw where North Street began and then sloped down toward the canal bed, the lumber district, the flats, the river. Brady's saloon was still on the corner. Was Brady alive? Pretty good pitcher. Played ball for Boston in 1912, same year Francis was with Washington. And when the King quit the game he opened the saloon. Two big-leaguers from Albany and they both wind up on the same street. Nick's delicatessen, new to Francis, was next to Brady's, and in front of it children in false faces—a clown, a spook, a monster—were playing hopscotch. One child hopped in and out of chalked squares, and Francis remembered it was Halloween, when spooks made house calls and the dead walked abroad.

"I used to live down at the foot of that street," Francis told Rudy, and then wondered why he'd bothered. He had no desire to tell Rudy anything intimate about his life. Yet working next to the simpleton all day, throwing dirt on dead people in erratic rhythm with him, had generated a bond that Francis found strange. Rudy, a friend for about two weeks, now seemed to Francis a fellow traveler on a journey to a nameless destination in another country. He was simple, hopeless and lost, as lost as Francis himself, though somewhat younger, dying of cancer, afloat in ignorance, weighted with stupidity, inane, sheeplike, and given to fits of weeping over his lostness; and yet there was something in him that buoyed Francis's spirit. They were both questing for the behavior that was proper to their station and their unutterable dreams. They both knew intimately the etiquette, the taboos, the protocol of bums. By their talk to each other they understood that they shared a belief in the brotherhood of the desolate; yet in the scars of their eyes they confirmed that no such fraternity had ever existed, that the only brotherhood they belonged to was the one that asked that enduring question: How do I get through the next twenty minutes? They feared drys, cops, jailers, bosses, moralists, crazies, truth-tellers, and one another. They loved storytellers, liars, whores, fighters, singers, collie dogs that wagged their tails, and generous bandits. Rudy, thought Francis: he's just a bum, but who ain't?

"You live there a long time?" Rudy asked.

"Eighteen years," Francis said. "The old lock was just down from my house."

"What kind of lock?"

"On the Erie Canal, you goddamn dimwit. I could throw a stone from my stoop twenty feet over the other side of the canal."

"I never saw the canal, but I seen the river."

"The river was a little ways further over. Still is. The lumber district's gone and all that's left is the flats where they filled the canal in. Jungle town been built up on 'em right down there. I stayed there one night last week with an old bo, a pal of mine. Tracks run right past it, same tracks I went west on out to Dayton to play ball. I hit .387 that year."

"What year was that?"

" 'Oh-one."

"I was five years old," Rudy said.

"How old are you now, about eight?"

They passed the old carbarns at Erie Street, all full of buses. Buildings a different color, and more of 'em, but it looks a lot like it looked in '16. The trolley full of scabs and soldiers left this barn that day in '01 and rocketed arrogantly down Broadway, the street supine and yielding all the way to downtown. But then at Columbia and Broadway the street changed its pose: it became volatile with the rage of strikers and their women, who trapped the car at that corner between two blazing bedsheets which

Francis helped to light on the overhead electric wire. Soldiers on horses guarded the trolley; troops with rifles rode on it. But every scabby-souled one of them was trapped between pillars of fire when Francis pulled back, wound up his educated right arm, and let fly that smooth round stone the weight of a baseball, and brained the scab working as the trolley conductor. The troops saw more stones coming and fired back at the mob, hitting two men who fell in fatal slumps; but not Francis, who ran down to the railroad tracks and then north along them till his lungs blew out. He pitched forward into a ditch and waited about nine years to see if they were on his tail, and they weren't, but his brother Chick and his buddies Patsy McCall and Martin Daugherty were; and when the three of them reached his ditch they all ran north, up past the lumberyards in the district, and found refuge with Iron Joe Farrell, Francis's father-in-law, who bossed the filtration plant that made Hudson River water drinkable for Albany folk. And after a while, when he knew for sure he couldn't stay around Albany because the scab was surely dead, Francis hopped a train going north, for he couldn't get a westbound without going back down into that wild city. But it was all right. He went north and then he walked awhile and found his way to some westbound tracks, and went west on them, all the way west to Dayton, O-hi-o.

That scab was the first man Francis Phelan ever killed. His name was Harold Allen and he was a single man from Worcester, Massachusetts, a member of the IOOF, of Scotch-Irish stock, twenty-nine years old, two years of college, veteran of the Spanish-American War who had seen no combat, an itinerant house painter who found work in Albany as a strikebreaker and who was now sitting across the aisle of the bus from Francis, dressed in a long black coat and a motorman's cap.

Why did you kill me? was the question Harold Allen's eyes put to Francis.

"Didn't mean to kill you," Francis said.

Was that why you threw that stone the size of a potato and broke open my skull? My brains flowed out and I died.

"You deserved what you got. Scabs get what they ask for. I was right in what I did."

Then you feel no remorse at all.

"You bastards takin' our jobs, what kind of man is that, keeps a man from feedin' his family?"

Odd logic coming from a man who abandoned his own family not only that summer but every spring and summer thereafter, when baseball season started. And didn't you finally abandon them permanently in 1916? The way I understand it, you haven't even been home for a visit in twenty-two years.

"There are reasons. That stone. The soldiers would've shot me. And I had to play ball–it's what I did. Then I dropped my baby son and he died and I couldn't face that."

A coward, he'll run.

"Francis is no coward. He had his reasons and they were goddamn good ones."

You have no serious arguments to justify what you did.

"I got arguments," Francis yelled, "I got arguments."

"Whatayou got arguments about?" Rudy asked.

"Down there," Francis said, pointing toward the tracks beyond the carbarns, "I was in this boxcar and didn't know where I was goin' except north, but it seemed I was safe. It wasn't movin' very fast or else I couldn't of got into it. I'm lookin' out, and up there ahead I see this young fella runnin' like hell, runnin' like I'd just run, and I see two guys chasin' him, and one of them two doin' the chasin' looks like a cop and he's shootin'. Stoppin' and shootin'. But this fella keeps runnin', and we're gettin' to him when I see another one right behind him. They're both headin' for the train, and I peek around the door, careful so's I don't got me shot, and I see the first one grab hold of a ladder on one of the cars, and he's up, he's up, and they're still shootin,' and then damn if we don't cross that road just about the time the second fella gets to the car I'm ridin' in, and he yells up to me: Help me, help me, and they're shootin' like sonsabitches at him and sure as hell I help him, they're gonna shoot at me too."

"What'd you do?" Rudy asked.

"I slid on my belly over to the edge of the car, givin' them shooters a thin target, and I give that fella a hand, and he's grabbin' at it, almost grabbin' it, and I'm almost gettin' a full purchase on him, and then whango bango, they shoot him right in the back and that's all she wrote. Katie bar the door. Too wet to plow. He's all done, that fella, and I roll around back in the car and don't find out till we get to Whitehall, when the other fella drops into my boxcar, that they both was prisoners and they was on their way to the county jail in Albany. But then there was this big trolley strike with shootin' and stuff because some guy threw a stone and killed a scab. And that got this mob of people in the street all mixed up and crazy and they was runnin' every which way and the deputies guardin' these two boys got a little careless and so off went the boys. They run and hid awhile and then lit out and run some more, about three miles or so, same as me, and them deputies picked up on 'em and kept right after them all the way. They never did get that first fella. He went to Dayton with me, 'preciated what I tried to do for his buddy and even stole two chickens when we laid over in some switchyards somewheres and got us a fine meal. We cooked it up right in the boxcar. He was a murderer, that fella. Strangled some lady in Selkirk and couldn't say why he done it. The one that got shot in the back, he was a horse thief."

"I guess you been mixed up in a lot of violence," Rudy said.

"If it draws blood or breaks heads," said Francis, "I know how it tastes."

The horse thief was named Aldo Campione, an immigrant from the town of Teramo in the Abruzzi. He'd come to America to seek his fortune and found work building the Barge Canal. But as a country soul he was distracted by an equine opportunity in the town of Coeymans, was promptly caught, jailed, transported to Albany for trial, and shot in the back escaping. His lesson to Francis was this: that life is full of caprice and missed connections, that thievery is wrong, especially if you get caught, that even Italians cannot outrun bullets, that a proffered hand in a moment of need is a beautiful thing. All this Francis knew well enough, and so the truest lesson of Aldo Campione resided not in intellected fact but in spectacle; for Francis can still remember Aldo's face as it came toward him. It looked like his own, which is perhaps why Francis put himself in jeopardy: to save his own face with his own hand. On came Aldo toward the open boxcar door. Out went the hand of Francis Phelan. It touched the curved fingers of Aldo's right hand. Francis's fingers curved and pulled. And there was tension. Tension! On came Aldo yielding to that tension, on and on and lift! Leap! Pull, Francis, pull! And then up, yes up! The grip was solid. The man was in the air, flying toward safety on the great right hand of Francis Phelan. And then whango bango and he let go. Whango bango and he's down, and he's rolling, and he's dead. Katie bar the door.

When the bus stopped at the corner of Broadway and Columbia Street, the corner where that infamous trolley was caught between flaming bedsheets, Aldo Campione boarded. He was clad in a white flannel suit, white shirt, and white necktie, and his hair was slicked down with brilliantine. Francis knew instantly that this was not the white of innocence but of humility. The man had been of low birth, low estate, and committed a low crime that had earned him the lowliest of deaths in the dust. Over there on the other side they must've give him a new suit. And here he came down the aisle and stopped at the seats where Rudy and Francis sat. He reached out his hand in a gesture to Francis that was ambiguous. It might have been a simple Abruzzian greeting. Or was it a threat, or a warning? It might have been an offer of belated gratitude, or even a show of compassion for a man like Francis who had lived long (for him), suffered much, and was inching toward death. It might have been a gesture of grace, urging, or even welcoming Francis into the next. And at this thought, Francis, who had raised his hand to meet Aldo's, withdrew it.

"I ain't shakin' hands with no dead horse thief," he said.

"I ain't no horse thief," Rudy said.

"Well you look like one," Francis said.

By then the bus was at Madison Avenue and Broadway, and Rudy and Francis stepped out into the frosty darkness of six o'clock on the final night of October 1938, the unruly night when grace is always in short supply, and the old and the new dead walk abroad in this land.

□ □ □

In the dust and sand of a grassless vacant lot beside the Mission of Holy Redemption, a human form lay prostrate under a lighted mission window. The sprawl of the figure arrested Francis's movement when he and Rudy saw it. Bodies in alleys, bodies in gutters, bodies anywhere, were part of his eternal landscape: a physical litany of the dead.

This one belonged to a woman who seemed to be doing the dead man's float in the dust: face down, arms forward, legs spread.

"Hey," Rudy said as they stopped. "That's Sandra."

"Sandra who?" said Francis.

"Sandra There-ain't-no-more. She's only got one name, like Helen. She's an Eskimo."

"You dizzy bastard. Everybody's an Eskimo or a Cherokee."

"No, that's the straight poop. She used to work up in Alaska when they were buildin' roads."

"She dead?"

Rudy bent down, picked up Sandra's hand and held it. Sandra pulled it away from him.

"No," Rudy said, "she ain't dead."

"Then you better get up outa there, Sandra," Francis said, "or the dogs'll eat your ass off."

Sandra didn't move. Her hair streamed out of her inertness, long, yellow-white wisps floating in the dust, her faded and filthy cotton housedress twisted above the back of her knees, revealing stockings so full of holes and runs that they had lost their integrity as stockings. Over her dress she wore two sweaters, both stained and tattered. She lacked a left shoe. Rudy bent over and tapped her on the shoulder.

"Hey Sandra, it's me, Rudy. You know me?"

"Hnnn," said Sandra.

"You all right? You sick or anything, or just drunk?"

"Dnnn," said Sandra.

"She's just drunk," Rudy said, standing up. "She can't hold it no more. She falls over."

"She'll freeze there and the dogs'll come along and eat her ass off," Francis said.

"What dogs?" Rudy asked.

"The dogs, the dogs. Ain't you seen them?"

"I don't see too many dogs. I like cats. I see a lotta cats."

"If she's drunk she can't go inside the mission," Francis said.

"That's right," said Rudy. "She comes in drunk, he kicks her right out. He hates drunk women more'n he hates us."

"Why the hell's he preachin' if he don't preach to people that need it?"

"Drunks don't need it," Rudy said. "How'd you like to preach to a room full of bums like her?"

"She a bum or just on a heavy drunk?"

"She's a bum."

"She looks like a bum."

"She's been a bum all her life."

"No," said Francis. "Nobody's a bum all their life. She hada been somethin' once."

"She was a whore before she was a bum."

"And what about before she was a whore?"

"I don't know," Rudy said. "She just talks about whorin' in Alaska. Before that I guess she was just a little kid."

"Then that's somethin'. A little kid's somethin' that ain't a bum or a whore."

Francis saw Sandra's missing shoe in the shadows and retrieved it. He set it beside her left foot, then squatted and spoke into her left ear.

"You gonna freeze here tonight, you know that? Gonna be frost, freezin' weather. Could even snow. You hear? You oughta get yourself inside someplace outa the cold. Look, I slept the last two nights in the weeds and it was awful cold, but tonight's colder already than it was either of them nights. My hands is half froze and I only been walkin' two blocks. Sandra? You hear what I'm sayin'? If I got you a cup of hot soup would you drink it? Could you? You don't look like you could but maybe you could. Get a little hot soup in, you don't freeze so fast. Or maybe you wanna freeze tonight, maybe that's why you're layin' in the goddamn dust. You don't even have any weeds to keep the wind outa your ears. I like them deep weeds when I sleep outside. You want some soup?"

Sandra turned her head and with one eye looked up at Francis.

"Who you?"

"I'm just a bum," Francis said. "But I'm sober and I can get you some soup."

"Get me a drink?"

"No, I ain't got money for that."

"Then soup."

"You wanna stand up?"

"No. I'll wait here."

"You're gettin' all dusty."

"That's good."

"Whatever you say," Francis said, standing up. "But watch out for them dogs."

She whimpered as Rudy and Francis left the lot. The night sky was black as a bat and the wind was bringing ice to the world. Francis admitted the futility of preaching to Sandra. Who could preach to Francis in the weeds? But that don't make it right that she can't go inside to get warm. Just because you're drunk don't mean you ain't cold.

"Just because you're drunk don't mean you ain't cold," he said to Rudy.

"Right," said Rudy. "Who said that?"

"I said that, you ape."

"I ain't no ape."

"Well you look like one."

From the mission came sounds made by an amateur organist of fervent aggression, and of several voices raised in praise of good old Jesus, where'd we all be without him? The voices belonged to the Reverend Chester, and to half a dozen men in shirt sleeves who sat in the front rows of the chapel area's folding chairs. Reverend Chester, a gargantuan man with a clubfoot, wild white hair, and a face flushed permanently years ago by a whiskey condition all his own, stood behind the lectern looking out at maybe forty men and one woman.

Helen.

Francis saw her as he entered, saw her gray beret pulled off to the left, recognized her old black coat. She held no hymnal as the others did, but sat with arms folded in defiant resistance to the possibility of redemption by any Methodist like Chester; for Helen was a Catholic. And any redemption that came her way had better be through her church, the true church, the only church.

"Jesus," the preacher and his shirt-sleeved loyalists sang, "the name that charms our fears, That bids our sorrows cease, 'Tis music in the sinners' ears, 'Tis life and health and peace . . ."

The remaining seven eighths of Reverend Chester's congregation, men hiding inside their overcoats, hats in their laps, if they had hats, their faces grimed and whiskered and woebegone, remained mute, or gave the lyrics a perfunctory mumble, or nodded already in sleep. The song continued: ". . . He breaks the power of canceled sin, He sets the prisoner free; His blood can make the foulest clean, His blood availed for me."

Well not me, Francis said to his unavailed-for self, and he smelled his own uncanceled stink again, aware that it had intensified since morning. The sweat of a workday, the sourness of dried earth on his hands and clothes, the putrid perfume of the cemetery air with its pretension to windblown purity, all this lay in foul encrustation atop the private pestilence of his being. When he threw himself onto Gerald's grave, the uprush of a polluted life all but asphyxiated him.

"Hear him, ye deaf; his praise, ye dumb, Your loosened

tongues employ; Ye blind, behold your Savior come; and leap, ye lame, for joy."

The lame and the halt put their hymnals down joylessly, and Reverend Chester leaned over his lectern to look at tonight's collection. Among them, as always, were good men and straight, men honestly without work, victims of a society ravaged by avarice, sloth, stupidity, and a God made wrathful by Babylonian excesses. Such men were merely the transients in the mission, and to them a preacher could only wish luck, send prayer, and provide a meal for the long road ahead. The true targets of the preacher were the others: the dipsos, the deadbeats, the wetbrains, and the loonies, who needed more than luck. What they needed was a structured way, a mentor and guide through the hells and purgatories of their days. Bringing the word, the light, was a great struggle today, for the decline of belief was rampant and the anti-Christ was on the rise. It was prophesied in Matthew and in Revelation that there would be less and less reverence for the Bible, greater lawlessness, depravity, and self-indulgence. The world, the light, the song, they would all die soon, for without doubt we were witnessing the advent of end times.

"Lost," said the preacher, and he waited for the word to resound in the sanctums of their damaged brains. "Oh lost, lost forever. Men and women lost, hopeless. Who will save you from your sloth? Who will give you a ride on the turnpike to salvation? Jesus will! Jesus delivers!"

The preacher screamed the word *delivers* and woke up half the congregation. Rudy, on the nod, flared into wakefulness with a wild swing of the left arm that knocked the hymnal out of Francis's grip. The book fell to the floor with a splat that brought Reverend Chester eye-to-eye with Francis. Francis nodded and the preacher gave him a firm and flinty smile in return.

The preacher then took the beatitudes for his theme. Blessed are the poor in spirit, for theirs is the kingdom of heaven. Blessed are the meek, for they shall inherit the earth. Blessed are they that mourn, for they shall be comforted.

"Oh yes, you men of skid row, brethren on the poor streets of the one eternal city we all dwell in, do not grieve that your spirit is low. Do not fear the world because you are of a meek and gentle nature. Do not feel that your mournful tears are in vain, for these things are the keys to the kingdom of God."

The men went swiftly back to sleep and Francis resolved he would wash the stink of the dead off his face and hands and hit Chester up for a new pair of socks. Chester was happiest when he was passing out socks to dried-out drunks. Feed the hungry, clothe the sober.

"Are you ready for peace of mind and heart?" the preacher asked. "Is there a man here tonight who wants a different life? God says: Come unto me. Will you take him at his word? Will you stand up now? Come to the front, kneel, and we will talk. Do this now and be saved. Now. Now. Now!"

No one moved.

"Then amen, brothers," said the preacher testily, and he left the lectern.

"Hot goddamn," Francis said to Rudy. "Now we get at that soup."

Then began the rush of men to table, the pouring of coffee, ladling of soup, cutting of bread by the mission's zealous volunteers. Francis sought out Pee Wee, a good old soul who managed the mission for Chester, and he asked him for a cup of soup for Sandra.

"She oughta be let in," Francis said. "She's gonna freeze out there."

"She was in before," Pee Wee said. "He wouldn't let her

stay. She was really shot, and you know him on that. He won't mind on the soup, but just for the hell of it, don't say where it's going."

"Secret soup," Francis said.

He took the soup out the back door, pulling Rudy along with him, and crossed the vacant lot to where Sandra lay as before. Rudy rolled her onto her back and sat her up, and Francis put the soup under her nose.

"Soup," he said.

"Gazoop," Sandra said.

"Have it." Francis put the cup to her lips and tipped the soup at her mouth. It dribbled down her chin. She swallowed none.

"She don't want it," Rudy said.

"She wants it," Francis said. "She's just pissed it ain't wine."

He tried again and Sandra swallowed a little.

"When I was sleepin' inside just now," Rudy said, "I remembered Sandra wanted to be a nurse. Or used to be a nurse. That right, Sandra?"

"No," Sandra said.

"No, what? Wanted to be a nurse or was a nurse?"

"Doctor," Sandra said.

"She wanted to be a doctor," Francis said, tipping in more soup.

"No," Sandra said, pushing the soup away. Francis put the cup down and slipped her ratty shoe onto her left foot. He lifted her, a feather, carried her to the wall of the mission, and propped her into a sitting position, her back against the building, somewhat out of the wind. With his bare hand he wiped the masking dust from her face. He raised the soup and gave her another swallow.

"Doctor wanted me to be a nursie," she said.

"But you didn't want it," Francis said.

"Did. But he died."

"Ah," said Francis. "Love?"

"Love," said Sandra.

Inside the mission, Francis handed the cup back to Pee Wee, who emptied it into the sink.

"She all right?" Pee Wee asked.

"Terrific," Francis said.

"The ambulance won't even pick her up anymore," Pee Wee said. "Not unless she's bleedin' to death."

Francis nodded and went to the bathroom, where he washed Sandra's dust and his own stink off his hands. Then he washed his face and his neck and his ears; and when he was finished he washed them all again. He sloshed water around in his mouth and brushed his teeth with his left index finger. He wet his hair and combed it with nine fingers and dried himself with a damp towel that was tied to the wall. Some men were already leaving by the time he picked up his soup and bread and sat down beside Helen.

"Where you been hidin'?" he asked her.

"A fat lot you care where anybody is or isn't. I could be dead in the street three times over and you wouldn't know a thing about it."

"How the hell could I when you walk off like a crazy woman, yellin' and stompin'."

"Who wouldn't be crazy around you, spending every penny we get. You go out of your mind, Francis."

"I got some money."

"How much?"

"Six bucks."

"Where'd you get it?"

"I worked all the damn day in the cemetery, fillin' up graves. Worked hard."

"Francis, you did?"

"I mean all day."

"That's wonderful. And you're sober. And you're eating."

"Ain't drinkin' no wine either. I ain't even smokin'."

"Oh that's so lovely. I'm very proud of my good boy."

Francis scarfed up the soup, and Helen smiled and sipped the last of her coffee. More than half the men were gone from table now, Rudy still eating with a partial mind across from Francis. Pee Wee and his plangently compassionate volunteers picked up dishes and carried them to the kitchen. The preacher finished his coffee and strode over to Francis.

"Glad to see you staying straight," the preacher said.

"Okay," said Francis.

"And how are you, little lady?" he asked Helen.

"I'm perfectly delightful," Helen said.

"I believe I've got a job for you if you want it, Francis," the preacher said.

"I worked today up at the cemetery."

"Splendid."

"Shovelin' dirt ain't my idea of that much of a job."

"Maybe this one is better. Old Rosskam the ragman came here today looking for a helper. I've sent him men from time to time and I thought of you. If you're serious about quitting the hooch you might put a decent penny together."

"Ragman," Francis said. "Doin' what, exactly?"

"Going house to house on the wagon. Rosskam himself buys the rags and bottles, old metal, junk, papers, no garbage. Carts it himself too, but he's getting on and needs another strong back."

"Where's he at?"

"Green Street, below the bridge."

"I'll go see him and I 'preciate it. Tell you what else I'd 'preciate's a pair of socks, if you can spare 'em. Ones I got are all rotted out."

"What size?"

"Tens. But I'll take nines, or twelves."

"I'll get you some tens. And keep up the good work,

Franny. Nice to see you're doing well too, little lady."

"I'm doing very well," Helen said. "Very exceptionally well." When he walked away she said: "He says it's nice I'm doing well. I'm doing just fine, and I don't need him to tell me I'm doing well."

"Don't fight him," Francis said. "He's givin' me some socks."

"We gonna get them jugs?" Rudy asked Francis. "Go somewheres and get a flop?"

"Jugs?" said Helen.

"That's what I said this mornin'," Francis said. "No, no jugs."

"With six dollars we could get a room and get our suitcase back," Helen said.

"I can't spend all six," Francis said. "I gotta give some to the lawyer. I figure I'll give him a deuce. After all, he got me the job and I owe him fifty."

"Where do you plan to sleep?" Helen asked.

"Where'd you sleep last night?"

"I found a place."

"Finny's car?"

"No, not Finny's car. I won't stay there anymore, you know that. I will absolutely not stay in that car another night."

"Then where'd you go?"

"Where did *you* sleep?"

"I slept in the weeds," Francis said.

"Well I found a bed."

"Where, goddamn it, where?"

"Up at Jack's."

"I thought you didn't like Jack anymore, or Clara either."

"They're not my favorite people, but they gave me a bed when I needed one."

"Somethin' to be said for that," Francis said.

Pee Wee came over with a second cup of coffee and sat across from Helen. Pee Wee was bald and fat and chewed cigars all day long without lighting them. He had cut hair in his younger days, but when his wife cleaned out their bank account, poisoned Pee Wee's dog, and ran away with the barber whom Pee Wee, by dint of hard work and superior tonsorial talent, had put out of business, Pee Wee started drinking and wound up on the bum. Yet he carried his comb and scissors everywhere to prove his talent was not just a bum's fantasy, and gave haircuts to other bums for fifteen cents, sometimes a nickel. He still gave haircuts, free now, at the mission.

When Francis came back to Albany in 1935, he met Pee Wee for the first time and they stayed drunk together for a month. When Francis turned up in Albany only weeks back to register for the Democrats at five dollars a shot, he met Pee Wee again. Francis registered to vote twenty-one times before the state troopers caught up with him and made him an Albany political celebrity. The pols had paid him fifty by then and still owed him fifty-five more that he'd probably never see. Pee Wee was off the juice when Francis met him the second time, and was full of energy, running the mission for Chester. Pee Wee was peaceful now, no longer the singing gin-drinker he used to be. Francis still felt good things about him, but now thought of him as an emotional cripple, dry, yeah, but at what cost?

"You see who's playin' over at The Gilded Cage?" Pee Wee asked Francis.

"I don't read the papers."

"Oscar Reo."

"You mean our Oscar?"

"The same."

"What's he doin'?"

"Singin' bartender. How's that for a comedown?"

"Oscar Reo who used to be on the radio?" Helen asked.

"That's the fella," said Pee Wee. "He blew the big time on booze, but he dried out and tends bar now. At least he's livin', even if it ain't what it was."

"Pee Wee and me pitched a drunk with him in New York. Two, three days, wasn't it, Pee?"

"Mighta been a week," Pee Wee said. "None of us was up to keepin' track. But he sang a million tunes and played piano everyplace they had one. Most musical drunk I ever see."

"I used to sing his songs," Helen said. " 'Hindustan Lover' and 'Georgie Is My Apple Pie' and another one, a grand ballad, 'Under the Peach Trees with You.' He wrote wonderful, happy songs and I sang them all when I was singing."

"I didn't know you sang," Pee Wee said.

"Well I most certainly sang, and played piano very well too. I was getting a classical education in music until my father died. I was at Vassar."

"Albert Einstein went to Vassar," Rudy said.

"You goofy bastard," said Francis.

"Went there to make a speech. I read it in the papers."

"He could have," Helen said. "Everybody speaks at Vassar. It just happens to be one of the three best schools in the world."

"We oughta go over and see old Oscar," Francis said.

"Not me," said Pee Wee.

"No," said Helen.

"What no?" Francis said. "You afraid we'd all get drunked up if we stopped in to say hello?"

"I'm not afraid of that."

"Then let's go see him. He's all right, Oscar."

"Think he'll remember you?" Pee Wee said.

"Maybe. I remember him."

"So do I."

"Then let's go."

"I wouldn't drink anything," Pee Wee said. "I ain't been in a bar in two years."

"They got ginger ale. You allowed to drink ginger ale?"

"I hope it's not expensive," Helen said.

"Just what you drink," Pee Wee said. "About usual."

"Is it snooty?"

"It's a joint, old-timey, but it pulls in the slummers. That's half the trade."

Reverend Chester stepped lively across the room and thrust at Francis a pair of gray woolen socks, his mouth a crescent of pleasure and his great chest heaving with beneficence.

"Try these for size," he said.

"I thank ya for 'em," said Francis.

"They're good and warm."

"Just what I need. Nothin' left of mine."

"It's fine that you're off the drink. You've got a strong look about you today."

"Just a false face for Halloween."

"Don't run yourself down. Have faith."

The door to the mission opened and a slim young man in bifocals and a blue topcoat two sizes small for him, his carroty hair a field of cowlicks, stood in its frame. He held the doorknob with one hand and stood directly under the inside ceiling light, casting no shadow.

"Shut the door," Pee Wee yelled, and the young man stepped in and shut it. He stood looking at all in the mission, his face a cracked plate, his eyes panicked and rabbity.

"That's it for him," Pee Wee said.

The preacher strode to the door and stood inches from the young man, studying him, sniffing him.

"You're drunk," the preacher said.

"I only had a couple."

"Oh no. You're in the beyond."

"Honest," said the young man. "Two bottles of beer."

"Where did you get the money for beer?"

"A fella paid me what he owed me."

"You panhandled it."

"No."

"You're a bum."

"I just had a drink, Reverend."

"Get your things together. I told you I wouldn't put up with this a third time. Arthur, get his bags."

Pee Wee stood up from the table and climbed the stairs to the rooms where the resident handful lived while they sorted out their lives. The preacher had invited Francis to stay if he could get the hooch out of his system. He would then have a clean bed, clean clothes, three squares, and a warm room with Jesus in it for as long as it took him to answer the question: What next? Pee Wee held the house record: eight months in the joint, and managing it after three, such was his zeal for abstention. No booze, no smoking upstairs (for drunks are fire hazards), carry your share of the work load, and then rise you must, rise you will, into the brilliant embrace of the just God. The kitchen volunteers stopped their work and came forward with solemnized pity to watch the eviction of one of their promising young men. Pee Wee came down with a suitcase and set it by the door.

"Give us a cigarette, Pee," the young man said.

"Don't have any."

"Well roll one."

"I said I don't have any tobacco."

"Oh."

"You'll have to leave now, Little Red," the preacher said.

Helen stood up and came over to Little Red and put a cigarette in his hand. He took it and said nothing. Helen struck a match and lit it for him, then sat back down.

"I don't have anyplace to go," Little Red said, blowing smoke past the preacher.

"You should have thought of that before you started drinking. You are a contumacious young man."

"I got noplace to put that bag. And I got a pencil and paper upstairs."

"Leave it here. Come and get your pencil and paper when you get that poison out of your system and you can talk sense about yourself."

"My pants are in there."

"They'll be all right. Nobody here will touch your pants."

"Can I have a cup of coffee?"

"If you found money for beer, you can find money for coffee."

"Where can I go?"

"I couldn't begin to imagine. Come back sober and you may have some food. Now get a move on."

Little Red grabbed the doorknob, opened the door, and took a step. Then he stepped back in and pointed at his suitcase.

"I got cigarettes there," he said.

"Then get your cigarettes."

Little Red undid the belt that held the suitcase together and rummaged for a pack of Camels. He rebuckled the belt and stood up.

"If I come back tomorrow . . ."

"We'll see about tomorrow," said the preacher, who grabbed the doorknob himself and pulled it to as he ushered Little Red out into the night.

"Don't lose my pants," Little Red called through the glass of the closing door.

□ □ □

Francis, wearing his new socks, was first out of the mission, first to cast an anxious glance around the corner of the building at Sandra, who sat propped where he had left her, her eyes sewn as tightly closed by the darkness as the eyes of a diurnal bird. Francis touched her firmly with a finger and she moved, but without opening her eyes. He looked up at the full moon, a silver cinder illuminating this night for bleeding women and frothing madmen, and which warmed him with the enormous shadow it thrust forward in his own path. When Sandra moved he leaned over and put the back of his hand against her cheek and felt the ice of her flesh.

"You got an old blanket or some old rags, any old bum's coat to throw over her?" he asked Pee Wee, who stood in the shadows considering the encounter.

"I could get something," Pee Wee said, and he loosened his keys and opened the door of the darkened mission: all lights off save the kitchen, which would remain bright until eleven, lockout time. Pee Wee opened the door and entered as Rudy, Helen, and Francis huddled around Sandra, watching her breathe. Francis had watched two dozen people suspire into death, all of them bums except for his father, and Gerald.

"Maybe if we cut her throat the ambulance'd take her," Francis said.

"She doesn't want an ambulance," Helen said. "She wants to sleep it all away. I'll bet she doesn't even feel cold."

"She's a cake of ice."

Sandra moved, turning her head toward the voices but without opening her eyes. "You got no wine?" she asked.

"No wine, honey," Helen said.

Pee Wee came out with a stone-gray rag that might once

have been a blanket and wrapped its rough doubleness around Sandra. He tucked it into the neck of her sweater, and with one end formed a cowl behind her head, giving her the look of a monastic beggar in sackcloth.

"I don't want to look at her no more," Francis said, and he walked east on Madison, the deepening chill aggravating his limp. Helen and Pee Wee fell in behind him, and Rudy after that.

"You ever know her, Pee Wee?" Francis asked. "I mean when she was in shape?"

"Sure. Everybody knew her. You took your turn. Then she got to givin' love parties, is what she called 'em, but she'd turn mean, first love you up and then bite you bad. Half-ruined enough guys so only strangers'd go with her. Then she stopped that and hung out with one bum name of Freddy and they specialized in one another about a year till he went somewheres and she didn't."

"Nobody suffers like a lover left behind," Helen said.

"Well that's a crock," Francis said. "Lots suffer ain't ever been in love even once."

"They don't suffer like those who have," said Helen.

"Yeah. Where's this joint, Pee Wee, Green Street?"

"Right. Couple of blocks. Where the old Gayety Theater used to be."

"I used to go there. Watch them ladies' ankles and cancanny crotches."

"Be nice, Francis," Helen said.

"I'm nice. I'm the nicest thing you'll see all week."

Goblins came at them on Green Street, hooded spooks, a Charlie Chaplin in whiteface, with derby, cane, and tash, and a girl wearing an enormous old bonnet with a full-sized bird on top of it.

"They gonna get us!" Francis said. "Look out!" He threw his arms in the air and shook himself in a fearful dance. The children laughed and spooked boo at him.

"Gee it's a nice night," Helen said. "Cold but nice and clear, isn't it, Fran?"

"It's nice," Francis said. "It's all nice."

□ □ □

The Gilded Cage door opened into the old Gayety lobby, now the back end of a saloon that mimicked and mocked the Bowery pubs of forty years gone. Francis stood looking toward a pair of monumental, half-wrapped breasts that heaved beneath a hennaed wig and scarlet lips. The owner of these spectacular possessions was delivering outward from an elevated platform a song of anguish in the city: You would not insult me, sir, if Jack were only here, in a voice so devoid of musical quality that it mocked its own mockery.

"She's terrible," Helen said. "Awful."

"She ain't that good," Francis said.

They stepped across a floor strewn with sawdust, lit by ancient chandeliers and sconces, all electric now, toward a long walnut bar with a shining brass bar rail and three gleaming spittoons. Behind the half-busy bar a man with high collar, string tie, and arm garters drew schooners of beer from a tap, and at tables of no significant location sat men and women Francis recognized: whores, bums, barflies. Among them, at other tables, sat men in business suits, and women with fox scarves and flyaway hats, whose presence was such that their tables this night were landmarks of social significance merely because they were sitting at them. Thus, The Gilded Cage was a museum of unnatural sociality, and the smile of the barman welcomed Francis, Helen, and Rudy, bums all, and Pee Wee, their clean-shirted friend, to the tableau.

"Table, folks?"

"Not while there's a bar rail," Francis said.

"Step up, brother. What's your quaff?"

"Ginger ale," said Pee Wee.

"I believe I'll have the same," said Helen.

"That beer looks tantalizin'," Francis said.

"You said you wouldn't drink," Helen said.

"I said wine."

The barman slid a schooner with a high collar across the bar to Francis and looked to Rudy, who ordered the same. The piano player struck up a medley of "She May Have Seen Better Days" and "My Sweetheart's the Man in the Moon" and urged those in the audience who knew the lyrics to join in song.

"You look like a friend of mine," Francis told the barman, drilling him with a smile and a stare. The barman, with a full head of silver waves and an eloquent white mustache, stared back long enough to ignite a memory. He looked from Francis to Pee Wee, who was also smiling.

"I think I know you two turks," the barman said.

"You thinkin' right," Francis said, "except the last time I seen you, you wasn't sportin' that pussy-tickler."

The barman stroked his silvery lip. "You guys got me drunk in New York."

"You got us drunk in every bar on Third Avenue," Pee Wee said.

The barman stuck out his hand to Francis.

"Francis Phelan," said Francis, "and this here is Rudy the Kraut. He's all right but he's nuts."

"My kind of fella," Oscar said.

"Pee Wee Packer," Pee Wee said with his hand out.

"I remember," said Oscar.

"And this is Helen," said Francis. "She hangs out with me, but damned if I know why."

"Oscar Reo's what I still go by, folks, and I really do remember you boys. But I don't drink anymore."

"Hey, me neither," said Pee Wee.

"I ain't turned it off yet," Francis said. "I'm waitin' till I retire."

"He retired forty years ago," Pee Wee said.

"That ain't true. I worked all day today. Gettin' rich. How you like my new duds?"

"You're a sport," Oscar said. "Can't tell you from those swells over there."

"Swells and bums, there ain't no difference," Francis said.

"Except swells like to look like swells," Oscar said, "and bums like to look like bums. Am I right?"

"You're a smart fella," Francis said.

"You still singin', Oscar?" Pee Wee asked.

"For my supper."

"Well goddamn it," Francis said, "give us a tune."

"Since you're so polite about it," Oscar said. And he turned to the piano man and said: " 'Sixteen' "; and instantly there came from the piano the strains of "Sweet Sixteen."

"Oh that's a wonderful song," Helen said. "I remember you singing that on the radio."

"How durable of you, my dear."

Oscar sang into the bar microphone and, with great resonance and no discernible loss of control from his years with the drink, he turned time back to the age of the village green. The voice was as commonplace to an American ear as Jolson's, or Morton Downey's; and even Francis, who rarely listened to the radio, or ever had a radio to listen to in either the early or the modern age, remembered its pitch and its tremolo from the New York binge, when this voice by itself was a chorale of continuous joy for all in earshot, or so it seemed to Francis at a distance of years. And further, the attention that the bums, the swells, the waiters, were giving the man, proved that this drunk was not dead, not dying, but living an epilogue to a notable life. And yet, and yet . . . here he was, disguised behind a mustache, another cripple, his ancient, weary eyes revealing to Francis the scars of a blood brother, a man for whom life had been a promise unkept in spite of great success, a promise now and forever unkeepable. The man was singing a song that had grown old not from time but from wear. The song is frayed. The song is worn out.

The insight raised in Francis a compulsion to confess his every transgression of natural, moral, or civil law; to relentlessly examine and expose every flaw of his own character, however minor. What was it, Oscar, that did you in? Would you like to tell us all about it? Do you know? It wasn't Gerald who did *me.* It wasn't drink and it wasn't baseball and it wasn't really Mama. What was it that went bust, Oscar, and how come nobody ever found out how to fix it for us?

When Oscar segued perfectly into a second song, his talent seemed awesome to Francis, and the irrelevance of talent to Oscar's broken life even more of a mystery. How does somebody get this good and why doesn't it mean anything? Francis considered his own talent on the ball field of a hazy, sunlit yesterday: how he could follow the line of the ball from every crack of the bat, zap after it like a chicken hawk after a chick, how he would stroke and pocket its speed no matter whether it was lined at him or sizzled erratically toward him through the grass. He would stroke it with the predatory curve of his glove and begin with his right hand even then, whether he was running or falling, to reach into that leather pocket, spear the chick with his educated talons, and whip it across to first or second base, or wherever it needed to go and you're out, man, you're out. No ball player anywhere moved his body any better than Franny Phelan, a damn fieldin' machine, fastest ever was.

Francis remembered the color and shape of his glove, its odor of oil and sweat and leather, and he wondered if Annie had kept it. Apart from his memory and a couple of clippings, it would be all that remained of a spent career that had blossomed and then peaked in the big leagues far too long after the best years were gone, but which brought with the peaking the promise that some belated and overdue glory was possible, that somewhere there was a hosannah to be cried in the name of Francis Phelan, one of the best sonsabitches ever to kick a toe into third base.

Oscar's voice quavered with beastly loss on a climactic line of the song: Blinding tears falling as he thinks of his lost pearl, broken heart calling, oh yes, calling, dear old girl. Francis turned to Helen and saw her crying splendid, cathartic tears: Helen, with the image of inexpungeable sorrow in her cortex, with a lifelong devotion to forlorn love, was weeping richly for all the pearls lost since love's old sweet song first was sung.

"Oh that was so beautiful, so beautiful," Helen said to Oscar when he rejoined them at the beer spigot. "That's absolutely one of my all-time favorites. I used to sing it myself."

"A singer?" said Oscar. "Where was that?"

"Oh everywhere. Concerts, the radio. I used to sing on the air every night, but that was an age ago."

"You should do us a tune."

"Oh never," said Helen.

"Customers sing here all the time," Oscar said.

"No, no," said Helen, "the way I look."

"You look as good as anybody here," Francis said.

"I could never," said Helen. But she was readying herself to do what she could never, pushing her hair behind her ear, straightening her collar, smoothing her much more than ample front.

"What'll it be?" Oscar said. "Joe knows 'em all."

"Let me think awhile."

Francis saw that Aldo Campione was sitting at a table at the far end of the room and had someone with him. That son of a bitch is following me, is what Francis thought. He fixed his glance on the table and saw Aldo move his hand in an ambiguous gesture. What are you telling me, dead man, and who's that with you? Aldo wore a white flower in the lapel of his white flannel suitcoat, a new addition since the bus. Goddamn dead people travelin' in packs, buyin' flowers. Francis studied the other man without recognition and felt the urge to walk over and take a closer look. But what if nobody's sittin' there? What if nobody sees these bozos but me? The flower girl came along with a full tray of white gardenias.

"Buy a flower, sir?" she asked Francis.

"Why not? How much?"

"Just a quarter."

"Give us one."

He fished a quarter out of his pants and pinned the gardenia on Helen's lapel with a pin the girl handed him. "It's been a while since I bought you flowers," he said. "You gonna sing up there for us, you gotta put on the dog a little."

Helen leaned over and kissed Francis on the mouth, which always made him blush when she did it in public. She was always a first-rate heller between the sheets, when there was sheets, when there was somethin' to do between them.

"Francis always bought me flowers," she said. "He'd get money and first thing he'd do was buy me a dozen roses, or a white orchid even. He didn't care what he did with the money as long as I got my flowers first. You did that for me, didn't you, Fran?"

"Sure did," said Francis, but he could not remember buying an orchid, didn't know what orchids looked like.

"We were lovebirds," Helen said to Oscar, who was smiling at the spectacle of bum love at his bar. "We had a beautiful apartment up on Hamilton Street. We had all the dishes anybody'd ever need. We had a sofa and a big bed and sheets and pillowcases. There wasn't anything we didn't have, isn't that right, Fran?"

"That's right," Francis said, trying to remember the place.

"We had flowerpots full of geraniums that we kept alive all winter long. Francis loved geraniums. And we had an icebox crammed full of food. We ate so well, both of us had to go on a diet. That was such a wonderful time."

"When was that?" Pee Wee asked. "I didn't know you ever stayed anyplace that long."

"What long?"

"I don't know. Months musta been if you had an apartment."

"I was here awhile, six weeks maybe, once."

"Oh we had it much longer than that," Helen said.

"Helen knows," Francis said. "She remembers. I can't call one day different from another."

"It was the drink," Helen said. "Francis wouldn't stop drinking and then we couldn't pay the rent and we had to give up our pillowcases and our dishes. It was Haviland china, the very best you could buy. When you buy, buy the best, my father taught me. We had solid mahogany chairs and my beautiful upright piano my brother had been keeping. He didn't want to give it up, it was so nice, but it was mine. Paderewski played on it once when he was in Albany in nineteen-oh-nine. I sang all my songs on it."

"She played pretty fancy piano," Francis said. "That's no joke. Why don't you sing us a song, Helen?"

"Oh I guess I will."

"What's your pleasure?" Oscar asked.

"I don't know. 'In the Good Old Summertime,' maybe."

"Right time to sing it," Francis said, "now that we're freezin' our ass out there."

"On second thought," said Helen, "I want to sing one for Francis for buying me that flower. Does your friend know 'He's Me Pal,' or 'My Man'?"

"You hear that, Joe?"

"I hear," said Joe the piano man, and he played a few bars of the chorus of "He's Me Pal" as Helen smiled and stood and walked to the stage with an aplomb and grace befitting her reentry into the world of music, the world she should never have left, oh why ever did you leave it, Helen? She climbed the three steps to the platform, drawn upward by familiar chords that now seemed to her to have always evoked joy, chords not from this one song but from an era of songs, thirty, forty years of songs that celebrated the splendors of love, and loyalty, and friendship, and family, and country, and the natural world. Frivolous Sal was a wild sort of devil, but wasn't she dead on the level too? Mary was a great pal, heaven-sent on Christmas morning, and love lingers on for her. The new-mown hay, the silvery moon, the home fires burning, these were sanctuaries of Helen's spirit, songs whose like she had sung from her earliest days, songs that endured for her as long as the classics she had committed to memory so indelibly in her youth, for they spoke to her, not abstractly of the aesthetic peaks of the art she had once hoped to master, but directly, simply, about the everyday currency of the heart and soul. The pale moon will shine on the twining of our hearts. My heart is stolen, lover dear, so please don't let us part. Oh love, sweet love, oh burning love–the songs told her–you are mine, I am yours, forever and a day. You spoiled the girl I used to be, my hope has gone away. Send me away with a smile, but remember: you're turning off the sunshine of my life.

Love.

A flood tide of pity rose in Helen's breast. Francis, oh sad man, was her last great love, but he wasn't her only one. Helen has had a lifetime of sadnesses with her lovers. Her first true love kept her in his fierce embrace for years, but then he loosened that embrace and let her slide down and down until the hope within her died. Hopeless Helen, that's who she was when she met Francis. And as she stepped up to the microphone on the stage of The Gilded Cage, hearing the piano behind her, Helen was a living explosion of unbearable memory and indomitable joy.

And she wasn't a bit nervous either, thank you, for she was a professional who had never let the public intimidate her when she sang in a church, or at musicales, or at weddings, or at Woolworth's when she sold song sheets, or even on the radio with that audience all over the city every night. Oscar Reo, you're not the only one who sang for Americans over the airwaves. Helen had her day and she isn't a bit nervous.

But she is . . . all right, yes, she is . . . a girl enveloped by private confusion, for she feels the rising of joy and sorrow simultaneously and she cannot say whether one or the other will take her over during the next few moments.

"What's Helen's last name?" Oscar asked.

"Archer," Francis said. "Helen Archer."

"Hey," said Rudy, "how come you told me she didn't have a last name?"

"Because it don't matter what anybody tells you," Francis said. "Now shut up and listen."

"A real old-time trouper now," said Oscar into the bar mike, "will give us a song or two for your pleasure, lovely Miss Helen Archer."

And then Helen, still wearing that black rag of a coat rather than expose the even more tattered blouse and skirt that she wore beneath it, standing on her spindle legs with her tumorous belly butting the metal stand of the microphone and giving her the look of a woman five months pregnant, casting boldly before the audience this image of womanly disaster and fully aware of the dimensions of this image, Helen then tugged stylishly at her beret, adjusting it forward over one eye. She gripped the microphone with a sureness that postponed her disaster, at least until the end of this tune, and sang then "He's Me Pal," a ditty really, short and snappy, sang it with exuberance and wit, with a tilt of the head, a roll of the eyes, a twist of the wrist that suggested the proud virtues. Sure, he's dead tough, she sang, but his love ain't no bluff. Wouldn't he share his last dollar with her? Hey, no millionaire will ever grab Helen. She'd rather have her pal with his fifteen a week. Oh Francis, if you only made just fifteen a week.

If you only.

The applause was full and long and gave Helen strength to begin "My Man," Fanny Brice's wonderful torch, and Helen Morgan's too. Two Helens. Oh Helen, you were on the radio, but where did it take you? What fate was it that kept you from the great heights that were yours by right of talent and education? You were born to be a star, so many said it. But it was others who went on to the heights and you were left behind to grow bitter. How you learned to envy those who rose when you did not, those who never deserved it, had no talent, no training. There was Carla, from high school, who could not even carry a tune but who made a movie with Eddie Cantor, and there was Edna, ever so briefly from Woolworth's, who sang in a Broadway show by Cole Porter because she learned how to wiggle her fanny. But ah, sweetness was Helen's, for Carla went off a cliff in an automobile, and Edna sliced her wrists and bled her life away in her lover's bathtub, and Helen laughed last. Helen is singing on a stage this very minute and just listen to the voice she's left with after all her troubles. Look at those well-dressed people out there hanging on her every note.

Helen closed her eyes and felt tears forcing their way

out and could not say whether she was blissfully happy or fatally sad. At some point it all came together and didn't make much difference anyway, for sad or happy, happy or sad, life didn't change for Helen. Oh, her man, how much she loves you. You can't imagine. Poor girl, all despair now. If she went away she'd come back on her knees. Some day. She's yours. Forevermore.

Oh thunder! Thunderous applause! And the elegant people are standing for Helen, when last did that happen? More, more, more, they yell, and she is crying so desperately now for happiness, or is it for loss, that it makes Francis and Pee Wee cry too. And even though people are calling for more, more, more, Helen steps delicately back down the three platform steps and walks proudly over to Francis with her head in the air and her face impossibly wet, and she kisses him on the cheek so all will know that this is the man she was talking about, in case you didn't notice when we came in together. This is the man.

By god that was great, Francis says. You're better'n anybody.

Helen, says Oscar, that was first-rate. You want a singing job here, you come round tomorrow and I'll see the boss puts you on the payroll. That's a grand voice you've got there, lady. A grand voice.

Oh thank you all, says Helen, thank you all so very kindly. It is so pleasant to be appreciated for your God-given talent and for your excellent training and for your natural presence. Oh I do thank you, and I shall come again to sing for you, you may be sure.

Helen closed her eyes and felt tears beginning to force their way out and could not say whether she was blissfully happy or devastatingly sad. Some odd-looking people were applauding politely, but others were staring at her with sullen faces. If they're sullen, then obviously they didn't think much of your renditions, Helen. Helen steps delicately back down the three steps, comes over to Francis, and keeps her head erect as he leans over and pecks her cheek.

"Mighty nice, old gal," he says.

"Not bad at all," Oscar says. "You'll have to do it again sometime."

Helen closed her eyes and felt tears forcing their way out and knew life didn't change. If she went away she'd come back on her knees. It is so pleasant to be appreciated.

Helen, you are like a blackbird, when the sun comes out for a little while. Helen, you are like a blackbird made sassy by the sun. But what will happen to you when the sun goes down again?

I do thank you.

And I shall come again to sing for you.

Oh sassy blackbird! Oh!

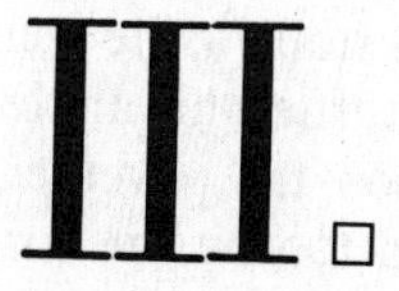

Rudy left them to flop someplace, half-drunk on six beers, and Francis, Helen, and Pee Wee walked back along Green Street to Madison and then west toward the mission. Walk Pee Wee home and go get a room at Palombo's Hotel, get warm, stretch out, rest them bones. Because Francis and Helen had money: five dollars and seventy-five cents. Two of it Helen had left from what Francis gave her last night; plus three-seventy-five out of his cemetery wages, for he spent little in The Gilded Cage, Oscar buying twice as many drinks as he took money for.

The city had grown quiet at midnight and the moon was as white as early snow. A few cars moved slowly on Pearl Street but otherwise the streets were silent. Francis turned up his suitcoat collar and shoved his hands into his pants pockets. Alongside the mission the moon illuminated Sandra, who sat where they had left her. They stopped to look at her condition. Francis squatted and shook her.

"You sobered up yet, lady?"

Sandra answered him with an enveloping silence. Francis pushed the cowl off her face and in the vivid moonlight saw the toothmarks on her nose and cheek and chin. He shook his head to clear the vision, then saw that one of her fingers and the flesh between forefinger and thumb on her left hand had been chewed.

"The dogs got her."

He looked across the street and saw a red-eyed mongrel waiting in the half-lit corner of an alley and he charged after it, picking up a stone as he went. The cur fled down the alley as Francis turned his ankle on a raised sidewalk brick and sprawled on the pavement. He picked himself up, he now bloodied too by the cur, and sucked the dirt out of the cuts.

As he crossed the street, goblins came up from Broadway, ragged and masked, and danced around Helen. Pee Wee, bending over Sandra, straightened up as the goblin dance gained in ferocity.

"Jam and jelly, big fat belly," the goblins yelled at Helen. And when she drew herself inward they only intensified the chant.

"Hey you kids," Francis yelled. "Let her alone."

But they danced on and a skull goblin poked Helen in the stomach with a stick. As she swung at the skull with her hand, another goblin grabbed her purse and then all scattered.

"Little bastards, devils," Helen cried, running after them. And Francis and Pee Wee too joined the chase, pounding through the night, no longer sure which one wore the skull mask. The goblins ran down alleys, around corners, and fled beyond capture.

Francis turned back to Helen, who was far behind him. She was weeping, gasping, doubled over in a spasm of loss.

"Sonsabitches," Francis said.

"Oh the money," Helen said, "the money."

"They hurt you with that stick?"

"I don't think so."

"That money ain't nothin'. Get more tomorrow."

"It was."

"Was what?"

"There was fifteen dollars in there besides the other."

"Fifteen? Where'd you get fifteen dollars?"

"Your son Billy gave it to me. The night he found us at Spanish George's. You were passed out and he gave us forty-five dollars, all the cash he had. I gave you thirty and kept the fifteen."

"I went through that pocketbook. I didn't see it."

"I pinned it inside the lining so you wouldn't drink it up. I wanted our suitcase back. I wanted our room for a week so I could rest."

"Goddamn it, woman, now we ain't got a penny. You and your sneaky goddamn ways."

Pee Wee came back from the chase empty-handed.

"Some tough kids around here," he said. "You okay, Helen?"

"Fine. just fine."

"You're not hurt?"

"Not anyplace you could see."

"Sandra," Pee Wee said. "She's dead."

"She's more than that," Francis said. "She's partly chewed away."

"We'll take her inside so they don't eat no more of her," Pee Wee said. "I'll call the police."

"You think it's all right to bring her inside?" Francis asked. "She's still got all that poison in her system."

Pee Wee said nothing and opened the mission door. Francis picked Sandra up from the dust and carried her inside. He put her down on an old church bench against the wall and covered her face with the scratchy blanket that had become her final gift from the world.

"If I had my rosary I'd say it for her," Helen said, sitting on a chair beside the bench and looking at Sandra's corpse. "But it was in my purse. I've carried that rosary for twenty years."

"I'll check the vacant lots and the garbage cans in the mornin'," Francis said. "It'll turn up."

"I'll bet Sandra prayed to die," Helen said.

"Hey," said Francis.

"I would if I was her. Her life wasn't human anymore."

Helen looked at the clock: twelve-ten. Pee Wee was calling the police.

"Today's a holy day of obligation," she said. "It's All Saints' Day."

"Yup," said Francis.

"I want to go to church in the morning."

"All right, go to church."

"I will. I want to hear mass."

"Hear it. That's tomorrow. What are we gonna do tonight? Where the hell am I gonna put you?"

"You could stay here," Pee Wee said. "All the beds are full but you can sleep down here on a bench."

"No," Helen said. "I'd rather not do that. We can go up to Jack's. He told me I could come back if I wanted."

"Jack said that?" Francis asked.

"Those were his words."

"Then let's shag ass. Jack's all right. Clara's a crazy bitch but I like Jack. Always did. You sure he said that?"

" 'Come back anytime,' he said as I was going out the door."

"All right. Then we'll move along, old buddy," Francis said to Pee Wee. "You'll figure it out with Sandra?"

"I'll do the rest," Pee Wee said.

"You know her last name?"

"No. Never heard it."

"Don't make much difference now."

"Never did," Pee Wee said.

□ □ □

Francis and Helen walked up Pearl Street toward State, the absolute center of the city's life for two centuries. One trolley car climbed State Street's violent incline and another came toward them, rocking south on Pearl. A man stepped out of the Waldorf Restaurant and covered his throat with his coat collar, shivered once, and walked on. The cold had numbed Francis's fingertips, frost was blooming on the roofs of parked cars, and the nightwalkers exhaled dancing plumes of vapor. From a manhole in the middle of State Street steam rose and vanished. Francis imagined the subterranean element at the source of this: a huge human head with pipes screwed into its ears, steam rising from a festering skull wound.

Aldo Campione, walking on the opposite side of North Pearl from Francis and Helen, raised his right hand in the same ambiguous gesture Francis had witnessed at the bar. As Francis speculated on the meaning, the man who had been sitting with Aldo stepped out of the shadows into a streetlight's glow, and Aldo's gesture then became clear: it introduced Francis to Dick Doolan, the bum who tried to cut off Francis's feet with a meat cleaver.

"I went to the kid's grave today," Francis said.

"What kid?"

"Gerald."

"Oh, you did?" she said. "Then that was the first time, wasn't it? It must've been."

"Right."

"You're thinking about him these days. You mentioned him last week."

"I never stop thinkin' about him."

"What's gotten into you?"

Francis saw the street that lay before him: Pearl Street, the central vessel of this city, city once his, city lost. The commerce along with its walls jarred him: so much new, stores gone out of business he never even heard of. Some things remained: Whitney's, Myers', the old First Church, which rose over Clinton Square, the Pruyn Library. As he walked, the cobblestones turned to granite, houses became stores, life aged, died, renewed itself, and a vision of what had been and what might have been intersected in an eye that could not really remember one or interpret the other. What would you give never to have left, Francis?

"I said, what's got into you?"

"Nothin's got into me. I'm just thinkin' about a bunch of stuff. This old street. I used to own this street, once upon a time."

"You should've sold it when you had the chance."

"Money. I ain't talkin' about money."

"I didn't think you were. That was a funny."

"Wasn't much funny. I said I saw Gerald's grave. I talked to him."

"Talked? How did you talk?"

"Stood and talked to the damn grass. Maybe I'm gettin' nutsy as Rudy. He can't hold his pants up, they fall over his shoes."

"You're not nutsy, Francis. It's because you're here. We shouldn't be here. We should go someplace else."

"Right. That's where we oughta go. Else."

"Don't drink any more tonight."

"Listen here. Don't you nag my ass."

"I want you straight, please. I want you straight."

"I'm the straightest thing you'll see all week. I am so straight. I'm the straightest thing you'll sweek. The thing that happened on the other side of the street. The thing that happened was Billy told me stuff about Annie. I never told you that. Billy told me stuff about Annie, how she never told I dropped him."

"Never told who, the police?"

"Never nobody. Never a damn soul. Not Billy, not Peg, not her brother, not her sisters. Ain't that the somethin'est thing you ever heard? I can't see a woman goin' through that stuff and not tellin' nobody about it."

"You've got a lot to say about those people."

"Not much to say."

"Maybe you ought to go see them."

"No, that wouldn't do no good."

"You'd get it out of your system."

"What out of my system?"

"Whatever it is that's in there."

"Never mind about my system. How come you wouldn't stay at the mission when you got an invite?"

"I don't want their charity."

"You ate their soup."

"I did not. All I had was coffee. Anyway, I don't like Chester. He doesn't like Catholics."

"Catholics don't like Methodists. What the hell, that's even. And I don't see any Catholic missions down here. I ain't had any Catholic soup lately."

"I won't do it and that's that."

"So freeze your ass someplace. Your flower's froze already."

"Let it freeze."

"You sang a song at least."

"Yes I did. I sang while Sandra was dying."

"She'da died no matter. Her time was up."

"No, I don't believe that. That's fatalism. I believe we die when we can't stand it anymore. I believe we stand as much as we can and then we die when we can, and Sandra decided she could die."

"I don't fight that. Die when you can. That's as good a sayin' as there is."

"I'm glad we agree on something," Helen said.

"We get along all right. You ain't a bad sort."

"You're all right too."

"We're both all right," Francis said, "and we ain't got a damn penny and noplace to flop. We on the bum. Let's get the hell up to Jack's before he puts the lights out on us."

Helen slipped her arm inside Francis's. Across the street Aldo Campione and Dick Doolan, who in the latter years of his life was known as Rowdy Dick, kept silent pace.

□ □ □

Helen pulled her arm away from Francis and tightened her collar around her neck, then hugged herself and buried her hands in her armpits.

"I'm chilled to my bones," she said.

"It's chilly, all right."

"I mean a real chill, a deep chill."

Francis put his arm around her and walked her up the steps of Jack's house. It stood on the east side of Ten Broeck Street, a three-block street in Arbor Hill named for a Revolutionary War hero and noted in the 1870s and 1880s as the place where a dozen of the city's arriviste lumber barons lived, all in a row, in competitive luxury. For their homes the barons built handsome brownstones, most of them now cut into apartments like Jack's, or into furnished rooms.

The downstairs door to Jack's opened without a key. Helen and Francis climbed the broad walnut staircase, still vaguely elegant despite the threadbare carpet, and Francis knocked. Jack opened the door and looked out with the expression of an ominous crustacean. With one hand he held the door ajar, with the other he gripped the jamb.

"Hey Jack," Francis said, "we come to see ya. How's chances for a bum gettin' a drink?"

Jack opened the door wider to look beyond Francis and when he saw Helen he let his arm fall and backed into the apartment. Kate Smith came at them, piped out of a small phonograph through the speaker of the radio. The Carolina moon was shining on somebody waiting for Kate. Beside the phonograph sat Clara, balancing herself on a chamber pot, propped on all sides with purple throw pillows, giving her the look of being astride a great animal. A red bedspread covered her legs, but it had fallen away at one side, revealing the outside of her naked left thigh, visible to the buttocks. A bottle of white fluid sat on the table by the phonograph, and on a smaller table on her other side a swinging rack cradled a gallon of muscatel, tiltable for pouring. Helen walked over to Clara and stood by her.

"Golly it's cold for this time of year, and they're calling for snow. Just feel my hands."

"This happens to be my home," Clara said hoarsely, "and I ain't about to feel your hands, or your head either. I don't see any snow."

"Have a drink," Jack said to Francis.

"Sure," Francis said. "I had a bowl of soup about six o'clock but it went right through me. I'm gonna have to eat somethin' soon."

"I don't care whether you eat or not," Jack said.

Jack went to the kitchen and Francis asked Clara: "You feelin' better?"

"No."

"She's got the runs," Helen said.

"I'll tell people what I got," Clara said.

"She lost her husband this week," Jack said, returning with two empty tumblers. He tilted the jug and half-filled both.

"How'd you find out?" Helen said.

"I saw it in the paper today," Clara said.

"I took her to the funeral this morning," Jack said. "We got a cab and went to the funeral home. They didn't even call her."

"He didn't look any different than when I married him."

"No kiddin'," Francis said.

"Outside of his hair was snow-white, that's all."

"Her kids were there," Jack said.

"The snots," Clara said.

"Sometimes I wonder what if I run off or dropped dead," Francis said. "Helen'd probably go crazy."

"Why if you dropped dead she'd bury you before you started stinkin', " Jack said. "That's all'd happen."

"What a heart you have," Francis said.

"You gotta bury your dead," Jack said.

"That's a rule of the Catholic church," said Helen.

"I'm not talkin' about the Catholic church," Francis said.

"Anyway, now she's a single girl," Jack said, "I'm gonna find out what Clara's gonna do."

"I'm gonna go right on livin' normal," Clara said.

"Normal is somethin'," Francis said. "What the hell is normal anyway, is what I'd like to know. Normal is cold. Goddamn it's cold tonight. My fingers. I rubbed myself to see if I was livin'. You know, I wanna ask you one question."

"No," Clara said.

"You said no. Whataya mean no?"

"What's he gonna ask?" Jack said. "Find out what he's gonna ask."

Clara waited.

"How's everythin' been goin'?" Francis asked.

□ □ □

Clara lifted the bottle of white fluid from the phonograph table, where the Kate Smith record was scratching in its final groove, and drank. She shook her head as it went down, and the greasy, uncombed stringlets of her hair leaped like whips. Her eyes hung low in their sockets, a pair of collapsing moons. She recapped the bottle and then swigged her muscatel to drive out the taste. She dragged on her cigarette, then coughed and spat venomously into a wadded handkerchief she held in her fist.

"Things ain't been goin' too good for Clara," Jack said, turning off the phonograph.

"I'm still trottin'," Clara said.

"Well you look pretty good for a sick lady," Francis said. "Look as good as usual to me."

Clara smiled over the rim of her wineglass at Francis.

"Nobody," said Helen, "asked how things are going for me, but I'll tell you. They're going just wonderful. Just wonderful."

"She's drunker than hell," Francis said.

"Oh I'm loaded to the gills," Helen said, giggling. "I can hardly walk."

"You ain't drunk even a nickel's worth," Jack said. "Franny's the drunk one. You're hopeless, right, Franny?"

"Helen'll never amount to nothin' if she stays with me," Francis said.

"I always thought you were an intelligent man," Jack said, and he swallowed half his wine, "but you can't be, you can't be."

"You could be mistaken," Helen said.

"Keep out of it," Francis told her, and he hooked a thumb at her, facing Jack. "There's enough right there to put you in the loony bin, just worryin' about where she's gonna live, where she's gonna stay."

"I think you could be a charmin' man," Jack said, "if you'd only get straight. You could have twenty dollars in your pocket at all times, make fifty, seventy-five a week, have a beautiful apartment with everything you want in it, all you want to drink, once you get straight."

"I worked today up at the cemetery," Francis said.

"Steady work?" asked Jack.

"Just today. Tomorrow I gotta see a fella needs some liftin' done. The old back's still tough enough."

"You keep workin' you'll have fifty in your pocket."

"I had fifty, I'd spend it on her," Francis said. "Or buy a pair of shoes. Other pair wore out and Harry over at the old clothes joint give 'em to me for a quarter. He seen me half barefoot and says, Francis you can't go around like that, and he give me these. But they don't fit right and I only got one of 'em laced. Twine there in the other one. I got a shoestring in my pocket but ain't put it in yet."

"You mean you got the shoelace and you didn't put it in the shoe?" Clara asked.

"I got it in my pocket," Francis said.

"Then put it in the shoe."

"I think it's in this pocket here. You know where it is, Helen?"

"Don't ask me."

"Look and see," Clara said.

"She wants me to put a shoestring in my shoe," Francis said.

"Right," said Clara.

Francis stopped fumbling in his pocket and let his hands fall away.

"I'm renegin'," he said.

"You're what?" Clara asked.

"I'm renegin' and I don't like to do that."

□ □ □

Francis put down his wine, walked to the bathroom, and sat on the toilet, cover down, trying to understand why he'd lied about a shoestring. He smelled the odor that came up from his fetid crotch and stood up then and dropped his trousers. He stepped out of them, then pulled off his shorts and threw them in the sink. He lifted the toilet cover and sat on the seat, and with Jack's soap and handfuls of water from the bowl, he washed his genitals and buttocks, and all their encrusted orifices, crevices, and secret folds. He rinsed himself, relathered, and rinsed again. He dried himself with one of Jack's towels, picked his shorts out of the sink, and mopped the floor with them where he had splashed water. Then he filled the sink with hot water and soaked the shorts. He soaped them and they separated into two pieces in his hands. He let the water out of the sink, wrung the shorts, and put them in his coat pocket. He opened the door a crack and called out: "Hey, Jack," and when Jack came, Francis hid his nakedness with a towel.

"Jack, old buddy, you got an old pair of shorts? Any old pair. Mine just ripped all to hell."

"I'll go look."

"Could I borry the use of your razor?"

"Help yourself."

Jack came back with the shorts and Francis put them on. Then, as Francis soaped his beard, Aldo Campione and Rowdy Dick Doolan entered the bathroom. Rowdy Dick, dapper in a three-piece blue-serge suit and a pearl-gray cap, sat on the toilet, cover down. Aldo made himself comfortable on the rim of the tub, his gardenia unintimidated by the chill of the evening. Jack's razor wouldn't cut Francis's three-day beard, and so he rinsed off the lather, soaked his face again in hot water, and relathered. While

Francis rubbed the soap deeply into his beard, Rowdy Dick studied him but could remember nothing of Francis's face. This was to be expected, for when last seen, it was night in Chicago, under a bridge not far from the railyards, and five men were sharing the wealth in 1930, a lean year. On the wall of the abutment above the five, as one of them had pointed out, a former resident of the space had inscribed a poem:

> Poor little lamb,
> He wakes up in the morning,
> His fleece all cold.
> He knows what's coming.
> Say, little lamb,
> We'll go on the bummer this summer.
> We'll sit in the shade
> And drink lemonade,
> The world'll be on the hummer.

Rowdy Dick remembered this poem as well as he remembered the laughter of his sister, Mary, who was striped dead, sleigh riding, under the rails of a horse-drawn sleigh; as clearly as he remembered the plaintive, dying frown of his brother, Ted, who perished from a congenital hole in the heart. They had been three until then, living with an uncle because their parents had died, one by one, and left them alone. And then there was Dick, truly alone, who grew up tough, worked the docks, and then found an easier home in the Tenderloin, breaking the faces of nasty drunks, oily pickpockets, and fat titty-pinchers. But that didn't last either. Nothing lasted for Rowdy Dick, and he went on the bum and wound up under the bridge with Francis Phelan and three other now-faceless men. What he did remember of Francis was his hand, which now held a razor that stroked the soapy cheek.

What Francis remembered was talking about baseball that famous night. He'd begun by reliving indelible memories of his childhood as a way of explaining, at leisurely pace since none of them had anyplace to go, the generation of his drive to become a third baseman. He had been, he was saying, a boy playing among men, witnessing their talents, their peculiarities, their capacity to dive for a grounder, smash a line drive, catch a fly—all with the very ease of breath itself. They had played in the Van Woert Street polo grounds (Mulvaney's goat pasture) and there were a heroic dozen and a half of them who came two or three evenings a week, some weeks, after work to practice; men in their late twenties and early thirties, reconstituting the game that had enraptured them in their teens. There was Andy Heffern, tall, thin, saturnine, the lunger who would die at Saranac, who could pitch but never run, and who played with a long-fingered glove that had no padding whatever in the pocket, only a wisp of leather that stood between the speed of the ball and Andy's most durable palm. There was Windy Evans, who played outfield in his cap, spikes, and jock, and who caught the ball behind his back, long flies he would outrun by twenty minutes, and then plop would go that dilatory fly ball into the peach basket of his glove; and Windy would leap and beam and tell the world: There's only a few of us left! And Red Cooley, the shortstop who was the pepper of Francis's ancient imagination, and who never stopped the chatter, who leaped at every ground ball as if it were the brass ring to heaven, and who, with his short-fingered glove, wanted for nothing to be judged the world's greatest living ball player, if only it hadn't been for the homegrown deference that kept him a prisoner of Arbor Hill for the rest of his limited life.

These reminiscences by Francis evoked from Rowdy Dick an envy that surpassed reason. Why should any man be so gifted not only with so much pleasurable history but also with a gift of gab that could mesmerize a quintet of bums around a fire under a bridge? Why were there no words that would unlock what lay festering in the heart of Rowdy Dick Doolan, who needed so desperately to express what he could never even know needed expression?

Well, the grand question went unanswered, and the magic words went undiscovered. For Rowdy Dick took vengeful focus on the shoes of the voluble Francis, which were both the most desirable and, except for the burning sticks and boards in the fire, the most visible objects under that Chicago bridge. And Rowdy Dick reached inside his shirt, where he kept the small meat cleaver he had carried ever since Colorado, and slid it out of its carrying case, which he had fashioned from cardboard, oilcloth, and string; and he told Francis then: I'm gonna cut your goddamn feet off; explaining this at first and instant lunge, but explaining, even then, rather too soon for achievement, for the reflexes of Francis were not so rubbery then as they might be now in Jack's bathroom. They were full of fiber and acid and cannonade; and before Rowdy Dick, who had drunk too much of the homemade hooch he had bought, unquestionably too cheaply for sanity, earlier in the day, could make restitution for his impetuosity, Francis deflected the cleaver, which was aimed no longer at his feet but at his head, losing in the process two thirds of a right index finger and an estimated one eighth of an inch of flesh from the approximate center of his nose. He bled then in a wild careen, and with diminished hand knocking the cleaver from Rowdy Dick's grip, he took hold of that same Rowdy Dick by pantleg and armpit and swung him, oh wrathful lambs, against the abutment where the poem was inscribed, swung him as a battering ram might be swung, and cracked Rowdy Dick's skull from left parietal to the squamous area of the occipital, rendering him bloody, insensible, leaking, and instantly dead.

What Francis recalled of this unmanageable situation was the compulsion to flight, the most familiar notion, after the desire not to aspire, that he had ever entertained. And after searching, as swiftly as he knew how, for his lost digital joints, and after concluding that they had flown too deeply into the dust and the weeds ever to be retrieved again by any hand of any man, and after pausing also, ever so briefly, for a reconnoitering, not of what might be recoverable of the nose but of what might be visually memorable because of its separation into parts, Francis began to run, and in so doing, reconstituted a condition that was as pleasurable to his being as it was natural: the running of bases after the crack of the bat, the running from accusation, the running from the calumny of men and women, the running from family, from bondage, from destitution of spirit through ritualistic straightenings, the running, finally, in a quest for pure flight as a fulfilling mannerism of the spirit.

He found his way to a freight yard, found there an empty boxcar with open door, and so entered into yet another departure from completion: the true and total story of his life thus far. It was South Bend before he got to a hospital, where the intern asked him: Where's the finger? And Francis said: In the weeds. And how about the nose? Where's that piece of the nose? If you'd only brought me that piece of the nose, we might be able to put it back together and you wouldn't even know it was gone.

All things had ceased to bleed by then, and so Francis was free once again from those deadly forces that so frequently sought to sever the line of his life.

He had stanched the flow of his wound.

He had stood staunchly irresolute in the face of capricious and adverse fate.

He had, oh wondrous man, stanched death its very self.

□ □ □

Francis dried his face with the towel, buttoned up his shirt, and put on his coat and trousers. He nodded an apology to Rowdy Dick for having taken his life and included in the nod the hope that Dick would understand it hadn't been intentional. Rowdy Dick smiled and doffed his cap, creating an eruption of brilliance around his dome. Francis could see the line of Dick's cranial fracture running through his hair like a gleaming river, and Francis understood that Rowdy Dick was in heaven, or so close to it that he was taking on the properties of an angel of the Lord. Dick put his cap on again and even the cap exuded a glow, like the sun striving to break through a pale, gray cloud. "Yes," said Francis, "I'm sorry I broke your head so bad, but I hope you remember I had my reasons," and he held up to Rowdy Dick his truncated finger. "You know, you can't be a priest when you got a finger missin'. Can't say mass with a hand like this. Can't throw a baseball either." He rubbed the bump in his nose with the stump of a finger. "Kind of a bump there, but what the hell. Doc put a big bandage on it, and it got itchy, so I ripped it off. Went back when it got infected, and the doc says, You shouldn'ta took off that bandage, because now I got to scrape it out and you'll have an even bigger bump there. I'da had a bump anyway. What the hell, little bump like that don't look too bad, does it? I ain't complainin'. I don't hold no grudges more'n five years."

"You all right in there, Francis?" Helen called. "Who are you talking to?"

Francis waved to Rowdy Dick, understanding that some debts of violence had been settled, but he remained full of the awareness of rampant martyrdom surrounding him: martyrs to wrath, to booze, to failure, to loss, to hostile weather. Aldo Campione gestured at Francis, suggesting that while there may be some inconsistency about it, prayers were occasionally answerable, a revelation that did very little to improve Francis's state of mind, for there had never been a time since childhood when he knew what to pray for.

"Hey bum," he said to Jack when he stepped out of the bathroom, "how about a bum gettin' a drink?"

"He ain't no bum," Clara said.

"Goddamn it, I know he ain't," Francis said. "He's a hell of a man. A workin' man."

"How come you shaved?" Helen asked.

"Gettin' itchy. Four days and them whiskers grow back inside again."

"It sure improves how you look," Clara said.

"That's the truth," said Jack.

"I knew Francis was handsome," Clara said, "but this is the first time I ever saw you clean shaved."

"I was thinkin' about how many old bums I know died in the weeds. Wake up covered with snow and some of 'em layin' there dead as hell, froze stiff. Some get up and walk away from it. I did myself. But them others are gone for good. You ever know a guy named Rowdy Dick Doolan in your travels?"

"Never did," Jack said.

"There was another guy, Pocono Pete, he died in Denver, froze like a brick. And Poocher Felton, he bought it in Detroit, pissed his pants and froze tight to the sidewalk. And a crazy bird they called Ward Six, no other name. They found him with a red icicle growin' out of his nose. All them old guys, never had nothin', never knew nothin', stupid, thievin', crazy. Foxy Phil Tooker, a skinny little runt, he froze all scrunched up, knees under his chin. 'Stead of straightenin' him out, they buried him in half a coffin. Lorda mercy, them geezers. I bet they all of 'em, dyin' like that, I bet they all wind up in heaven, if they ever got such a place."

"I believe when you're dead you go in the ground and

that's the end of it," Jack said. "Heaven never made no sensicality to me whatsoever."

"You wouldn't get in anyhow," Helen said. "They've got your reservations someplace else."

"Then I'm with him," Clara said. "Who'd want to be in heaven with all them nuns? God what a bore."

Francis knew Clara less than three weeks, but he could see the curve of her life: sexy kid likes the rewards, goes pro, gets restless, marries and makes kids, chucks that, pro again, sickens, but really sick, gettin' old, gettin' ugly, locks onto Jack, turns monster. But she's got most of her teeth, not bad; and that hair: you get her to a beauty shop and give her a marcel, it'd be all right; put her in new duds, high heels and silk stockin's; and hey, look at them titties, and that leg: the skin's clear on it.

Clara saw Francis studying her and gave him a wink. "I knew a fella once, looked a lot like you. I had the hots for him."

"I'll bet you did," Helen said.

"He loved what I gave him."

"Clara never lacked for boyfriends," Jack said. "I'm a lucky man. But she's pretty sick. That's why you can't stay. She eats a lot of toast."

"Oh I could make some toast," Helen said, standing up from her chair. "Would you like that?"

"If I feel like eatin' I'll make my own toast," Clara said. "And I'm gettin' ready to go to bed. Make sure you lock the door when you go out."

Jack grabbed Francis by the arm and pulled him toward the kitchen, but not before Francis readjusted his vision of Clara sitting in the middle of her shit machine, sending up a silent reek from her ruined guts and their sewerage.

□ □ □

When Jack and Francis came back into the living room Francis was smoking one of Jack's cigarettes. He dropped it as he reached for the wine, and Helen groaned.

"Everything fallin' on the floor," Francis said. "I don't blame you for throwin' these bums out if they can't behave respectable."

"It's gettin' late for me," Jack said. "I used to get by on two, three hours' sleep, but no more."

"I ain't stayed here in how long now?" Francis asked. "Two weeks, ain't it?"

"Oh come on, Francis," Clara said. "You were here not four days ago. And Helen last night. And last Sunday you were here."

"Sunday we left," Helen said.

"I flopped here two nights, wasn't it?" Francis said.

"Six," Jack said. "Like a week."

"I beg to differ with you," Helen said.

"It was over a week," Jack said.

"I know different," said Helen.

"From Monday to Sunday."

"Oh no."

"It's a little mixed up," Francis said.

"He's got a lot of things mixed up," Helen said. "I hope you don't get your food mixed up like that down at the diner."

"No," Jack said.

"You know, you're very insultin'," Francis said to Helen.

"It was a week," Jack said.

"You're a liar," Helen said.

"Don't call me a liar because I know so."

"Haven't you got any brains at all?" Francis said. "You supposed to be a college woman, you supposed to be this and that."

"I am a college woman."

"You know what I thought," Jack said, "was for you to stay here, Franny, till you get work, till you pick up a little bankroll. You don't have to give me nothin'."

"Shake hands on it," Helen said.

"I don't know about the proposition now," Jack said.

"Because I'm a bum," Francis said.

"No, I wouldn't put it that way." Jack poured more wine for Francis.

"I knew he didn't mean it," Helen said.

"I'm gonna tell you," Francis said. "I always thought a lot of Clara."

"You're drunk, Francis," Helen screamed, standing up again. "Stay drunk for the rest of your life. I'm leaving you, Francis. You're crazy. All you want is to guzzle wine. You're insane!"

"What'd I say?" Francis asked. "I said I liked Clara."

"Nothin' wrong about that," Jack said.

"I don't mind about that," Helen said, sitting down.

"I don't know what to do with that woman," Francis said.

"Do you even know if you're staying here tonight?" Helen asked.

"No, he's not," Jack said. "Take him with you when you go."

"We're going," Helen said.

"Clara's too sick, Francis," said Jack.

Francis sipped his wine, put it on the table, and struck a tap dancer's pose.

"How you like these new duds of mine, Clara? You didn't tell me how swell I look, all dressed up."

"You look sharp," Clara said.

"You can't keep up with Francis."

"Don't waste your time, Francis," Helen said.

"You're getting very hostile, you know that? Listen, you want to sleep with me in the weeds tonight?"

"I never slept in the weeds," Helen said.

"Never?" asked Clara.

"No, never," said Helen.

"Oh yes," Francis said. "She slept in the coaches with me, and the fields."

"Never. You made that up, Francis."

"We been through the valley together," Francis said.

"Maybe you have," said Helen. "I've never gone that far down and I don't intend to go that far down."

"It ain't far to go. She slept in Finny's car night before last."

"That's the last time. If it came to that, I'd get in touch with my people."

"You really ought to get in touch with them, dearie," said Clara.

"My people are very high class. My brother is a very well-to-do lawyer but I don't like to ask him for anything."

"Sometimes you have to," Jack said. "You oughta move in with him."

"Then Francis'd be out. No, I've got Francis. We'd get married tomorrow if only he could get a divorce, wouldn't we, Fran."

"That's right, honey."

"We battle sometimes, but only when he drinks. Then he goes haywire."

"You oughta get straight, Franny," Jack said. "You could have twenty bucks in your pocket at all times. They need men like you. You could have everything you want. A new Victrola like that one right there. That's a honey."

"I had all that shit," Francis said.

"It's late," Clara said.

"Yeah, people," said Jack. "Gotta hit the hay."

"Fix me a sandwich, will ya?" Francis asked. "To take out."

"No," Clara said.

Helen rose, screaming, and started for Clara. "You forget when you were hungry."

"Sit down and shut up," Francis said.

"I won't shut up. I remember when she came to my place years ago, begging for food. I know her a long time. I'm honest in what I know."

"I never begged," said Clara.

"He only asked for a sandwich," said Helen.

"I'm gonna give him a sandwich," Jack said.

"Jack don't want you to come back again," Francis said to Helen.

"I don't want to ever come back again," Helen said.

"He asked for a sandwich," Jack said, "I'll give him a sandwich."

"I knew you would," Francis told him.

"Damn right I'll give you a sandwich."

"Damn right," Francis said, "and I knew it."

"I don't want to be bothered," Clara said.

"Sharp cheese. You like sharp cheese?"

"My favorite," Francis said.

Jack went to the kitchen and came back into a silent room with a sandwich wrapped in waxed paper. Francis took it and put it in his coat. Helen stood in the doorway.

"Good night, pal," Francis said to Jack.

"Best of luck," Jack said.

"See you around," Francis said to Clara.

"Toodle-oo," said Clara.

□ □ □

On the street, Francis felt the urge to run. Ten Broeck Street, in the direction they were walking, inclined downward toward Clinton Avenue, and he felt the gravitational fall driving him into a trot that would leave her behind to solve her own needs. The night seemed colder than before, and clearer too, the moon higher in its sterile solitude. North Pearl Street was deserted, no cars, no people at this hour, one-forty-five by the great clock on the First

Church. They had walked three blocks without speaking and now they were heading back toward where they had begun, toward the South End, the mission, the weeds.

"Where the hell you gonna sleep now?" Francis asked.

"I can't be sure, but I wouldn't stay there if they gave me silk sheets and mink pillows. I remember her when she was whoring and always broke. Now she's so high and mighty. I had to speak my piece."

"You didn't accomplish anything."

"Did Jack really say that they don't want me anymore?"

"Right. But they asked me to stay. Clara thinks you're a temptation to Jack. The way I figure, if I give her some attention she won't worry about you, but you're so goddamn boisterous. Here. Have a piece of sandwich."

"It'd choke me."

"It won't choke you. You'll be glad for it."

"I'm not a phony."

"I'm not a phony either."

"You're not, eh?"

"You know what I'll do?" He grabbed her collar and her throat and screamed into her eyes. "I'll knock you right across that goddamn street! You don't bullshit me one time. Be a goddamn woman! That's the reason you can't flop with nobody. I can go up there right now and sleep. Jack said I could stay."

"He did not."

"He certainly did. But they don't want you. I asked for a sandwich. Did I get it?"

"You're really stupendous and colossal."

"Listen"–and he still held her by the collar–"you squint your eyes at me and I'll knock you over that goddamn automobile. You been a pain in the ass to me for nine years. They don't want you because you're a pain in the ass."

Headlights moved north on Pearl Street, coming toward

them, and Francis let go of her. She did not move, but stared at him.

"You got some goddamn eyes, you know?" He was screaming. "I'll black 'em for you. You're a horse's ass! You know what I'll do? I'll rip that fuckin' coat off and put you in rags."

She did not move her body or her eyes.

"I'm gonna eat this sandwich. Whole hunk of cheese."

"I don't want it."

"By god I do. I'll be hungry tomorrow. It won't choke me. I'm thankful for everything."

"You're a perfect saint."

"Listen. Straighten up or I'm gonna kill you."

"I won't eat it. It's rat food."

"I'm gonna kill you!" Francis screamed. "Goddamn it, you hear what I said? Don't drive me insane. Be a goddamn woman and go the fuck to bed somewhere."

They walked, not quite together, toward Madison Avenue, south again on South Pearl, retracing their steps. Francis brushed Helen's arm and she moved away from him.

"You gonna stay at the mission with Pee Wee?"

"No."

"Then you gonna stay with me?"

"I'm going to call my brother."

"Good. Call him. Call him a couple of times."

"I'll have him meet me someplace."

"Where you gonna get the nickel to make the call?"

"That's my business. God, Francis, you were all right till you started on the wine. Wine, wine, wine."

"I'll get some cardboard. We'll go to that old building."

"The police keep raiding that place. I don't want to go to jail. I don't know why you didn't stay with Jack and Clara since you were so welcome."

"You're a woman for abuse."

They walked east on Madison, past the mission. Helen

did not look in. When they reached Green Street she stopped.

"I'm going down below," she said.

"Who you kiddin'?" Francis said. "You got noplace to go. You'll be knocked on the head."

"That wouldn't be the worst ever happened to me."

"We got to find something. Can't leave a dog out like this."

"Shows you what kind of people they are up there."

"Stay with me."

"No, Francis. You're crazy."

He grabbed the hair at the back of her head, then held her whole head in both hands.

"You're gonna hit me," she said.

"I won't hit ya, babe. I love ya some. Are ya awful cold?"

"I don't think I've been warm once in two days."

Francis let go of her and took off his suitcoat and put it around her shoulders.

"No, it's too cold for you to do that," she said. "I've got this coat. You can't be in just a shirt."

"What the hell's the difference. Coat ain't no protection."

She handed him back the coat. "I'm going," she said.

"Don't walk away from me," Francis said. "You'll be lost in the world."

But she walked away. And Francis leaned against the light pole on the corner, lit the cigarette Jack had given him, fingered the dollar bill Jack had slipped him in the kitchen, ate what was left of the cheese sandwich, and then threw his old undershorts down the sewer.

□ □ □

Helen walked down Green Street to a vacant lot, where she saw a fire in an oil drum. From across the street she could see five coloreds around the fire, men and women.

On an old sofa in the weeds just beyond the drum, she saw a white woman lying underneath a colored man. She walked back to where Francis waited.

"I couldn't stay outside tonight," she said. "I'd die."

Francis nodded and they walked to Finny's car, a 1930 black Oldsmobile, dead and wheelless in an alley off John Street. Two men were asleep in it, Finny in the front passenger seat.

"I don't know that man in back," Helen said.

"Yeah you do," said Francis. "That's Little Red from the mission. He won't bother you. If he does I'll pull out his tongue."

"I don't want to get in there, Francis."

"It's warm, anyhow. Cold in them weeds, honey, awful cold. You walk the streets alone, they'll pinch you quicker'n hell."

"You get in the back."

"No. No room in there for the likes of me. Legs're too long."

"Where will you go?"

"I'll find me some of them tall weeds, get outa the wind."

"Are you coming back?"

"Sure, I'll be back. You get a good sleep and I'll see you here or up at the mission in the ayem."

"I don't want to stay here."

"You got to, babe. It's what there is."

Francis opened the passenger door and shook Finny.

"Hey bum. Move over. You got a visitor."

Finny opened his eyes, heavy with wine. Little Red was snoring.

"Who the hell are you?" Finny said.

"It's Francis. Move over and let Helen in."

"Francis." Finny raised his head.

"I'll get you a jug tomorrow for this, old buddy," Francis said. "She's gotta get in outa this weather."

"Yeah," said Finny.

"Never mind yeah, just move your ass over and let her sit. She can't sleep behind that wheel, condition her stomach's in."

"Unnngghh," said Finny, and he slid behind the wheel.

Helen sat on the front seat, dangling her legs out of the car. Francis stroked her cheek with three fingertips and then let his hand fall. She lifted her legs inside.

"You don't have to be scared," Francis said.

"I'm not scared," Helen said. "Not that."

"Finny won't let nothin' happen to you. I'll kill the son of a bitch if he does."

"She knows," Finny said. "She's been here before."

"Sure," said Francis. "Nothing can happen to you."

"No."

"See you in the mornin'."

"Sure."

"Keep the faith," Francis said.

And he closed the car door.

□ □ □

He walked with an empty soul toward the north star, magnetized by an impulse to redirect his destiny. He had slept in the weeds of a South End vacant lot too many times. He would do it no more. Because he needed to confront the ragman in the morning, he would not chance arrest by crawling into a corner of one of the old houses on lower Broadway where the cops swept through periodically with their mindless net. What difference did it make whether four or six or eight lost men slept under a roof and out of the wind in a house with broken stairs and holes in the floors you could fall through to death, a house that for five or maybe ten years had been inhabited only by pigeons? What difference?

He walked north on Broadway, past Steamboat Square, where as a child he'd boarded the riverboats for outings to

Troy, or Kingston, or picnics on Lagoon Island. He passed the D & H building and Billy Barnes's Albany *Evening Journal*, a building his simpleminded brother Tommy had helped build in 1913. He walked up to Maiden Lane and Broadway, where Keeler's Hotel used to be, and where his brother Peter sometimes spent the night when he was on the outs with Mama. But Keeler's burned the year after Francis ran away and now it was a bunch of stores. Francis had rowed down Broadway to the hotel, Billy in the rowboat with him, in 1913 when the river rose away the hell and gone up and flooded half of downtown. The kid loved it. Said he liked it better'n sleigh ridin'. Gone. What the hell ain't gone? Well, me. Yeah, me. Ain't a whole hell of a lot of me left, but I ain't gone entirely. Be goddiddley-damned if I'm gonna roll over and die.

Francis walked half an hour due north from downtown, right into North Albany. At Main Street he turned east toward the river, down Main Street's little incline past the McGraw house, then past the Greenes', the only coloreds in all North Albany in the old days, past the Daugherty house, where Martin still lived, no lights on, and past the old Wheelbarrow, Iron Joe Farrell's old saloon, all boarded up now, where Francis learned how to drink, where he watched cockfights in the back room, and where he first spoke to Annie Farrell.

He walked toward the flats, where the canal used to be, long gone and the ditch filled in. The lock was gone and the lockhouse too, and the towpath all grown over. Yet incredibly, as he neared North Street, he saw a structure he recognized. Son of a bitch. Welt the Tin's barn, still standing. Who'd believe it? Could Welt the Tin be livin'? Not likely. Too dumb to live so long. Was it in use? Still a barn? Looks like a barn. But who keeps horses now?

The barn was a shell, with a vast hole in the far end of the roof where moonlight poured cold fire onto the ancient splintered floor. Bats flew in balletic arcs around the streetlamp outside, the last lamp on North Street; and the ghosts of mules and horses snorted and stomped for Francis. He scuffed at the floorboards himself and found them solid. He touched them and found them dry. One barn door canted on one hinge, and Francis calculated that if he could move the door a few feet to sleep in its lee, he would be protected from the wind on three sides. No moonlight leaked through the roof above this corner, the same corner where Welt the Tin had hung his rakes and pitchforks, all in a row between spaced nails.

Francis would reclaim this corner, restore all rakes and pitchforks, return for the night the face of Welt the Tin as it had been, reinvest himself with serendipitous memories of a lost age. On a far shelf in the moonlight he saw a pile of papers and a cardboard box. He spread the papers in his chosen corner, ripped the box at its seams, and lay down on the flattened pile.

He had lived not seventy-five feet from where he now lay.

Seventy-five feet from this spot, Gerald Phelan died on the 26th of April, 1916.

In Finny's car Helen would probably be pulling off Finny, or taking him in her mouth. Finny would be unequal to intercourse, and Helen would be too fat for a toss in the front seat. Helen would be equal to any such task. He knew, though she had never told him, that she once had to fuck two strangers to be able to sleep in peace. Francis accepted this cuckoldry as readily as he accepted the onus of pulling the blanket off Clara and penetrating whatever dimensions of reek necessary to gain access to a bed. Fornication was standard survival currency everywhere, was it not?

Maybe I won't survive tonight after all, Francis thought as he folded his hands between his thighs. He drew his knees up toward his chest, not quite so high as Foxy Phil Tooker's, and considered the death he had caused in this life, and was perhaps causing still. Helen is dying and Francis is perhaps the principal agent of hastening her death, even as his whole being tonight has been directed to keeping her from freezing in the dust like Sandra. I don't want to die before you do, Helen, is what Francis thought. You'll be like a little kid in the world without me.

He thought of his father flying through the air and knew the old man was in heaven. The good leave us behind to think about the deeds they did. His mother would be in purgatory, probably for goddamn ever. She wasn't evil enough for hell, shrew of shrews that she was, denier of life. But he couldn't see her ever getting a foot into heaven either, if they ever got such a place.

The new and frigid air of November lay on Francis like a blanket of glass. Its weight rendered him motionless and brought peace to his body, and the stillness brought a cessation of anguish to his brain. In a dream he was only just beginning to enter, horns and mountains rose up out of the earth, the horns–ethereal, trumpets–sounding with a virtuosity equal to the perilousness of the crags and cornices of the mountainous pathways. Francis recognized the song the trumpets played and he floated with its melody. Then, yielding not without trepidation to its coded urgency, he ascended bodily into the exalted reaches of the world where the song had been composed so long ago. And he slept.

# IV.

Francis stood in the junkyard driveway, looking for old Rosskam. Gray clouds that looked like two flying piles of dirty socks blew swiftly past the early-morning sun, the world shimmered in a sudden blast of incandescence, and Francis blinked. His eyes roved over a cemetery of dead things: rusted-out gas stoves, broken wood stoves, dead iceboxes, and bicycles with twisted wheels. A mountain of worn-out rubber tires cast its shadow on a vast plain of rusty pipes, children's wagons, toasters, automobile fenders. A three-sided shed half a block long sheltered a mountain range of cardboard, paper, and rags.

Francis stepped into this castoff world and walked toward a wooden shack, small and tilted, with a swayback horse hitched to a four-wheeled wooden wagon in front of it. Beyond the wagon a small mountain of wagon wheels rose alongside a sprawling scatter of pans, cans, irons, pots, and kettles, and a sea of metal fragments that no longer had names.

Francis saw probably Rosskam, framed in the shack's only window, watching him approach. Francis pushed open the door and confronted the man, who was short, filthy, and sixtyish, a figure of visible sinew, moon-faced, bald, and broad-chested, with fingers like the roots of an oak tree.

"Howdy," Francis said.

"Yeah," said Rosskam.

"Preacher said you was lookin' for a strong back."

"It could be. You got one, maybe?"

"Stronger than some."

"You can pick up an anvil?"

"You collectin' anvils, are you?"

"Collect everything."

"Show me the anvil."

"Ain't got one."

"Then I'd play hell pickin' it up."

"How about the barrel. You can pick that up?"

He pointed to an oil drum, half full of wood scraps and junk metal. Francis wrapped his arms around it and lifted it, with difficulty.

"Where'd you like it put?"

"Right where you got it off."

"You pick up stuff like this yourself?" Francis asked.

Rosskam stood and lifted the drum without noticeable strain, then held it aloft.

"You got to be in mighty fair shape, heftin' that," said Francis. "That's one heavy item."

"You call this heavy?" Rosskam said, and he heaved the drum upward and set its bottom edge on his right shoulder. Then he let it slide to chest level, hugged it, and set it down.

"I do a lifetime of lifting," he said.

"I see that clear. You own this whole shebang here?"

"All. You still want to work?"

"What are you payin'?"

"Seven dollar. And work till dark."

"Seven. That ain't much for back work."

"Some might even bite at it."

"It's worth eight or nine."

"You got better, take it. People feed families all week on seven dollar."

"Seven-fifty."

"Seven."

"All right, what the hell's the difference?"

"Get up the wagon."

Two minutes in the moving wagon told Francis his tailbone would be grieving by day's end, if it lasted that long. The wagon bounced over the granite blocks and the trolley tracks, and the men rode side by side in silence through the bright streets of morning. Francis was glad for the sunshine, and felt rich seeing the people of his old city rising for work, opening stores and markets, moving out into a day of substance and profit. Clearheadedness always brought optimism to Francis; a long ride on a freight when there was nothing to drink made way for new visions of survival, and sometimes he even went out and looked for work. But even as he felt rich, he felt dead. He had not found Helen and he had to find her. Helen was lost again. The woman makes a goddamn career out of being lost. Probably went to mass someplace. But why didn't she come back to the mission for coffee, and for Francis? Why the hell should Helen always make Francis feel dead?

Then he remembered the story about Billy in the paper and he brightened. Pee Wee read it first and gave it to him. It was a story about Francis's son Billy, written by Martin Daugherty, the newspaperman, who long ago lived next door to the Phelans on Colonie Street. It was the story of Billy getting mixed up in the kidnapping of the nephew of

Patsy McCall, the boss of Albany's political machine. They got the nephew back safely, but Billy was in the middle because he wouldn't inform on a suspected kidnapper. And there was Martin's column defending Billy, calling Patsy McCall a very smelly bag of very small potatoes for being rotten to Billy.

"So how do you like it?" Rosskam said.

"Like what?" said Francis.

"Sex business," Rosskam said. "Women stuff."

"I don't think much about it anymore."

"You bums, you do a lot of dirty stuff up the heinie, am I right?"

"Some like it that way. Not me."

"How do you like it?"

"I don't even like it anymore, I'll tell you the truth. I'm over the hill."

"A man like you? How old? Fifty-five? Sixty-two?"

"Fifty-eight," said Francis.

"Seventy-one here," said Rosskam. "I go over no hills. Four, five times a night I get it in with the old woman. And in the daylight, you never know."

"What's the daylight?"

"Women. They ask for it. You go house to house, you get offers. This is not a new thing in the world."

"I never went house to house," Francis said.

"Half my life I go house to house," said Rosskam, "and I know how it is. You get offers."

"You probably get a lot of clap, too."

"Twice all my life. You use the medicine, it goes away. Those ladies, they don't do it so often to get disease. Hungry is what they got, not clap."

"They bring you up to bed in your old clothes?"

"In the cellar. They love it down the cellar. On the woodpile. In the coal. On top the newspapers. They follow me down the stairs and bend over the papers to show me their bubbies, or they up their skirts on the stairs ahead of me, showing other things. Best I ever got lately was on top of four ash cans. Very noisy, but some woman. The things she said you wouldn't repeat. Hot, hotsy, oh my. This morning we pay her a visit, up on Arbor Hill. You wait in the wagon. It don't take long, if you don't mind."

"Why should I mind? It's your wagon, you're the boss."

"That's right. I am the boss."

They rode up to Northern Boulevard and started down Third Street, all downhill so as not to kill the horse. House by house they went, carting out old clocks and smashed radios, papers always, two boxes of broken-backed books on gardening, a banjo with a broken neck, cans, old hats, rags.

"Here," old Rosskam said when they reached the hot lady's house. "If you like, watch by the cellar window. She likes lookers and I don't mind it."

Francis shook his head and sat alone on the wagon, staring down Third Street. He could have reconstructed this street from memory. Childhood, young manhood were passed on the streets of Arbor Hill, girls discovering they had urges, boys capitalizing on this discovery. In the alleyways the gang watched women undress, and one night they watched the naked foreplay of Mr. and Mrs. Ryan until they put out the light. Joey Kilmartin whacked off during that show. The old memory aroused Francis sexually. Did he want a woman? No. Helen? No, no. He wanted to watch the Ryans again, getting ready to go at it. He climbed down from the wagon and walked into the alley of the house where Rosskam's hot lady lived. He walked softly, listening, and he heard groaning, inaudible words, and the sound of metal fatigue. He crouched down and peered in the cellar window at the back of the house, and there they were on the ash cans, Rosskam's pants hanging from his shoes, on top of a lady with her dress up to her neck. When Francis brought the scene into focus, he could hear their words.

"Oh boyoboy," Rosskam was saying, "oh boyoboy."

"Hey I love it," said the hot lady. "Do I love it? Do I love it?"

"You love it," said Rosskam. "Oh boyoboy."

"Gimme that stick," said the hot lady. "Gimme it, gimme it, gimme, gimme, gimme that stick."

"Oh take it," said Rosskam. "Oh take it."

"Oh gimme it," said the hot lady. "I'm a hot slut. Gimme it."

"Oh boyoboy," said Rosskam.

The hot lady saw Francis at the window and waved to him. Francis stood up and went back to the wagon, conjuring memories against his will. Bums screwing in boxcars, women gang-banged in the weeds, a girl of eight raped, and then the rapist kicked half to death by other bums and rolled out of the moving train. He saw the army of women he had known: women upside down, women naked, women with their skirts up, their legs open, their mouths open, women in heat, women sweating and grunting under and over him, women professing love, desire, joy, pain, need. Helen.

He met Helen at a New York bar, and when they found out they were both from Albany, love took a turn toward the sun. He kissed her and she tongued him. He stroked her body, which was old even then, but vital and full and without the tumor, and they confessed a fiery yearning for each other. Francis hesitated to carry it through, for he had been off women eight months, having finally and with much discomfort rid himself of the crabs and a relentless, pusy drip. Yet the presence of Helen's flaming body kept driving away his dread of disease, and finally, when he saw they were going to be together for much more than a one-nighter, he told her: I wouldn't touch ya, babe. Not till I got me a checkup. She told him to wear a sheath but he said he hated them goddamn things. Get us a blood test, that's what we'll do, he told her, and they pooled their money and went to the hospital and both got a clean bill and then took a room and made love till they wore out. Love, you are my member rubbed raw. Love, you are an unstoppable fire. You burn me, love. I am singed, blackened. Love, I am ashes.

□ □ □

The wagon rolled on and Francis realized it was heading for Colonie Street, where he was born and raised, where his brothers and sisters still lived. The wagon wheels squeaked as they moved and the junk in the back rattled and bounced, announcing the prodigal's return. Francis saw the house where he grew up, still the same colors, brown and tan, the vacant lot next to it grown tall with weeds where the Daugherty house and the Brothers' School had stood until they burned.

He saw his mother and father alight from their honeymoon carriage in front of the house and, with arms entwined, climb the front stoop. Michael Phelan wore his trainman's overalls and looked as he had the moment before the speeding train struck him. Kathryn Phelan, in her wedding dress, looked as she had when she hit Francis with an open hand and sent him sprawling backward into the china closet.

"Stop here a minute, will you?" Francis said to Rosskam, who had uttered no words since ascending from his cellar of passion.

"Stop?" Rosskam said, and he reined the horse.

The newlyweds stepped across the threshold and into the house. They climbed the front stairs to the bedroom they would share for all the years of their marriage, the room that now was also their shared grave, a spatial duality as reasonable to Francis as the concurrence of this moment both in the immediate present of his fifty-eighth year of life and in the year before he was born: that year of sacramental consummation, 1879. The room had about it the familiarity of his young lifetime. The oak bed and the two oak dressers were as rooted to their positions in the room as the trees that shaded the edge of the Phelan burial plot. The room was redolent of the blend of maternal and paternal odors, which separated themselves when Francis buried his face deeply in either of the personal pillows, or opened a drawer full of private garments, or inhaled the odor of burned tobacco in a cold pipe, say, or the fragrance of a cake of Pears' soap, kept in a drawer as a sachet.

In their room Michael Phelan embraced his new wife of fifty-nine years and ran a finger down the crevice of her breasts; and Francis saw his mother-to-be shudder with what he assumed was the first abhorrent touch of love. Because he was the firstborn, Francis's room was next to theirs, and so he had heard their nocturnal rumblings for years; and he well knew how she perennially resisted her husband. When Michael would finally overcome her, either by force of will or by threatening to take their case to the priest, Francis would hear her gurgles of resentment, her moans of anguish, her eternal arguments about the sinfulness of all but generative couplings. For she hated the fact that people even knew that she had committed intercourse in order to have children, a chagrin that was endlessly satisfying to Francis all his life.

Now, as her husband lifted her chemise over her head, the virginal mother of six recoiled with what Francis recognized for the first time to be spiritually induced terror, as visible in her eyes in 1879 as it was in the grave. Her skin was as fresh and pink as the taffeta lining of her coffin, but she was, in her youthfully rosy bloom, as lifeless as the spun silk of her magenta burial dress. She has been dead all her life, Francis thought, and for the first time in years he felt pity for this woman, who had been spayed by self-neutered nuns and self-gelded priests. As she yielded her fresh body to her new husband out of obligation, Francis felt the iron maiden of induced chastity piercing her everywhere, tightening with the years until all sensuality was strangulated and her body was as bloodless and cold as a granite angel.

She closed her eyes and fell back on the wedding bed like a corpse, ready to receive the thrust, and the old man's impeccable blood shot into her aged vessel with a passionate burst that set her writhing with the life of newly conceived death. Francis watched this primal pool of his own soulish body squirm into burgeoning matter, saw it change and grow with the speed of light until it was the size of an infant, saw it then yanked roughly out of the maternal cavern by his father, who straightened him, slapped him into being, and swiftly molded him into a bestial weed. The body sprouted to wildly matured growth and stood fully clad at last in the very clothes Francis was now wearing. He recognized the toothless mouth, the absent finger joints, the bump on the nose, the mortal slouch of this newborn shade, and he knew then that he would be this decayed self he had been so long in becoming, through all the endless years of his death.

□ □ □

"Giddap," said Rosskam to his horse, and the old nag clomped on down the hill of Colonie Street.

"Raaaa-aaaaaags," screamed Rosskam. "Raaaa-aaaa-aags." The scream was a two-noted song, C and B-flat, or maybe F and E-flat. And from a window across the street from the Phelan house, a woman's head appeared.

"Goooo-ooooooo," she called in two-noted answer. "Raaaag-maaan."

Rosskam pulled to a halt in front of the alley alongside her house.

"On the back porch," she said. "Papers and a washtub and some old clothes."

Rosskam braked his wagon and climbed down.

"Well?" he said to Francis.

"I don't want to go in," Francis said. "I know her."

"So what's that?"

"I don't want her to see me. Mrs. Dillon. Her husband's a railroad man. I know them all my life. My family lives in that house over there. I was born up the street. I don't want people on this block to see me looking like a bum."

"But you're a bum."

"Me and you know that, but they don't. I'll cart anything, I'll cart it all the next time you stop. But not on this street. You understand?"

"Sensitive bum. I got a sensitive bum working for me."

While Rosskam went for the junk alone, Francis stared across the street and saw his mother in housedress and apron surreptitiously throwing salt on the roots of the young maple tree that grew in the Daugherty yard but had the temerity to drop twigs, leaves, and pods onto the Phelan tomato plants and flowers. Kathryn Phelan told her near-namesake, Katrina Daugherty, that the tree's droppings and shade were unwelcome at the Phelans'. Katrina trimmed what she could of the tree's low branches and asked Francis, a neighborhood handyman at seventeen, to help her trim the higher ones; and he did: climbed aloft and sawed living arms off the vigorous young tree. But for every branch cut, new life sprouted elsewhere, and the tree thickened to a lushness unlike that of any other tree on Arbor Hill, infuriating Kathryn Phelan, who increased her dosage of salt on the roots, which waxed and grew under and beyond the wooden fence and surfaced ever more brazenly on Phelan property.

Why do you want to kill the tree, Mama? Francis asked.

And his mother said it was because the tree had no right insinuating itself into other people's yards. If we want a tree in the yard we'll plant our own, she said, and threw more salt. Some leaves withered on the tree and one branch died entirely. But the salting failed, for Francis saw the tree now, twice its old size, a giant thing in the world, rising high out of the weeds and toward the sun from what used to be the Daugherty yard.

On this high noon in 1938, under the sun's full brilliance, the tree restored itself to its half size of forty-one years past, a July morning in 1897 when Francis was sitting on a middle branch, sawing the end off a branch above him. He heard the back door of the Daughertys' new house open and close, and he looked down from his perch to see Katrina Daugherty, carrying her small shopping bag, wearing a gray sun hat, gray satin evening slippers, and nothing else. She descended the five steps of the back piazza and strode toward the new barn, where the Daugherty landau and horse were kept.

"Mrs. Daugherty?" Francis called out, and he leaped down from the tree. "Are you all right?"

"I'm going downtown, Francis," she said.

"Shouldn't you put something on? Some clothes?"

"Clothes?" she said. She looked down at her naked self and then cocked her head and widened her eyes into quizzical rigidity.

"Mrs. Daugherty," Francis said, but she gave no response, nor did she move. From the piazza railing that he was building, Francis lifted a piece of forest-green canvas he would eventually install as an awning on a side window, and wrapped the naked woman in it, picking her up in his arms then, and carrying her into her house. He sat her on the sofa in the back parlor and, as the canvas slid slowly away from her shoulders, he searched the house for a garment and found a housecoat hanging behind the pantry door. He stood her up and shoved her arms into the housecoat, tied its belt at her waist, covering her body fully, and undid the chin ribbon that held her hat. Then he sat her down again on the sofa.

He found a bottle of Scotch whiskey in a cabinet and poured her an inch in a goblet from the china closet, held it to her lips, and cajoled her into tasting it. Whiskey is magic and will cure all your troubles. Katrina sipped it and smiled and said, "Thank you, Francis. You are very thoughtful," her eyes no longer wide, the glaze gone from them, her rigidity banished, and the softness of her face and body restored.

"Are you feeling better?" he asked her.

"I'm fine, fine indeed. And how are *you*, Francis?"

"Do you want me to go and get your husband?"

"My husband? My husband is in New York City, and rather difficult to reach, I'm afraid. What did you want with my husband?"

"Someone in your family you'd like me to get, maybe? You seem to be having some kind of spell."

"Spell? What do you mean, spell?"

"Outside. In the back."

"The back?"

"You came out without any clothes on, and then you went stiff."

"Now really, Francis, do you think you should be so familiar?"

"I put that housecoat on you. I carried you indoors."

"You carried me?"

"Wrapped in canvas. That there." And he pointed to the canvas on the floor in front of the sofa. Katrina stared at the canvas, put her hand inside the fold of her housecoat, and felt her naked breast. In her face, when she again looked up at him, Francis saw lunar majesty, a chilling fusion of beauty and desolation. At the far end of the front parlor, observing all from behind a chair, Francis saw also the forehead and eyes of Katrina Daugherty's nine-year-old son, Martin.

□ □ □

A month passed, and on a day when Francis was doing finishing work on the doors of the Daugherty carriage barn, Katrina called out to him from the back porch and beckoned him into the house, then to the back parlor, where she sat again on the same sofa, wearing a long yellow afternoon frock with a soft collar. She looked like a sunbeam to Francis as she motioned him into a chair across from the sofa.

"May I make you some tea, Francis?"

"No, ma'am."

"Would you care for one of my husband's cigars?"

"No, ma'am. I don't use 'em."

"Have you none of the minor vices? Do you perhaps drink whiskey?"

"I've had a bit but the most I drink of is ale."

"Do you think I'm mad, Francis?"

"Mad? How do you mean that?"

"Mad. Mad as the Red Queen. Peculiar. Crazy, if you like. Do you think Katrina is crazy?"

"No, ma'am."

"Not even after my spell?"

"I just took it as a spell. A spell don't have to be crazy."

"Of course you're correct, Francis. I am not crazy. With whom have you talked about that day's happenings?"

"No one, ma'am."

"No one? Not even your family?"

"No, ma'am, no one."

"I sensed you hadn't. May I ask why?"

Francis dropped his eyes, spoke to his lap. "Could be, people wouldn't understand. Might figure it the wrong way."

"How wrong?"

"Might figure they was some goin's on. People with no clothes isn't what you'd call reg'lar business."

"You mean people would make something up? Conjure an imaginary relationship between us?"

"Might be they would. Most times they don't need that much to start their yappin'."

"So you've been protecting us from scandal with your silence."

"Yes, ma'am."

"Would you please not call me ma'am. It makes you sound like a servant. Call me Katrina."

"I couldn't do that."

"Why couldn't you?"

"It's more familiar than I oughta get."

"But it's my name. Hundreds of people call me Katrina."

Francis nodded and let the word sit on his tongue. He tried it out silently, then shook his head. "I can't get it out," he said, and he smiled.

"Say it. Say Katrina."

"Katrina."

"So there, you've gotten it out. Say it again."

"Katrina."

"Fine. Now say: May I help you, Katrina?"

"May I help you, Katrina?"

"Splendid. Now I want never to be called anything else again. I insist. And I shall call you Francis. That is how we were designated at birth and our baptisms reaffirmed it. Friends should dispense with formality, and you, who have saved me from scandal, you, Francis, are most certainly my friend."

□ □ □

From the perspective of his perch on the junk wagon Francis could see that Katrina was not only the rarest bird in his life, but very likely the rarest bird ever to nest on Colonie Street. She brought to this street of working-class Irish a posture of elegance that had instantly earned her glares of envy and hostility from the neighbors. But within a year of residence in her new house (a scaled-down copy of the Elk Street mansion in which she had been born and nurtured like a tropical orchid, and where she had lived until she married Edward Daugherty, the writer, whose work and words, whose speech and race, were anathema to Katrina's father, and who, as a compromise for his bride, built the replica that would maintain her in her cocoon, but built it in a neighborhood where he would never be an outlander, and built it lavishly until he ran out of capital and was forced to hire neighborhood help, such as Francis, to finish it), her charm and generosity, her absence of pretension, and her abundance of the human virtues transformed most of her neighbors' hostility into fond attention and admiration.

Her appearance, when she first set foot in the house next door to his, stunned Francis; her blond hair swept upward into a soft wreath, her eyes a dark and shining brown, the stately curves and fullness of her body carried so regally, her large, irregular teeth only making her beauty more singular. This goddess, who had walked naked across his life, and whom he had carried in his arms, now sat on the sofa and with eyes wide upon him she leaned forward and posed the question: "Are you in love with anyone?"

"No, m– no. I'm too young."

Katrina laughed and Francis blushed.

"You are such a handsome boy. You must have many girls in love with you."

"No," said Francis. "I never been good with girls."

"Why ever not?"

"I don't tell 'em what they want to hear. I ain't big with talk."

"Not all girls want you to talk to them."

"Ones I know do. Do you like me? How much? Do you like me better'n Joan? Stuff like that. I got no time for stuff like that."

"Do you dream of women?"

"Sometimes."

"Have you ever dreamt of me?"

"Once."

"Was it pleasant?"

"Not all that much."

"Oh my. What was it?"

"You couldn't close your eyes. You just kept lookin' and never blinked. It got scary."

"I understand the dream perfectly. You know, a great poet once said that love enters through the eyes. One must be careful not to see too much. One must curb one's appetites. The world is much too beautiful for most of us. It can destroy us with its beauty. Have you ever seen anyone faint?"

"Faint? No."

"No, what?"

"No, Katrina."

"Then I shall faint for you, dear Francis."

She stood up, walked to the center of the room, looked directly at Francis, closed her eyes, and collapsed on the rug, her right hip hitting the floor first and she then falling backward, right arm outstretched over her head, her face toward the parlor's east wall. Francis stood up and looked down at her.

"You did that pretty good," he said.

She did not move.

"You can get up now," he said.

But still she did not move. He reached down and took her left hand in his and tugged gently. She did not move. He took both her hands and tugged. She did not move voluntarily, nor did she open her eyes. He pulled her to a sitting position but she remained limp, with closed eyes. He lifted her off the floor in his arms and put her on the sofa. When he sat her down she opened her eyes and sat fully erect. Francis still had one arm on her back.

"My mother taught me that," Katrina said. "She said it was useful in strained social situations. I performed it once in a pageant and won great applause."

"You did it good," Francis said.

"I can do a cataleptic fit quite well also."

"I don't know what that is."

"It's when you stop yourself in a certain position and do not move. Like this."

And suddenly she was rigid and wide-eyed, unblinking.

☐ ☐ ☐

A week after that, Katrina passed by Mulvaney's pasture on Van Woert Street, where Francis was playing baseball, a pickup game. She stood on the turf, just in from the street, across the diamond from where Francis danced and chattered as the third-base pepper pot. When he saw her he stopped chattering. That inning he had no fielding chances. The next inning he did not come to bat. She watched through three innings until she saw him catch a line drive and then tag a runner for a double play; saw him also hit a long fly to the outfield that went for two bases. When he reached second base on the run, she walked home to Colonie Street.

□ □ □

She called him to lunch the day he installed the new awnings. After the first day she always chose a time to talk with him when her husband was elsewhere and her son in school. She served lobster *gratiné*, asparagus with hollandaise, and Blanc de Blancs. Only the asparagus, without sauce, had Francis ever tasted before. She served it at the dining-room table, without a word, then sat across from him and ate in silence, he following her lead.

"I like this," he finally said.

"Do you? Do you like the wine?"

"Not very much."

"You will learn to like it. It is exquisite."

"If you say so."

"Have you had any more dreams of me?"

"One. I can't tell it."

"But you must."

"It's crazy."

"Dreams must be. Katrina is not crazy. Say: May I help you, Katrina?"

"May I help you, Katrina?"

"You may help me by telling me your dream."

"What it is, is you're a little bird, but you're just like you always are too, and a crow comes along and eats you up."

"Who is the crow?"

"Just a crow. Crows always eat little birds."

"You are protective of me, Francis."

"I don't know."

"What does your mother know of me? Does she know you and I have talked as friends?"

"I wouldn't tell her. I wouldn't tell her anything."

"Good. Never tell your mother anything about me. She is your mother and I am Katrina. I will always be Katrina in your life. Do you know that? You will never know another like me. There can be no other like me."

"I sure believe you're right."

"Do you ever want to kiss me?"

"Always."

"What else do you want to do with me?"

"I couldn't say."

"You may say."

"Not me. I'd goddamn die."

When they had eaten, Katrina filled her own and Francis's wineglasses and set them on the octagonal marble-topped table in front of the sofa where she always sat; and he sat in what had now become his chair. He drank all of the wine and she refilled his glass as they talked of asparagus and lobster and she taught him the meaning of *gratiné*, and why a French word was used to describe a dish made in Albany from a lobster caught in Maine.

"Wondrous things come from France," she said to him, and by this time he was at ease in the suffusion of wine and pleasure and possibility, and he gave her his fullest attention. "Do you know Saint Anthony of Egypt, Francis? He is of your faith, a faith I cherish without embracing. I speak of him because of the way he was tempted with the flesh and I speak too of my poet, who frightens me because he sees what men should not see in women. He is dead these thirty years, my poet, but he sees through me still with his image of a caged woman ripping apart the body of a living rabbit with her teeth. Enough, says her keeper, you should not spend all you receive in one day, and he pulls the rabbit from her, letting some of its intestines dangle from her teeth. She remains hungry, with only a taste of what might nourish her. Oh, little Francis, my rabbit, you must not fear me. I shall not rip you to pieces and let your sweet intestines dangle from my teeth. Beautiful Francis of sweet excellence in many things, beautiful young man whom I covet, please do not speak ill of me. Do not say Katrina was made for the fire of *luxuria*, for you must understand that I am Anthony and am tempted by the devil with the sweetness of yourself in my house, in my kitchen, in my yard, in my tree of trees, sweet Francis who carried me naked in his arms."

"I couldn't let you go out in the street with no clothes on," Francis said. "You'd get arrested."

"I know you couldn't," Katrina said. "That's precisely why I did it. But what I do not know is what will be the consequence of it. I do not know what strengths I have to confront the temptations I bring into my life so willfully. I only know that I love in ten thousand directions and that I must not; for that is the lot of the harlot. My poet says that caged woman with the rabbit in her teeth is the true and awful image of this life, and not the woman moaning aloud her dirge of unattainable hopes . . . dead, so dead, how sad. Of course you must know I am not dead. I am merely a woman in self-imposed bondage to a splendid man, to a mannerism of life which he calls a sacrament and I call a magnificent prison. Anthony lived as a hermit, and I too have thought of this as a means of thwarting the enemy. But my husband worships me, and I him, and we equally worship our son of sons. You see, there has never been a magnificence of contact greater than that which exists within this house. We are a family of reverence, of achievement, of wounds sweetly healed. We yearn for the touch, the presence of each other. We cannot live without these things. And yet you are here and I dream of you and long for the pleasures you cannot speak of to me, of joys beyond the imaginings of your young mind. I long for the pleasures of Mademoiselle Lancet, who pursued doctors as I pursue my young man of tender breath, my beautiful Adonis of Arbor Hill. The Mademoiselle cherished all her doctors did and were. The blood on their aprons was a badge of their achievement in the operating room, and she embraced it as I embrace your swan's throat with its necklace of dirt, the haunting pain of young ignorance in your eyes. Do you believe there is a God, Francis? Of course you do and so do I, and I believe he loves me and will cherish me in heaven, as I will cherish him. We shall be lovers. God made me in his image, and so why should I not believe that God too is an innocent monster, loving the likes of me, this seductress of children, this caged animal with blood and intestines in her teeth, embracing her own bloody aprons and then kneeling at the altar of all that is holy in the penitential pose of all hypocrites. Did you ever dream, Francis, when I called you out of our tree, that you would enter such a world as I inhabit? Would you kiss me if I closed my eyes? If I fainted would you undo the buttons of my dress to let me breathe easier?"

□ □ □

Katrina died in 1912 in the fire that began in the Brothers' School and then made the leap to the Daugherty house. Francis was absent from the city when she died, but he learned the news from a newspaper account and returned for her funeral. He did not see her in her coffin, which was closed to mourners. Smoke, not fire, killed her, just as the ashes and not the flames of her sensuality had finally smothered her desire; so Francis believed.

In the immediate years after her death, Katrina's grave in the Albany Rural Cemetery, where Protestants entered the underworld, grew wild with dandelions and became a curiosity to the manicurists of the cemetery's floral tapestry. In precisely the way Katrina and Francis had trimmed the maple tree, only to see it grow ever more luxuriant, so was it that the weeding of her burial plot led to an intensity of weed growth: as if the severing of a single root were cause for the birth of a hundred rootlings. Such was its growth that the grave, in the decade after her death, became an attraction for cemetery tourists, who marveled at the midspring yellowing of her final residence on earth. The vogue passed, though the flowers remain even today; and it is now an historical marvel that only the very old remember, or that the solitary wanderer discovers when rambling among the gravestones, and generally attributes to a freakish natural effusion.

□ □ □

"So," said Rosskam, "did you have a nice rest?"

"It ain't rest what I'm doin'," said Francis. "You got all the stuff from back there?"

"All," said Rosskam, throwing an armful of old clothes into the wagon. Francis looked them over, and a clean, soft-collared, white-on-white shirt, one sleeve half gone, caught his eye.

"That shirt," he said. "I'd like to buy it." He reached into the wagon and lifted it from the pile. "You take a quarter for it?"

Rosskam studied Francis as he might a striped blue toad.

"Take it out of my pay," Francis said. "Is it a deal?"

"For what is it a bum needs a clean shirt?"

"The one I got on stinks like a dead cat."

"Tidy bum. Sensitive, tidy bum on my wagon."

□ □ □

Katrina unwrapped the parcel on the dining-room table, took Francis by the hand, and pulled him up from his chair. She unbuttoned the buttons of his blue workshirt.

"Take that old thing off," she said, and held the gift aloft, a white-on-white silk shirt whose like was as rare to

Francis as the *fruits de mer* and Château Pontet-Canet he had just consumed.

When his torso was naked, Katrina stunned him with a kiss, and with an exploration of the whole of his back with her fingertips. He held her as he would a crystal vase, fearful not only of her fragility but of his own. When he could again see her lips, her eyes, the sanctified valley of her mouth, when she stood inches from him, her hands gripping his naked back, he cautiously brought his own fingers around to her face and neck. Emulating her, he explored the exposed regions of her shoulders and her throat, letting the natural curve of her collar guide him to the top button of her blouse. And then slowly, as if the dance of their fingers had been choreographed, hers crawled across her own chest, brushing past his, which were carefully at work at their gentlest of chores, and she pushed the encumbering chemise strap down over the fall of her left shoulder. His own fingers then repeated the act on her right shoulder and he trembled with pleasure, and sin, and with, even now, the still unthinkable possibilities that lay below and beneath the boundary line her fallen clothing demarcated.

"Do you like my scar?" she asked, and she lightly touched the oval white scar with a ragged pink periphery, just above the early slope of her left breast.

"I don't know," Francis said. "I don't know about likin' scars."

"You are the only man besides my husband and Dr. Fitzroy who has ever seen it. I can never again wear a low-necked dress. It is such an ugly thing that I do believe my poet would adore it. Does it offend you?"

"It's there. Part of you. That's okay by me. Anything you do, or got, it's okay by me."

"My adorable Francis ."

"How'd you ever get a thing like that?"

"A burning stick flew through the air and pierced me cruelly during a fire. The Delavan Hotel fire."

"Yeah. I heard you were in that. You're lucky you didn't get it in the neck."

"Oh I'm a very lucky woman indeed," Katrina said, and she leaned into him and held him again. And again they kissed.

He commanded his hands to move toward her breasts but they would not. They would only hold tight to their grip on her bare arms. Only when she moved her own fingers forward from the blades of his back toward the hollows of his arms did his own fingers dare move toward the hollows of hers. And only when she again inched back from him, letting her fingers tweeze and caress the precocious hair on his chest, did he permit his own fingers to savor the curving flow, the fleshy whiteness, the blooded fullness of her beautiful breasts, culminating his touch at their roseate tips, which were now being so cleverly cataleptic for him.

When Francis put the new shirt on and threw the old one into the back of Rosskam's wagon, he saw Katrina standing on her front steps, across the street, beckoning to him. She led him into a bedroom he had never seen and where a wall of flame engulfed her without destroying even the hem of her dress, the same dress she wore when she came to watch him play baseball on that summer day in 1897. He stood across the marriage bed from her, across a bridge of years of love and epochs of dream.

Never a woman like Katrina: who had forced him to model that shirt for her, then take it home so that someday she would see him walking along the street wearing it and relive this day; forced him first to find a hiding place for it outside his house while he schemed an excuse as to why a seventeen-year-old boy of the working classes should come to own a shirt that only sublime poets, or stage actors, or unthinkably wealthy lumber barons could afford. He invented the ruse of a bet: that he had played poker at a downtown sporting club with a man who ran out of dollars and put up his new shirt as collateral; and Francis had inspected the shirt, liked it, accepted the bet, and then won the hand with a full house.

His mother did not seem to believe the story. But neither did she connect the gift to Katrina. Yet she found ways to slander Katrina in Francis's presence, knowing that he had formed an allegiance, if not an affection, for not only a woman, but the woman who owned the inimical tree.

She is impudent, arrogant. (Wrong, said Francis.)

Slovenly, a poor housekeeper. (Go over and look, said Francis.)

Shows off by sitting in the window with a book. (Francis, knowing no way to defend a book, fumed silently and left the room.)

In the leaping windows of flame that engulfed Katrina and her bed, Francis saw naked bodies coupled in love, writhing in lascivious embrace, kissing in sweet agony. He saw himself and Katrina in a ravenous lunge that never was, and then in a blissful stroking that might have been, and then in a sublime fusion of desire that would always be.

Did they love? No, they never loved. They always loved. They knew a love that Katrina's poet would abuse and befoul. And they befouled their imaginations with a mutation of love that Katrina's poet would celebrate and consecrate. Love is always insufficient, always a lie. Love, you are the clean shirt of my soul. Stupid love, silly love.

Francis embraced Katrina and shot into her the impeccable blood of his first love, and she yielded up not a being but a word: clemency. And the word swelled like the mercy of his swollen member as it rose to offer her the enduring, erubescent gift of retributive sin. And then this woman interposed herself in his life, hiding herself in the deepest center of the flames, smiling at him with all the lewd beauty of her dreams; and she awakened in him the urge for a love of his own, a love that belonged to no other man, a love he would never have to share with any man, or boy, like himself.

"Giddap," Rosskam called out.

And the wagon rolled down the hill as the sun moved toward its apex, and the horse turned north off Colonie Street.

# V. □

Tell me, pretty maiden, are there any more at home like you? There are a few, kind sir, and dum-de-dum and dum-dum too.

So genteel, so quaint.

Helen hummed, staring at the wall in the light of the afternoon sun. In her kimono (only ten-cent-store silk, alas, but it did have a certain elegance, so much like the real thing no one would ever know; no one but Francis had ever seen her in it, or ever would; no one had seen her take it ever so cleverly off the rack in Woolworth's): in her kimono, and naked beneath it, she sank deeper into the old chair that was oozing away its stuffing; and she stared at the dusty swan in the painting with the cracked glass, swan with the lovely white neck, lovely white back: swan was, was.

Dah dah-dah,
Dah dah-de-dah-dah,
Dah dah-de-dah-dah,

Dah dah dah,

She sang. And the world changed.

Oh the lovely power of music to rejuvenate Helen. The melody returned her to that porcelain age when she aspired so loftily to a classical career. Her plan, her father's plan before it was hers, was for her to follow in her grandmother's footsteps, carry the family pride to lofty pinnacles: Vassar first, then the Paris Conservatory if she was truly as good as she seemed, then the concert world, then the entire world. If you love something well enough, Grandmother Archer told Helen when the weakness was upon her, you will die for it; for when we love with all our might, our silly little selves are already dead and we have no more fear of dying. Would you die for your music? Helen asked. And her grandmother said: I believe I already have. And in a month she was very unkindly cut down forever.

Swan was, was.

Helen's first death.

Her second came to her in a mathematics class at Vassar when she was a freshman of two months. Mrs. Carmichael, who was pretty and young and wore high shoes and walked with a limp, came for Helen and brought her to the office. A visitor, said Mrs. Carmichael, your uncle Andrew: who told Helen her father was ill,

And on the train up from Poughkeepsie changed that to dead,

And in the carriage going up State Street hill from the Albany depot added that the man had,

Incredibly,

Thrown himself off the Hawk Street viaduct.

Helen, confusing fear with grief, blocked all tears until two days after the funeral, when her mother told her that there will be no more Vassar for you, child; that Brian Archer killed himself because he had squandered his fortune; that what money remained would not be wasted in educating a foolish girl like Helen but would instead finance her brother Patrick's final year in Albany Law School; for a lawyer can save the family. And whatever could a classical pianist do for it?

Helen had been in the chair hours, it seemed, though she had no timepiece for such measurement. But it did seem an hour at least since crippled old Donovan came to the door and said: Helen, are you all right? You been in there all day. Don't you wanna eat something? I'm makin' some coffee, you want some? And Helen said: Oh thank you, old cripple, for remembering I still have a body now that I've all but forgotten it. And no, no thank you, no coffee, kind sir. Are there any more at home like you?

*Freude, schöner Götterfunken,*
*Tochter aus Elysium!*

The day had all but begun with music. She left Finny's car humming the "Te Deum"; why, she could not say. But at six o'clock, when it was still dark and Finny and the other man were both snoring, it became the theme of her morning pathway. As she walked she considered the immediate future for herself and her twelve dollars, the final twelve dollars of her life capital, money she never intended to tell Francis about, money tucked safely in her brassiere.

Don't touch my breasts, Finny, they're too sore, she had said again and again, afraid he would feel the money. Finny acceded and explored her only between the thighs, trying mightily to ejaculate, and she, Lord have mercy on her, tried to help him. But Finny could not ejaculate, and he fell back in exhaustion and dry indifference and then slept, as Helen did not, could not; for sleep seemed to be a thing of the past.

What for weeks she had achieved in her time of rest was only an illustrated wakefulness that hovered at the edge of dream: angels rejoicing, multitudes kneeling before the Lamb, worms all, creating a great butterfly of angelic hair, Helen's joyous vision.

Why was Helen joyous in her sleeplessness? Because she was able to recede from evil love and bloodthirsty spiders. Because she had mastered the trick of escaping into music and the pleasures of memory. She pulled on her bloomers, slid sideways out of the car, and walked out into the burgeoning day, the morning star still visible in her night's vanishing sky. Venus, you are my lucky star.

Helen walked to the church with head bowed. She was picking her steps when the angel appeared (and she still in her kimono) and called out to her: *Drunk with fire, o heav'n-born Goddess, we invade thy haildom!*

How nice.

The church was Saint Anthony's, Saint Anthony of Padua, the wonder-working saint, hammer of heretics, ark of the testament, finder of lost articles, patron of the poor and of pregnant and barren women. It was the church where the Italians went to preserve their souls in a city where Italians were the niggers and micks of a new day. Helen usually went to the Cathedral of the Immaculate Conception a few blocks up the hill, but her tumor felt so heavy, a great rock in her belly, that she chose Saint Anthony's, not such a climb, even if she did fear Italians. They looked so dark and dangerous. And she did not care much for their food, especially their garlic. And they seemed never to die. They eat olive oil all day long, Helen's mother had instructed her, and that's what does it; did you ever in all your life see a sick Italian?

The sound of the organ resonated out from the church before the mass began, and on the sidewalk Helen knew the day boded well for her, with such sanctified music greeting her at the dawning. There were three dozen people in the church, not many for a holy day of obligation. Not everybody feels obligations the way Helen feels them, but then again, it is only ten minutes to seven in the morning.

Helen walked all the way to the front and sat in the third pew of center-aisle left, in back of a man who looked like Walter Damrosch. The candle rack caught her eye and she rose and went to it and dropped in the two pennies she carried in her coat pocket, all the change she had. The organist was roaming free through Gregorian hymns as Helen lit a candle for Francis, offering up a Hail Mary so he would be given divine guidance with his problem. The poor man was so guilty.

Helen was giving help of her own to Francis now by staying away from him. She had made this decision while holding Finny's stubby, bloodless, and uncircumcised little penis in her hand. She would not go to the mission, would not meet Francis in the morning as planned. She would stay out of his life, for she understood that by depositing her once again with Finny, and knowing precisely what that would mean for her, Francis was willfully cuckolding himself, willfully debasing her, and, withal, separating them both from what still survived of their mutual love and esteem.

Why did Helen let Francis do this to them?

Well, she is subservient to Francis, and always has been. It was she who, by this very subservience, had perpetuated his relationship to her for most of their nine years together. How many times had she walked away from him? Scores upon scores. How many times, always knowing where he'd be, had she returned? The same scores, but minus one now.

The Walter Damrosch man studied her movements at the candle rack, just as she remembered Damrosch himself studying the score of the Ninth Symphony at Harmanus Bleecker Hall when she was sixteen. Listen to it carefully, her father had told her. It's what Debussy said: the magical blossoming of a tree whose leaves burst forth all at once. It was the first time, her father said, that the human voice ever entered into a symphonic creation. Perhaps, my Helen, you too will create a great musical work of art one day. One never knows the potential within any human breast.

A bell jingled as the priest and two altar boys emerged from the sacristy and the mass began. Helen, without her rosary to say, searched for something to read and found a *Follow the Mass* pamphlet on the pew in front of her. She read the ordinary of the mass until she came to the Lesson, in which John sees God's angel ascending from the rising of the sun, and God's angel sees four more angels, to whom it is given to hurt the earth and the sea; and God's angel tells those four bad ones: Hurt not the earth, nor the sea, nor the trees . . .

Helen closed the pamphlet.

Why would angels be sent to hurt the earth and the sea? She had never read that passage before that she could remember, but it was so dreadful. Angel of the earthquake, who splits the earth. Sargasso angel, who chokes the sea with weeds.

Helen could not bear to think such things, and so cast her eyes to others hearing the mass and saw a boy, perhaps nine, who might have been hers and Francis's if she'd had a child instead of a miscarriage, the only fertilization her womb had ever accepted. In front of the boy a kneeling woman with the palsy and twisted bones held on to the front of the pew with both her crooked hands. Calm her trembling, oh Lord, straighten her bones, Helen prayed. And then the priest read the gospel. Blessed are they who mourn, for they shall be comforted. Blessed are ye when they shall revile you, and persecute you, and speak all that is evil against you, untruly, for my sake: be glad and rejoice, for your reward is very great in heaven.

Rejoice. Yes.

*Oh embrace now, all you millions,*
*With one kiss for all the world.*

Helen could not stand through the entire gospel. A weakness came over her and she sat down. When mass ended she would try to put something in her stomach. A cup of coffee, a bite of toast.

Helen turned her head and counted the house, the church now more than a third full, a hundred and fifty maybe. They could not all be Italians, since one woman looked rather like Helen's mother, the imposing Mrs. Mary Josephine Nurney Archer in her elegant black hat. Helen had that in common with Francis: both had mothers who despised them.

It was twenty-one years before Helen discovered, folded in a locked diary, the single sheet of paper that was her father's final will, never known to exist and written when he knew he was going to kill himself, leaving half the modest residue of his fortune to Helen, the other half to be divided equally between her mother and brother.

Helen read the will aloud to her mother, a paralytic then, nursed toward the grave for ten years by Helen alone, and received in return a maternal smile of triumph at having stolen Helen's future, stolen it so that mother and son might live like peahen and peacock, son grown now into a political lawyer noted for his ability to separate widows from their inheritances, and who always hangs up when Helen calls.

Helen never got even with you for what you, without understanding, did to her, Patrick. Not even you, who profited most from it, understood Mother's duplicitous thievery. But Helen did manage to get even with Mother; left her that very day and moved to New York City, leaving brother dear to do the final nursing, which he accomplished by putting the old cripple into what Helen likes to think of now as the poorhouse, actually the public nursing home, and having her last days paid for by Albany County.

Alone and unloved in the poorhouse.

Where did your plumage go, Mother?

But Helen. Dare you be so vindictive? Did you not have tailfeathers of your own once, however briefly, however long ago? Just look at yourself sitting there staring at the bed with its dirty sheets beckoning to you. Your delicacy resists those sheets, does it not? Not only because of their dirt but because you also resist lying on your back with nothing of beauty to respond to, only the cracked plaster and peeling ceiling paint; whereas by sitting in the chair you can at least look at Grandmother Swan, or even at the blue cardboard clock on the back of the door, which might help you to estimate the time of your life: WAKE ME AT: as if any client of this establishment ever had, or ever would, use such a sign, as if crippled Donovan would ever see it if they did use it, or seeing it, heed it. The clock said ten minutes to eleven. Pretentious.

When you sit at the edge of the bed in a room like this, and hold on to the unpolished brass of the bed, and look at those dirty sheets and the soft cocoons of dust in the corner, you have the powerful impulse to go to the bathroom, where you were just sick for more than half an hour, and wash yourself. No. You have the impulse to go to the genuine bath farther down the hall, with the bathtub where you so often swatted and drowned the cockroaches before you scrubbed that tub, scrub, scrub, scrub. You would walk down the hall to the bath in your Japanese kimono with your almond soap inside your pink bathtowel and the carpets would be thick and soft under the soft soles of your slippers, which you kept under the bed when you were a child; the slippers with the brown wool tassel on the top and the soft yellow lining like a kid glove, that came in the Whitney's box under the Christmas tree. Santa Claus shops at Whitney's.

When you really don't care anymore about Whitney's, or Santa Claus, or shoes, or feet, or even Francis, when that which you thought would last as long as breath itself has worn out and you are a woman like Helen, you hold tightly to the brass, as surely as you would walk down the hall in bare feet, or in shoes with one broken strap, walk on filthy, threadbare carpet and wash under your arms and between your old breasts with the washcloth to keep down the body odor, if you had anyone to keep down the odor for.

Of course Helen is putting on airs with this thought, being just like her mother, washing out the washcloth with the cold water, all there is, and only after washing the cloth twice would she dare to use it on her face. And then she would (yes, she would, can you imagine? can you remember?) dab herself all over with the Madame Pompadour body powder, and touch her ears with the Violet de Paris perfume, and give her hair sixty strokes that way, sixty strokes this way, and say to her image in the mirror that pretty is as pretty does. Arthur loved her pretty.

Helen saw a man who looked a little bit like Arthur, going bald the way he always was, when she was leaving Saint Anthony's Church after mass. It wasn't Arthur, because Arthur was dead, and good enough for him. When she was nineteen, in 1906, Helen went to work in Arthur's piano store, selling only sheet music at first, and then later demonstrating how elegant the tone of Arthur's pianos could be when properly played.

Look at her sitting there at the Chickering upright, playing "Won't You Come Over to My House?" for that fashionable couple with no musical taste. Look at her there at the Steinway grand, playing a Bach suite for the handsome woman who knows her music. Look how both parties are buying pianos, thanks to magical Helen.

But then, one day when she is twenty-seven and her life is over, when she knows at last that she will never marry, and probably never go further with her music than the boundaries of the piano store, Helen thinks of Schubert, who never rose to be anything more than a children's music teacher, poor and sick, getting only fifteen or twenty cents for his songs, and dead at thirty-one; and on this awful day Helen sits down at Arthur's grand piano and plays "Who Is Silvia?" and then plays all she can remember of the flight of the raven from *Die Winterreise.*

The Schubert blossom,
Born to bloom unseen,
Like Helen.

Did Arthur do that?

Well, he kept her a prisoner of his love on Tuesdays and Thursdays, when he closed early, and on Friday nights too, when he told his wife he was rehearsing with the Mendelssohn Club. There is Helen now, in that small room on High Street, behind the drawn curtains, sitting naked in bed while Arthur stands up and puts on his dressing gown, expostulating no longer on sex but now on the *Missa Solemnis*, or was it Schubert's lieder, or maybe the glorious Ninth, which Berlioz said was like the first rays of the rising sun in May?

It was really all three, and much, much more, and Helen listened adoringly to the wondrous Arthur as his semen flowed out of her, and she aspired exquisitely to embrace all the music ever played, or sung, or imagined.

In her nakedness on that continuing Tuesday and

Thursday and unchanging Friday, Helen now sees the spoiled seed of a woman's barren dream: a seed that germinates and grows into a shapeless, windblown weed blossom of no value to anything, even its own species, for it produces no seed of its own; a mutation that grows only into the lovely day like all other wild things, and then withers, and perishes, and falls, and vanishes.

The Helen blossom.

One never knows the potential within the human breast.

One would never expect Arthur to abandon Helen for a younger woman, a tone-deaf secretary, a musical illiterate with a big bottom.

Stay on as long as you like, my love, Arthur told Helen; for there has never been a saleswoman as good as you.

Alas, poor Helen, loved for the wrong talent by angelic Arthur, to whom it was given to hurt Helen: who educated her body and soul and then sent them off to hell.

Helen walked from Saint Anthony's Church to South Pearl Street and headed north in search of a restaurant. She envisioned herself sitting at one of the small tables in the Primrose Tea Room on State Street, where they served petite watercress sandwiches, with crusts cut off, tea in Nippon cups and saucers, and tiny sugar cubes in a silver bowl with ever-so-delicate silver tongs.

But she settled for the Waldorf Cafeteria, where coffee was a nickel and buttered toast a dime. Discreetly, she took one of the dollar bills out of her brassiere and held it in her left fist inside her coat pocket. She let go of it only long enough to carry the coffee and toast to a table, and then she clutched it anew, a dollar with a fifteen-cent hole in it now. Eleven-eighty-five all she had left. She sweetened and creamed her coffee and sipped at it. She ate half a piece of toast and a bite of another and left the rest. She drank all the coffee, but food did not want to go down.

She paid her check and walked back out onto North

Pearl, clutching her change, wondering about Francis and what she should do now. The air had a bite to it, in spite of the warming sun, driving her mind indoors. And so she walked toward the Pruyn Library, a haven. She sat at a table, shivering and hugging herself, warming slowly but deeply chilled. She dozed willfully, in flight to the sun coast where the white birds fly, and a white-haired librarian shook her awake and said: "Madam, the rules do not allow sleeping in here," and she placed a back issue of *Life* magazine in front of Helen, and from the next table picked up the morning *Times-Union* on a stick and gave it to her, adding: "But you may stay as long as you like, my dear, if you choose to read." The woman smiled at Helen through her pince-nez and Helen returned the smile. There are nice people in the world and sometimes you meet them. Sometimes.

Helen looked at *Life* and found a picture of a two-block-long line of men and women in dark overcoats and hats, their hands in their pockets against the cold of a St. Louis day, waiting to pick up their relief checks. She saw a photo of Millie Smalls, a smiling Negro laundress who earned fifteen dollars a week and had just won $150,000 on her Irish Sweepstakes ticket.

Helen closed the magazine and looked at the newspaper. Fair and warmer, the weatherman said. He's a liar. Maybe up to fifty today, but yesterday it was thirty-two. Freezing. Helen shivered and thought of getting a room. Dewey leads Lehman in Crosley poll. Dr. Benjamin Ross of Albany's Dudley Observatory says Martians can't attack earth, and adds: "It is difficult to imagine a rocket-ship or space ship reaching earth. Earth is a very small target and in all probability a Martian space ship would miss it altogether." Albany's Mayor Thacher denies false registration of 5,000 voters in 1936. Woman takes poison after son is killed trying to hop freight train.

Helen turned the page and found Martin Daugherty's story about Billy Phelan and the kidnapping. She read it and began to cry, not absorbing any of it, but knowing the family was taking Francis away from her. If Francis and Helen still had a house together, he would never leave her. Never. But they hadn't had a house since early 1930. Francis was working as a fixit man in the South End then, wearing a full beard so nobody'd know it was him, and calling himself Bill Benson. Then the fixit shop went out of business and Francis started drinking again. After a few months of no job, no chance of one, he left Helen alone. "I ain't no good to you or anybody else," he said to her during his crying jag just before he went away. "Never amounted to nothin' and never will."

How insightful, Francis. How absolutely prophetic of you to see that you would come to nothing, even in Helen's eyes. Francis is somewhere now, alone, and even Helen doesn't love him anymore. Doesn't. For everything about love is dead now, wasted by weariness. Helen doesn't love Francis romantically, for that faded years ago, a rose that bloomed just once and then died forever. And she doesn't love Francis as a companion, for he is always screaming at her and leaving her alone to be fingered by other men. And she certainly doesn't love him as a love thing, because he can't love that way anymore. He tried so hard for so long, harder and longer than you could ever imagine, Finny, but all it did was hurt Helen to see it. It didn't hurt Helen physically because that part of her is so big now, and so old, that nothing can ever hurt her there anymore.

Even when Francis was strong he could never reach all the way up, because she was deeper. She used to need something exceptionally big, bigger than Francis. She had that thought the first time, when she began playing with men after Arthur, who was so big, but she never got what she needed. Well, perhaps once. Who was that? Helen can't remember the face that went with the once. She can't remember anything now but how that night, that once, something in her was touched: a deep center no one had touched before, or has touched since. That was when she thought: This is why some girls become professionals, because it is so good, and there would always be somebody else, somebody new, to help you along.

But a girl like Helen could never really do a thing like that, couldn't just open herself to any man who came by with the price of another day. Does anyone think Helen was ever that kind of a girl?

Ode to Joy, please.

*Freude, schöner Götterfunken,*
*Tochter aus Elysium!*

Helen's stomach rumbled and she left the library to breathe deeply of the therapeutic morning air. As she walked down Clinton Avenue and then headed south on Broadway, a vague nausea rose in her and she stopped between two parked cars to hold on to a phone pole, ready to vomit. But the nausea passed and she walked on, past the railroad station, until the musical instruments in the window of the Modern Music Shop caught her attention. She let her eyes play over the banjos and ukuleles, the snare drum and the trombone, the trumpet and violin. Phonograph records stood on shelves, above the instruments: Benny Goodman, the Dorsey Brothers, Bing Crosby, John McCormack singing Schubert, Beethoven's "Appassionata."

She went into the store and looked at, and touched, the instruments. She looked at the rack of new song sheets: "The Flat Foot Floogie," "My Heart Belongs to Daddy," "You Must Have Been a Beautiful Baby." She walked to the counter and asked the young man with the slick brown hair: "Do you have Beethoven's Ninth Symphony?" She paused. "And might I see that Schubert album in your window?"

"We do, and you may," said the man, and he found them and handed them to her and pointed her to the booth where she could listen to the music in private.

She played the Schubert first, John McCormack inquiring: Who is Silvia? What is she? That all our swains commend her? . . . Is she as kind as she is fair? And then, though she absolutely loved McCormack, adored Schubert, she put them both aside for the fourth movement of the *Choral* Symphony.

*Joy, thou spark from flame immortal,*
*Daughter of Elysium!*

The words tumbled at Helen in the German and she converted them to her own joyful tongue.

*He that's won a noble woman,*
*Let him join our jubilee!*

Oh the rapture she felt. She grew dizzy at the sounds: the oboes, the bassoons, the voices, the grand march of the fugal theme. Scherzo. Molto vivace.

Helen swooned.

A young woman customer saw her fall and was at her side almost instantly. Helen came to with her head in the young woman's lap, the young clerk fanning her with a green record jacket. Beethoven, once green, green as a glade. The needle scratched in the record's end groove. The music had stopped, but not in Helen's brain. It rang out still, the first rays of the rising sun in May.

"How you feeling, ma'am," the clerk asked.

Helen smiled, hearing flutes and violas.

"I think I'm all right. Will you help me up?"

"Rest a minute," the girl said. "Get your bearings first. Would you like a doctor?"

"No, no thank you. I know what it is. I'll be all right in a minute or two."

But she knew now that she would have to get the room and get it immediately. She did not want to collapse crossing the street. She needed a place of her own, warm and dry, and with her belongings near her. The clerk and the young woman customer helped her to her feet and stood by as she settled herself again on the bench of the listening booth. When the young people were reassured that Helen was fully alert and probably not going to collapse again, they left her. And that's when she slipped the record of the fourth movement inside her coat, under her blouse, and let it rest on the slope of her tumor her doctor said was benign. But how could anything so big be benign? She pulled her coat around her as tightly as she could without cracking the record, said her thank yous to both her benefactors, and walked slowly out of the store.

Her bag was at Palombo's Hotel and she headed for there: all the way past Madison Avenue. Would she make it to the hotel without a collapse? Well, she did. She was exhausted but she found crippled old Donovan in his rickety rocker, and his spittoon at his feet, on the landing between the first and second floors, all there was of a lobby in this establishment. She said she wanted to redeem her bag and rent a room, the same room she and Francis always took whenever it was empty. And it was empty.

Six dollars to redeem the bag, old Donovan told her, and a dollar and a half for one night, or two-fifty for two nights running. Just one, Helen said, but then she thought: What if I don't die tonight? I will need it tomorrow too.

And so she took the bargain rate, which left her with three dollars and thirty-five cents.

Old Donovan gave her the key to the second-floor room and went to the cellar for her suitcase.

"Ain't seen ya much," Donovan said when he brought the bag to her room.

"We've been busy," Helen said. "Francis got a job."

"A job? Ya don't say."

"We're all quite organized now, you might describe it. It's just possible that we'll rent an apartment up on Hamilton Street."

"You're back in the chips. Mighty good. Francis comin' in tonight?"

"He might be, and he might not be," said Helen. "It all depends on his work, and how busy he might or might not be."

"I get it," said Donovan.

She opened the suitcase and found the kimono and put it on. She went then to wash herself, but before she could wash she vomited; sat on the floor in front of the toilet bowl and vomited until there was nothing left to come up; and then she retched dryly for five minutes, finally taking sips of water so there would be something to bring up. And Francis thought she was just being contrary, refusing Jack's cheese sandwich.

Finally it passed, and she rinsed her mouth and her stinging eyes and did, oh yes, did wash herself, and then padded back along the threadbare carpet to her room, where she sat in the chair at the foot of the bed, staring at the swan and remembering nights in this room with Francis.

Clara, that cheap whore, rolled that nice young man in the brown suit and then came in here to hide. If you're gonna sleep with a man, sleep with him, Francis said. Be a goddamn woman. If you're gonna roll a man, roll him.

But don't sleep with him and then roll him. Francis had such nice morals. Oh Clara, why in heaven's name do you come in here with your trouble? Haven't we got trouble enough of our own without you? All Clara got was fourteen dollars. But that is a lot.

Helen propped her Beethoven record against the pillow in the center of the bed and studied its perfection. Then she rummaged in the suitcase to see and touch all that was in it: another pair of bloomers, her rhinestone butterfly, her blue skirt with the rip in it, Francis's safety razor and his penknife, his old baseball clippings, his red shirt, and his left brown shoe, the right one lost; but one shoe's better than none, ain't it? was Francis's reasoning. Sandra lost a shoe but Francis found it for her. Francis was very thoughtful. Very everything. Very Catholic, though he pretended not to be. That was why Francis and Helen could never marry.

Wasn't it nice the way Helen and Francis put their religion in the way of marriage?

Wasn't that an excellent idea?

For really, Helen wanted to fly free in the same way Francis did. After Arthur she knew she would always want to be free, even if she had to suffer for it.

Arthur, Arthur, Helen no longer blames you for anything. She knows you were a man of frail allegiance in a way that Francis never was; knows too that she allowed you to hurt her.

Helen remembers Arthur's face and how relieved it was, how it smiled and wished her luck the day she said she was leaving to take a job playing piano for silent films and vaudeville acts. Moving along in the world willfully, that's what Helen was doing then (and now). A will to grace, if you would like to call it that, however elusive that grace has proven to be.

Was this willfulness a little deceit Helen was playing on herself?

Was she moving, instead, in response to impulses out of that deep center?

Why was it, really, that things never seemed to work out?

Why was Helen's life always turning into some back alley, like a wandering old cat?

What is Helen?

Who is Silvia, please?

Please?

Helen stands up and holds the brass. Helen's feet are like fine brass. She is not unpolished like the brass of this bed. Helen is the very polished person who is standing at the end of the end bed in the end room of the end hotel of the end city of the end.

And when a person like Helen comes to an ending of something, she grows nostalgic and sentimental. She has always appreciated the fine things in life: music, kind words, gentility, flowers, sunshine, and good men. People would feel sad if they knew what Helen's life might have been like had it gone in another direction than the one that brought her to this room.

People would perhaps even weep, possibly out of some hope that women like Helen could go on living until they found themselves, righted themselves, discovered ever-unfolding joy instead of coming to lonely ends. People would perhaps feel that some particular thing went wrong somewhere and that if it had only gone right it wouldn't have brought a woman like Helen so low.

But that is the error; for there are no women like Helen.

Helen is no symbol of lost anything, wrong-road-taken kind of person, if-they-only-knew-then kind of person.

Helen is no pure instinct deranged, no monomaniacal yearning out of a deep center that wants everything, even the power to destroy itself.

Helen is no wandering cat in its ninth termination.

For since Helen was born, and so elegantly raised by her father, and so exquisitely self-developed, she has been making her own decisions based on rational thinking, reasonably current knowledge, intuition about limitations, and the usual instruction by friends, lovers, enemies, and others. Her head was never injured, and her brain, contrary to what some people might think, is not pickled. She did not miss reading the newspapers, although she has tapered off somewhat in recent years, for now all the news seems bad. She always listened to the radio and kept up on the latest in music. And in the winter in the library she read novels about women and love: Helen knows all about Lily Bart and Daisy Miller. Helen also cared for her appearance and kept her body clean. She washed her underthings regularly and wore earrings and dressed modestly and carried her rosary until they stole it. She did not sleep when sleep was not called for. She went through her life feeling: I really do believe I am doing the more-or-less right thing. I believe in God. I salute the flag. I wash my armpits and between my legs, and what if I did drink too much? Whose business is that? Who knows how much I didn't drink?

They never think of that sort of thing when they call a woman like Helen a drunken old douchebag. Why would anyone (like that nasty Little Red in the back of Finny's car) ever want to revile Helen that way? When she hears people say such things about her, Helen then plays the pretend game. She dissembles. Helen remembers that word even though Francis thinks she has forgotten her education. But she has not. She is not a drunk and not a whore. Her attitude is: I flew through my years and I never let a man use me for money. I went Dutch lots of times. I would let them buy the drinks but that's because it's the man's place to buy drink.

And when you're a woman like Helen who hasn't turned out to be a whore, who hasn't led anybody into sin . . . (Well, there were some young boys in her life occasionally, lonely in the bars like Helen so often was, but they seemed to know about sin already. Once.)

Once.

Was once a boy?

Yes, with a face like a priest.

Oh Helen, how blasphemous of you to have such a thought. Thank God you never loved up a priest. How would you ever explain that?

Because priests are good.

And so when Helen holds the brass, and looks at the clock that still says ten minutes to eleven, and thinks of slippers and music and the great butterfly and the white pebble with the hidden name, she has this passing thought for priests. For when you were raised like Helen was, you think of priests as holding the keys to the door of redemption. No matter how many sins you have committed (sands of the desert, salt of the sea), you are bound to come to the notion of absolution at the time of brass holding and clock watching, and to the remembering of how you even used to put Violet de Paris on your brassiere so that when he opened your dress to kiss you there, he wouldn't smell any sweat.

But priests, Helen, have nothing whatsoever to do with brassieres and kissing, and you should be ashamed to have put them all in the same thought. Helen does truly regret such a thought, but after all, it has been a most troubled time for her and her religion. And even though she prayed at mass this morning, and has prayed intermittently throughout the day ever since, even though she prayed in Finny's car last night, saying her Now I Lay Me Down to Sleeps when there was no sleep or chance of it, then the point is that, despite all prayer, Helen has no compulsion to confess her sins to gain absolution.

Helen has even come to the question of whether or not she is really a Catholic, and to what a Catholic really is these days. She thinks that, truly, she may not be one anymore. But if she isn't, she certainly isn't anything else either. She certainly isn't a Methodist, Mr. Chester.

What brought her to this uncertainty is the accumulation of her sins, and if you must call them sins, then there is certainly quite an accumulation. But Helen prefers to call them decisions, which is why she has no compulsion to confess them. On the other hand, Helen wonders whether anyone is aware of how really good a life she lived. She never betrayed anybody, and that, in the end, is what counts most with her. She admits she is leaving Francis, but no one could call that a betrayal. One might, perhaps, call it an abdication, the way the King of England abdicated for the woman he loved. Helen is abdicating for the man she used to love so he can be as free as Helen wants him to be, as free as she always was in her own way, as free as the two of them were even when they were most perfectly locked together. Didn't Francis beg on the street for Helen when she was sick in '33? Why, he never begged even for himself before that. If Francis could become a beggar out of love, why can't Helen abdicate for the same reason?

Of course the relationships Helen had with Arthur and Francis were sinful in the eyes of some. And she admits that certain other liberties she has taken with the commandments of God and the Church might also loom large against her when the time of judgment comes (brass and clock, brass and clock). But even so, there will be no priests coming to see her, and she is surely not going out to see them. She is not going to declare to anyone for any reason that loving Francis was sinful when it was very probably–no, very certainly–the greatest thing in her life, greater, finally, than loving Arthur, for Arthur failed of honor.

And so when crippled Donovan knocks again at eleven

o'clock and asks if Helen needs anything, she says no, no thank you, old cripple, I don't need anything or anybody anymore. And old Donovan says: The night man's just comin' on, and so I'm headin' home. I'll be here in the mornin'. And Helen says: Thank you, Donovan, thank you ever so much for your concern, and for saying good night to me. And after he goes away from the door she lets go of the brass and thinks of Beethoven, Ode to Joy,

And hears the joyous multitudes advancing,

Dah dah-dah,

Dah dah-de-dah-dah,

And feels her legs turning to feathers and sees that her head is floating down to meet them as her body bends under the weight of so much joy,

Sees it floating ever so slowly

As the white bird glides over the water until it comes to rest on the Japanese kimono

That has fallen so quietly,

So softly,

Onto the grass where the moonlight grows.

# VI.

First came the fire in a lower Broadway warehouse, near the old Fitzgibbon downtown ironworks. It rose in its own sphere, in an uprush into fire's own perfection, and great flames violated the sky. Then, as Francis and Rosskam halted behind trucks and cars, Rosskam's horse snorty and balky with elemental fear, the fire touched some store of thunder and the side of the warehouse blew out in a great rising cannon blossom of black smoke, which the wind carried toward them. Motorists rolled up their windows, but the vulnerable lights of Francis, Rosskam, and the horse smarted with evil fumes.

Ahead of them a policeman routed traffic into a U-turn and sent it back north. Rosskam cursed in a foreign language Francis didn't recognize. But that Rosskam was cursing was unmistakable. As they turned toward Madison Avenue, both men's faces were astream with stinging tears.

They were now pulling an empty wagon, fresh from dumping the day's first load of junk back at Rosskam's yard. Francis had lunched at the yard on an apple Rosskam gave him, and had changed into his new white-on-white shirt, throwing his old blue relic onto Rosskam's rag mountain. They had then set out on the day's second run, heading for the deep South End of the city, until the fire turned them around at three o'clock.

Rosskam turned up Pearl Street and the wagon rolled along into North Albany, the smoke still rising into the heavens below and behind them. Rosskam called out his double-noted ragman's dirge and caught the attention of a few cluttered housewives. From the backyard of an old house near Emmett Street, Francis hauled out a wheelless wheelbarrow with a rust hole through its bottom. As he heaved it upward into the wagon, the odor of fire still in his nostrils, he confronted Fiddler Quain, sitting on an upended metal chamber pot that had been shot full of holes by some backyard marksman.

The Fiddler, erstwhile motorman, now wearing a tan tweed suit, brown polka-dot bow tie, and sailor straw hat, smiled coherently at Francis for the first time since that day on Broadway in 1901 when they both ignited the kerosene-soaked sheets that trapped the strikebreaking trolley car.

When a soldier split the Fiddler's skull with a rifle butt, the sympathetic mob spirited him away to safety before he could be arrested. But the blow left the man mindless for a dozen years, cared for by his spinster sister, Martha. Martyred herself by his wound, Martha paraded the Fiddler through the streets of North Albany, a heroic vegetable, so the neighbors could see the true consequences of the smartypants trolley strike.

Francis offered to be a bearer at the Fiddler's funeral in 1913, but Martha rejected him; for she believed it was Francis's firebrand style that had seduced the Fiddler into violence that fated morning. Your hands have done enough damage, she told Francis. You'll not touch my brother's coffin.

Pay her no mind, the Fiddler told Francis from his perch on the riddled pot. I don't blame you for anything. Wasn't I ten years your elder? Couldn't I make up my own mind?

But then the Fiddler gave Francis a look that loosened a tide of bafflement, as he said solemnly: It's those traitorous hands of yours you'll have to forgive.

Francis brushed rust off his fingers and went behind the house for more dead metal. When he returned with an armload, the scab Harold Allen, wearing a black coat and a motorman's cap, was sitting with the Fiddler, who had his boater in his lap now. When Francis looked at the pair of them, Harold Allen doffed his cap. Both men's heads were laid open and bloody, but not bleeding, their unchanging wounds obviously healed over and as much a part of their aerial bodies as their eyes, which burned with an entropic passion common among murdered men.

Francis threw the old junk into the wagon and turned away. When he turned back to verify the images, two more men were sitting in the wheelless wheelbarrow. Francis could call neither of them by name, but he knew from the astonishment in the hollows of their eyes that they were the shopper and haberdasher, bystanders both, who had been killed by the soldiers' random retaliatory fire after Francis opened Harold Allen's skull with the smooth stone.

"I'm ready," said Francis to Rosskam. "You ready?"

"What's the big hurry-up?" Rosskam asked.

"Nothin' else to haul. Shouldn't we be movin'?"

"He's impatient too, this bum," Rosskam said, and he climbed aboard the wagon.

Francis, feeling the eyes of the four shades on him, gave them all the back of his neck as the wagon rolled north on

Pearl Street, Annie's street. Getting closer. He pulled up the collar of his coat against a new bite in the wind, the western sky graying with ominous clouds. It was almost three-thirty by the Nehi clock in the window of Elmer Rivenburgh's grocery. First day of early winter. If it rains tonight and we're outside, we freeze our ass once and for all.

He rubbed his hands together. Were they the enemies? How could a man's hands betray him? They were full of scars, calluses, split fingernails, ill-healed bones broken on other men's jaws, veins so bloated and blue they seemed on the verge of explosion. The hands were long-fingered, except where there was no finger, and now, with accreting age, the fingers had thickened, like the low-growing branches of a tree.

Traitors? How possible?

"You like your hands?" Francis asked Rosskam.

"*Like*, you say? Do I like my hands?"

"Yeah. You like 'em?"

Rosskam looked at his hands, looked at Francis, looked away.

"I mean it," Francis said. "I got the idea that my hands do things on their own, you know what I mean?"

"Not yet," said Rosskam.

"They don't need me. They do what they goddamn please."

"Ah ha," said Rosskam. He looked again at his own gnarled hands and then again at Francis. "Nutsy," he said, and slapped the horse's rump with the reins. "Giddap," he added, changing the subject.

Francis remembered Skippy Maguire's left hand, that first summer away at Dayton. Skippy was Francis's roommate, a pitcher: tall and lefty, a man who strutted when he walked; and on the mound he shaped up like a king of the hill. Why, when he wanted to, Skippy could strut standin' still. But then his left hand split open, the fingers first and then the palm. He pampered the hand: greased it, sunned it, soaked it in Epsom salts and beer, but it wouldn't heal. And when the team manager got impatient, Skippy ignored the splits and pitched ten minutes in a practice session, which turned the ball red and tore the fingers and the palm into a handful of bloody pulp. The manager told Skippy he was stupid and took him and his useless hand off the payroll.

That night Skippy cursed the manager, got drunker than usual, started a fire in the coal stove even though it was August, and when it was roaring, reached in and picked up a handful of flaming coal. And he showed that goddamn Judas of a hand a thing or two. The doc had to cut off three fingers to save it.

Well, Francis may be a little nutsy to people like Rosskam, but he wouldn't do anything like Skippy did. Would he? He looked at his hands, connecting scars to memories. Rowdy Dick got the finger. The jagged scar behind the pinky . . . a violent thirst gave him that one, the night he punched out a liquor store window in Chinatown to get at a bottle of wine. In a fight on Eighth Avenue with a bum who wanted to screw Helen, Francis broke the first joint on his middle finger and it healed crookedly. And a wild man in Philadelphia out to steal Francis's hat bit off the tip of the left thumb.

But Francis got 'em. He avenged all scars, and he lived to remember every last one of them dickie birds too, most of 'em probably dead now, by their own hand maybe. Or the hand of Francis?

Rowdy Dick.

Harold Allen.

The latter name suddenly acted as a magical key to history for Francis. He sensed for the first time in his life the workings of something other than conscious will within himself: insight into a pattern, an overview of all the violence in his history, of how many had died or been maimed by his hand, or had died, like that nameless pair of astonished shades, as an indirect result of his violent ways. He limped now, would always limp with the metal plate in his left leg, because a man stole a bottle of orange soda from him. He found the man, a runt, and retrieved the soda. But the runt hit him with an ax handle and splintered the bone. And what did Francis do? Well the runt was too little to hit, so Francis shoved his face into the dirt and bit a piece out of the back of his neck.

There are things I never wanted to learn how to do, is one thought that came to Francis.

And there are things I did without needin' to learn.

And I never wanted to know about them either.

Francis's hands, as he looked at them now, seemed to be messengers from some outlaw corner of his psyche, artificers of some involuntary doom element in his life. He seemed now to have always been the family killer; for no one else he knew of in the family had ever lived as violently as he. And yet he had never sought that kind of life.

But you set out to kill *me*, Harold Allen said silently from the back of the wagon.

"No," answered Francis without turning. "Not kill anybody. Just do some damage, get even. Maybe bust a trolley window, cause a ruckus, stuff like that."

But you knew, even that early in your career, how accurate your throw could be. You were proud of that talent. It was what you brought to the strike that day, and it was why you spent the morning hunting for stones the same weight as a baseball. You aimed at me to make yourself a hero.

"But not to kill you."

Just to knock out an eye, was it?

Francis now remembered the upright body of Harold

Allen on the trolley, indisputably a target. He remembered the coordination of vision with arm movement, of distance with snap of wrist. For a lifetime he had remembered precisely the way Harold Allen crumpled when the stone struck his forehead at the hairline. Francis had not heard, but had forever after imagined, the sound the stone (moving at maybe seventy miles an hour?) made when it hit Harold Allen's skull. It made the skull sound as hollow, as tough, and as explodable, he decided, as a watermelon hit with a baseball bat.

Francis considered the evil autonomy of his hands and wondered what Skippy Maguire, in his later years, had made of his own left hand's suicidal impulse. Why was it that suicide kept rising up in Francis's mind? Wake up in the weeds outside Pittsburgh, half frozen over, too cold to move, flaked out 'n' stiffer than a chunk of old iron, and you say to yourself: Francis, you don't ever want to put in another night, another mornin', like this one was. Time to go take a header off the bridge.

But after a while you stand up, wipe the frost out of your ear, go someplace to get warm, bum a nickel for coffee, and then start walkin' toward somewheres else that ain't near no bridge.

Francis did not understand this flirtation with suicide, this flight from it. He did not know why he hadn't made the big leap the way Helen's old man had when he knew he was done in. Too busy, maybe, figurin' out the next half hour. No way for Francis ever to get a real good look past the sunset, for he's the kind of fella just kept runnin' when things went bust; never had the time to stop anyplace easy just to die.

But he never wanted to run off all that much either. Who'd have figured his mother would announce to the family at Thanksgiving dinner, just after Francis married Annie, that neither he nor his common little woman would ever be welcome in this house again? The old bat relented after two years and Francis was allowed visiting privileges. But he only went once, and not even inside the door then, for he found out that privileges didn't extend to most uncommon Annie at his side.

And so family contact on Colonie Street ended for Francis in a major way. He vacated the flat he'd rented nine doors up the block, moved to the North End to be near Annie's family, and never set foot again in the goddamned house until the old battle-ax (sad, twisted, wrongheaded, pitiable woman) died.

Departure.

Flight of a kind, the first.

Flight again, when he killed the scab.

Flight again, every summer until it was no longer possible, in order to assert the one talent that gave him full and powerful ease, that let him dance on the earth to the din of brass bands, raucous cheers, and the voluptuous approval of the crowd. Flight kept Francis sane during all those years, and don't ask him why. He loved living with Annie and the kids, loved his sister, Mary, and half-loved his brothers Peter and Chick and his moron brother, Tommy, too, who all came to visit him at his house when he was no longer welcome at theirs.

He loved and half-loved lots of things about Albany.
But then one day it's February again,
And it won't be long now till the snow gets gone again,
And the grass comes green again,
And then the dance music rises in Francis's brain,
And he longs to flee again,
And he flees.

□ □ □

A man stepped out of a small apartment house behind Sacred Heart Church and motioned to Rosskam, who reined the horse and climbed down to negotiate for new junk. Francis, on the wagon, watched a group of children coming out of School 20 and crossing the street. A woman whom Francis took to be their teacher stood a few steps into the intersection with raised hand to augment the stopping power of the red light, even though there were no automobiles in sight, only Rosskam's wagon, which was already standing still. The children, their secular school day ended, crossed like a column of ants into the custody of two nuns on the opposite corner, gliding black figures who would imbue the pliant young minds with God's holy truth: Blessed are the meek. Francis remembered Billy and Peg as children, similarly handed over from the old school to this same church for instruction in the ways of God, as if anybody could ever figure that one out.

At the thought of Billy and Peg, Francis trembled. He was only a block away from where they lived. And he knew the address now, from the newspaper. I'll come by of a Sunday and bring a turkey, Francis had told Billy when Billy first asked him to come home. And Billy's line was: Who the fuck wants a turkey? Yeah, who does? Francis answered then. But his answer now was: I sorta do.

Rosskam climbed back on the wagon, having made no deal with the man from the apartment house, who wanted garbage removed.

"Some people," said Rosskam to the rear end of his horse, "they don't know junk. It ain't garbage. And garbage, it ain't junk."

The horse moved forward, every clip clop of its hooves tightening the bands around Francis's chest. How would he do it? What would he say? Nothing to say. Forget it. No, just knock at the door. Well, I'm home. Or maybe just: How's chances for a cupacoffee; see what that brings. Don't ask no favors or make no promises. Don't apologize. Don't cry. Make out it's just a visit. Get the news, pay respects, get gone.

But what about the turkey?

"I think I'm gonna get off the wagon up ahead a bit," Francis told Rosskam, who looked at him with a squinty eye. "Gettin' near the end of the day anyway, 'bout an hour or so left before it starts gettin' dark, ain't that right?" He looked up at the sky, gray but bright, with a vague hint of sun in the west.

"Quit before dark?" Rosskam said. "You don't quit before dark."

"Gotta see some people up ahead. Ain't seen 'em in a while."

"So go."

" 'Course I want my pay for what I done till now."

"You didn't work the whole day. Come by tomorrow, I'll figure how much."

"Worked most of the day. Seven hours, must be, no lunch."

"Half a day you worked. Three hours yet before dark."

"I worked more'n half a day. I worked more'n seven hours. I figure you can knock off a dollar. That'd be fair. I'll take six 'stead of seven, and a quarter out for the shirt. Five-seventy-five."

"Half a day you work, you get half pay. Three-fifty."

"No sir."

"No? I am the boss."

"That's right. You are the boss. And you're one strong fella too. But I ain't no dummy, and I know when I'm bein' skinned. And I want to tell you right now, Mr. Rosskam, I'm mean as hell when I get riled up." He held out his right hand for inspection. "If you think I won't fight for what's mine, take a look. That hand's seen it all. I mean the worst. Dead men took their last ride on that hand. You get me?"

Rosskam reined the horse, braked the wagon, and looped the reins around a hook on the footboard. The wagon stood in the middle of the block, immediately across Pearl Street from the main entrance to the school. More children were exiting and moving in ragged columns toward the church. Blessed are the many meek. Rosskam studied Francis's hand, still outstretched, with digits gone, scars blazing, veins pounding, fingers curled in the vague beginnings of a fist.

"Threats," he said. "You make threats. I don't like threats. Five-twenty-five I pay, no more."

"Five-seventy-five. I say five-seventy-five is what's fair. You gotta be fair in this life."

From inside his shirt Rosskam pulled out a change purse which hung around his neck on a leather thong. He opened it and stripped off five singles, from a wad, counted them twice, and put them in Francis's outstretched hand, which turned its palm skyward to receive them. Then he added the seventy-five cents.

"A bum is a bum," Rosskam said. "I hire no more bums."

"I thank ye," Francis said, pocketing the cash.

"You I don't like," Rosskam said.

"Well I sorta liked you," Francis said. "And I ain't really a bad sort once you get to know me." He leaped off the wagon and saluted Rosskam, who pulled away without a word or a look, the wagon half full of junk, empty of shades.

□ □ □

Francis walked toward the house with a more pronounced limp than he'd experienced for weeks. The leg pained him, but not excessively. And yet he was unable to lift it from the sidewalk in a normal gait. He walked exceedingly slowly and to a passerby he would have seemed to be lifting the leg up from a sidewalk paved with glue. He could not see the house half a block away, only a gray porch he judged to be part of it. He paused, seeing a chubby middle-aged woman emerging from another house. When she was about to pass him he spoke.

"Excuse me, lady, but d'ya know where I could get me a nice little turkey?"

The woman looked at him with surprise, then terror, and retreated swiftly up her walkway and back into the house. Francis watched her with awe. Why, when he was sober, and wearing a new shirt, should he frighten a woman with a simple question? The door reopened and a shoeless bald man in an undershirt and trousers stood in the doorway.

"What did you ask my wife?" he said.

"I asked if she knew where I could get a turkey."

"What for?"

"Well," said Francis, and he paused, and scuffed one foot, "my duck died."

"Just keep movin', bud."

"Gotcha," Francis said, and he limped on.

He hailed a group of schoolboys crossing the street toward him and asked: "Hey fellas, you know a meat market around here?"

"Yeah, Jerry's," one said, "up at Broadway and Lawn."

Francis saluted the boy as the others stared. When Francis started to walk they all turned and ran ahead of him. He walked past the house without looking at it, his gait improving a bit. He would have to walk two blocks to the market, then two blocks back. Maybe they'd have a turkey for sale. Settle for a chicken? No.

By the time he reached Lawn Avenue he was walking well, and by Broadway his gait, for him, was normal. The floor of Jerry's meat market was bare wood, sprinkled with sawdust and extraordinarily clean. Shining white display cases with slanted and glimmering glass offered rows of splendid livers, kidneys, and bacon, provocative steaks and chops, and handsomely ground sausage and hamburg to Francis, the lone customer.

"Help you?" a white-aproned butcher asked. His hair

was so black that his facial skin seemed bleached.

"Turkey," Francis said. "I'd like me a nice dead turkey."

"It's the only kind we carry," the butcher said. "Nice and dead. How big?"

"How big they come?"

"So big you wouldn't believe it."

"Gimme a try."

"Twenty-five, twenty-eight pounds?"

"How much those big fellas sell for?"

"Depends on how much they weigh."

"Right. How much a pound, then?"

"Forty-four cents."

"Forty-four. Say forty." He paused. "You got maybe a twelve-pounder?"

The butcher entered the white meat locker and came out with a turkey in each hand. He weighed one, then another.

"Ten pounds here, and this is twelve and a half."

"Give us that big guy," Francis said, and he put the five singles and change on the white counter as the butcher wrapped the turkey in waxy white paper. The butcher left him twenty-five cents change on the counter.

"How's business, pal?" Francis asked.

"Slow. No money in the world."

"They's money. You just gotta go get it. Lookit that five bucks I just give ye. I got me that this afternoon."

"If I go out to get money, who'll mind the store?"

"Yeah," said Francis, "I s'pose some guys just gotta sit and wait. But it's a nice clean place you got to wait in."

"Dirty butchers go out of business."

"Keep the meat nice and clean, is what it is."

"Right. Good advice for everybody. Enjoy your dead turkey."

□ □ □

He walked down Broadway to King Brady's saloon and then stared down toward the foot of North Street, toward Welt the Tin's barn and the old lock, long gone, a daylight look at last. A few more houses stood on the street now, but it hadn't changed so awful much. He'd looked briefly at it from the bus, and again last night in the barn, but despite the changes time had made, his eyes now saw only the vision of what had been so long ago; and he gazed down on reconstituted time: two men walking up toward Broadway, one of them looking not unlike himself at twenty-one. He understood the cast of the street's incline as the young man stepped upward, and upward, and upward toward where Francis stood.

The turkey's coldness penetrated his coat, chilling his arm and his side. He switched the package to his other arm and walked up North Third Street toward their house. They'll figure I want 'em to cook the turkey, he thought. Just tell 'em: Here's a turkey, cook it up of a Sunday.

Kids came toward him on bikes. Leaves covered the sidewalks of Walter Street. His leg began to ache, his feet again in the glue. Goddamn legs got a life of their own too. He turned the corner, saw the front stoop, walked past it. He turned at the driveway and stopped at the side door just before the garage. He stared at the dotted white curtain behind the door's four small windowpanes, looked at the knob, at the aluminum milkbox. He'd stole a whole gang of milk outa boxes just like it. Bum. Killer. Thief. He touched the bell, heard the steps, watched the curtain being pulled aside, saw the eye, watched the door open an inch.

"Howdy," he said.

"Yes?"

Her.

"Brought a turkey for ye."

"A turkey?"

"Yep. Twelve-and-a-half-pounder." He held it aloft with one hand.

"I don't understand."

"I told Bill I'd come by of a Sunday and bring a turkey. It ain't Sunday but I come anyway."

"Is that you, Fran?"

"It ain't one of them fellas from Mars."

"Well my God. My God, my God." She opened the door wide.

"How ya been, Annie? You're lookin' good."

"Oh come in, come in." She went up the five stairs ahead of him. Stairs to the left went into the cellar, where he thought he might first enter, carry out some of their throwaways to Rosskam's wagon before he made himself known. Now he was going into the house itself, closing the side door behind him. Up five stairs with Annie watching and into the kitchen, she backing away in front of him. She's staring. But she's smiling. All right.

"Billy told us he'd seen you," she said. She stopped in the center of the kitchen and Francis stopped too. "But he didn't think you'd ever come. My oh my, what a surprise. We saw the story about you in the paper."

"Hope it didn't shame you none."

"We all thought it was funny. Everybody in town thought it was funny, registering twenty times to vote."

"Twenty-one."

"Oh my, Fran. Oh my, what a surprise this is."

"Here. Do somethin' with this critter. It's freezin' me up."

"You didn't have to bring anything. And a turkey. What it must've cost you."

"Iron Joe always used to tell me: Francis, don't come by empty-handed. Hit the bell with your elbow."

She had store teeth in her mouth. Those beauties gone. Her hair was steel-gray, only a trace of the brown left, and her chin was caved in a little from the new teeth. But that smile was the same, that honest-to-god smile. She'd put on weight: bigger breasts, bigger hips; and her shoes turned over at the counters. Varicose veins through the stocking too, hands all red, stains on her apron. That's what housework does to a pretty kid like she was.

Like she was when she came into The Wheelbarrow.

The canalers' and lumbermen's saloon that Iron Joe ran at the foot of Main Street.

Prettiest kid in the North End. Folks always said that about pretty girls.

But she was.

Came in lookin' for Iron Joe,

And Francis, working up to it for two months,

Finally spoke to her.

Howdy, he'd said.

Two hours later they were sitting between two piles of boards in Kibbee's lumberyard with nobody to see them, holding hands and Francis saying goopy things he swore to himself he'd never say to anybody.

And then they kissed.

Not just then, but some hours or maybe even days later, Francis compared that kiss to Katrina's first, and found them as different as cats and dogs. Remembering them both now as he stood looking at Annie's mouth with its store teeth, he perceived that a kiss is as expressive of a way of life as is a smile, or a scarred hand. Kisses come up from below, or down from above. They come from the brain sometimes, sometimes from the heart, and sometimes just from the crotch. Kisses that taper off after a while come only from the heart and leave the taste of sweetness. Kisses that come from the brain tend to try to work things out inside other folks' mouths and don't hardly register. And kisses from the crotch and the brain put together, with maybe a little bit of heart, like Katrina's, well they are the kisses that can send you right around the bend for your whole life.

But then you get one like that first whizzer on Kibbee's lumber pile, one that come out of the brain and the heart and the crotch, and out of the hands on your hair, and out of those breasts that weren't all the way blown up yet, and out of the clutch them arms give you, and out of time itself, which keeps track of how long it can go on without you gettin' even slightly bored the way you got bored years later with kissin' almost anybody but Helen, and out of fingers (Katrina had fingers like that) that run themselves around and over your face and down your neck, and out of the grip you take on her shoulders, especially on them bones that come out of the middle of her back like angel wings, and out of them eyes that keep openin' and closin' to make sure that this is still goin' and still real and not just stuff you dream about and when you know it's real it's okay to close 'em again, and outa that tongue, holy shit, that tongue, you gotta ask where she learned that because nobody ever did that that good except Katrina who was married and with a kid and had a right to know, but Annie, goddamn, Annie, where'd you pick that up, or maybe you been gidzeyin' heavy on this lumber pile regular (No, no, no, I know you never, I always knew you never), and so it is natural with a woman like Annie that the kiss come out of every part of her body and more, outa that mouth with them new teeth Francis is now looking at, with the same lips he remembers and doesn't want to kiss anymore except in memory (though that could be subject to change), and he sees well beyond the mouth into a primal location in this woman's being, a location that evokes in him not only the memory of years but decades and even more, the memory of epochs, aeons, so that he is sure that no matter where he might have sat with a woman and felt this way, whether it was in some ancient cave or some bogside shanty, or on a North Albany lumber pile, he and she would both know that there was something in each of them that had to stop being one and become two, that had to swear that forever after there would never be another (and there never has been, quite), and that there would be allegiance and sovereignty and fidelity and other such tomfool horseshit that people destroy their heads with when what they are saying has nothing to do with time's forevers but everything to do with the simultaneous recognition of an eternal twain, well sir, then both of them, Francis and Annie, or the Francises and Annies of any age, would both know in that same instant that there was something between them that had to stop being two and become one.

Such was the significance of that kiss.

Francis and Annie married a month and a half later.

Katrina, I will love you forever.

However, something has come up.

□ □ □

"The turkey," Annie said. "You'll stay while I cook it."

"No, that'd take one long time. You just have it when you want to. Sunday, whenever."

"It wouldn't take too long to cook. A few hours is all. Are you going to run off so soon after being away so long?"

"I ain't runnin' off."

"Good. Then let me get it into the oven right now. When Peg comes home we can peel potatoes and onions and Danny can go get some cranberries. A turkey. Imagine that. Rushing the season."

"Who's Danny?"

"You don't know Danny. Naturally, you don't. He's Peg's boy. She married George Quinn. You know George, of course, and they have the boy. He's ten."

"Ten."

"In fourth grade and smart as a cracker."

"Gerald, he'd be twenty-two now."

"Yes, he would."

"I saw his grave."

"You did? When?"

"Yesterday. Got a day job up there and tracked him down and talked there awhile."

"Talked?"

"Talked to Gerald. Told him how it was. Told him a bunch of stuff."

"I'll bet he was glad to hear from you."

"May be. Where's Bill?"

"Bill? Oh, you mean Billy. We call him Billy. He's taking a nap. He got himself in trouble with the politicians and he's feeling pretty low. The kidnapping. Patsy McCall's nephew was kidnapped. Bindy McCall's son. You must've read about it."

"Yeah, I did, and Martin Daugherty run it down for me too, awhile back."

"Martin wrote about Billy in the paper this morning."

"I seen that too. Nice write-up. Martin says his father's still alive."

"Edward. He is indeed, living down on Main Street. He lost his memory, poor man, but he's healthy. We see him walking with Martin from time to time. I'll go wake Billy and tell him you're here."

"No, not yet. Talk a bit."

"Talk. Yes, all right. Let's go in the living room."

"Not me, not in these clothes. I just come off workin' on a junk wagon. I'd dirty up the joint somethin' fierce."

"That doesn't matter at all. Not at all."

"Right here's fine. Look out the window at the yard there. Nice yard. And a collie dog you got."

"It is nice. Danny cuts the grass and the dog buries his bones all over it. There's a cat next door he chases up and down the fence."

"The family changed a whole lot. I knew it would. How's your brother and sisters?"

"They're fine, I guess. Johnny never changes. He's a committeeman now for the Democrats. Josie got very fat and lost a lot of her hair. She wears a switch. And Minnie was married two years and her husband died. She's very lonely and lives in a rented room. But we all see one another."

"Billy's doin' good."

"He's a gambler and not a very good one. He's always broke."

"He was good to me when I first seen him. He had money then. Bailed me outa jail, wanted to buy me a new suit of clothes. Then he give me a hefty wad of cash and acourse I blew it all. He's tough too, Billy. I liked him a whole lot. He told me you never said nothin' to him and Peg about me losin' hold of Gerald."

"No, not until the other day."

"You're some original kind of woman, Annie. Some original kind of woman."

"Nothing to be gained talking about it. It was over and done with. Wasn't your fault any more than it was my fault. Wasn't anybody's fault."

"No way I can thank you for that. That's something thanks don't even touch. That's something I don't even know–"

She waved him silent.

"Never mind that," she said. "It's over. Come, sit, tell me what finally made you come see us."

He sat down on the backless bench in the breakfast nook and looked out the window, out past the geranium plant with two blossoms, out at the collie dog and the apple tree that grew in this yard but offered shade and blossoms and fruit to two other yards adjoining, out at the flower beds and the trim grass and the white wire fence that enclosed it all. So nice. He felt a great compulsion to confess all his transgressions in order to be equal to this niceness he had missed out on; and yet he felt a great torpor in his tongue, akin to what he had felt in his legs when he walked on the glue of the sidewalks. His brain, his body seemed to be in a drugged sleep that allowed perception without action. There was no way he could reveal all that had brought him here. It would have meant the recapitulation not only of all his sins but of all his fugitive and fallen dreams, all his random movement across the country and back, all his returns to this city only to leave again without ever coming to see her, them, without ever knowing why he didn't. It would have meant the anatomizing of his compulsive violence and his fear of justice, of his time with Helen, his present defection from Helen, his screwing so many women he really wanted nothing to do with, his drunken ways, his morning-after sicknesses, his sleeping in the weeds, his bumming money from strangers not because there was a depression but first to help Helen and then because it was easy: easier than working. Everything was easier than coming home, even reducing yourself to the level of social maggot, streetside slug.

But then he came home.

He is home now, isn't he?

And if he is, the question on the table is: Why is he?

"You might say it was Billy," Francis said. "But that don't really get it. Might as well ask the summer birds why they go all the way south and then come back north to the same old place."

"Something must've caught you."

"I say it was Billy gettin' me outa jail, goin' my bail, then invitin' me home when I thought I'd never get invited after what I did, and then findin' what you did, or didn't do is more like it, and not ever seein' Peg growin' up, and wantin' some of that. I says to Billy I want to come home when I can do something' for the folks, but he says just come home and see them and never mind the turkey, you can do that for them. And here I am. And the turkey too."

"But something changed in you," Annie said. "It was the woman, wasn't it? Billy meeting her?"

"The woman."

"Billy told me you had another wife. Helen, he said."

"Not a wife. Never a wife. I only had one wife."

Annie, her arms folded on the breakfast table across from him, almost smiled, which he took to be a sardonic response. But then she said: "And I only had one husband. I only had one man."

Which froze Francis's gizzard.

"That's what the religion does," he said, when he could talk.

"It wasn't the religion."

"Men must've come outa the trees after you, you were such a handsome woman."

"They tried. But no man ever came near me. I wouldn't have it. I never even went to the pictures with anybody except neighbors, or the family."

"I couldn'ta married again," Francis said. "There's some things you just can't do. But I did stay with Helen. That's the truth, all right. Nine years on and off. She's a good sort, but helpless as a baby. Can't find her way across the street if you don't take her by the hand. She nursed me when I was all the way down and sick as a pup. We got on all right. Damn good woman, I say that. Came from good folks. But she can't find her way across the damn street."

Annie stared at him with a grim mouth and sorrowful eyes.

"Where is she now?"

"Somewheres, goddamned if I know. Downtown somewheres, I suppose. You can't keep track of her. She'll drop dead in the street one of these days, wanderin' around like she does."

"She needs you."

"Maybe so."

"What do you need, Fran?"

"Me? Huh. Need a shoelace. All I got is a piece of twine in that shoe for two days."

"Is that all you need?"

"I'm still standin'. Still able to do a day's work. Don't do it much, I admit that. Still got my memory, my memories. I remember you, Annie. That's an enrichin' thing. I remember Kibbee's lumber pile the first day I talked to you. You remember that?"

"Like it was this morning."

"Old times."

"Very old."

"Jesus Christ, Annie, I missed everybody and everything, but I ain't worth a goddamn in the world and never was. Wait a minute. Let me finish. I can't finish. I can't even start. But there's somethin'. Somethin' to say about this. I got to get at it, get it out. I'm so goddamned sorry, and I know that don't cut nothin'. I know it's just a bunch of shitass words, excuse the expression. It's nothin' to what I did to you and the kids. I can't make it up. I knew five, six months after I left that it'd get worse and worse and no way ever to fix it, no way ever to go back. I'm just hangin' out now for a visit, that's all. Just visitin' to see you and say I hope things are okay. But I got other things goin' for me, and I don't know the way out of anything. All there is is this visit. I don't want nothin', Annie, and that's the honest-to-god truth, I don't want nothin' but the look of everybody. Just the look'll do me. Just the way things look out in that yard. It's a nice yard. It's a nice doggie. Damn, it's nice. There's plenty to say, plenty of stuff to say, explain, and such bullshit, excuse the expression again, but I ain't ready to say that stuff, I ain't ready to look at you while you listen to it, and I bet you ain't ready to hear it if you knew what I'd tell you. Lousy stuff, Annie, lousy stuff. Just gimme a little time, gimme a sandwich too, I'm hungry as a damn bear. But listen, Annie, I never stopped lovin' you and the kids, and especially you, and that don't entitle me to nothin', and I don't want nothin' for sayin' it, but I went my whole life rememberin' things here that were like nothin' I ever saw anywhere in Georgia or Louisiana or Michigan, and I been all over, Annie, all over, and there ain't nothin' in the world like your elbows sittin' there on the table across from me, and that apron all full of stains. Goddamn, Annie. Goddamn. Kibbee's was just this mornin'. You're right about that. But it's old times too, and I ain't askin' for nothin' but a sandwich and a cupa tea. You still use the Irish breakfast tea?"

□ □ □

The talk that passed after what Francis said, and after the silence that followed it, was not important except as it moved the man and the woman closer together and physically apart, allowed her to make him a Swiss cheese sandwich and a pot of tea and begin dressing the turkey: salting, peppering, stuffing it with not quite stale enough bread but it'll have to do, rubbing it with butter and sprinkling it with summer savory, mixing onions in with the dressing, and turkey seasoning too from a small tin box with a red and yellow turkey on it, fitting the bird into a dish for which it seemed to have been groomed and killed to order, so perfect was the fit.

And too, the vagrant chitchat allowed Francis to stare out at the yard and watch the dog and become aware that the yard was beginning to function as the site of a visitation, although nothing in it except his expectation when he looked out at the grass lent credence to that possibility.

He stared and he knew that he was in the throes of flight, not outward this time but upward. He felt feathers growing from his back, knew soon he would soar to regions unimaginable, knew too that what had brought him home was not explicable without a year of talking, but a scenario nevertheless took shape in his mind: a pair of kings on a pair of trolley cars moving toward a single track, and the trolleys, when they meet at the junction, do not wreck each other but fuse into a single car inside which the kings rise up against each other in imperial intrigue, neither in control, each driving the car, a careening thing, wild, anarchic, dangerous to all else, and then Billy leaps aboard and grabs the power handle and the kings instantly yield control to the wizard.

He give me a Camel cigarette when I was coughin' my lungs up, Francis thought.

He knows what a man needs, Billy does.

□ □ □

Annie was setting the dining-room table with a white linen tablecloth, with the silver Iron Joe gave them for their wedding, and with china Francis did not recognize, when Daniel Quinn arrived home. The boy tossed his schoolbag in a corner of the dining room, then stopped in midmotion when he saw Francis standing in the doorway to the kitchen.

"Hulooo," Francis said to him.

"Danny, this is your grandfather," Annie said. "He just came to see us and he's staying for dinner." Daniel stared at Francis's face and slowly extended his right hand. Francis shook it.

"Pleased to meet you," Daniel said.

"The feeling's mutual, boy. You're a big lad for ten."

"I'll be eleven in January."

"You comin' from school, are ye?"

"From instructions, religion."

"Oh, religion. I guess I just seen you crossin' the street

and didn't even know it. Learn anything, did you?"

"Learned about today. All Saints' Day."

"What about it?"

"It's a holy day. You have to go to church. It's the day we remember the martyrs who died for the faith and nobody knows their names."

"Oh yeah," Francis said. "I remember them fellas."

"What happened to your teeth?"

"Daniel."

"My teeth," Francis said. "Me and them parted company, most of 'em. I got a few left."

"Are you Grampa Phelan or Grampa Quinn?"

"Phelan," Annie said. "His name is Francis Aloysius Phelan."

"Francis Aloysius, right," said Francis with a chuckle. "Long time since I heard that."

"You're the ball player," Danny said. "The big-leaguer. You played with the Washington Senators."

"Used to. Don't play anymore."

"Billy says you taught him how to throw an inshoot."

"He remembers that, does he?"

"Will you teach me?"

"You a pitcher, are ye?"

"Sometimes. I can throw a knuckle ball."

"Change of pace. Hard to hit. You get a baseball, I'll show you how to hold it for an inshoot." And Daniel ran into the kitchen, then the pantry, and emerged with a ball and glove, which he handed to Francis. The glove was much too small for Francis's hand but he put a few fingers inside it and held the ball in his right hand, studied its seams. Then he gripped it with his thumb and one and a half fingers.

"What happened to your finger?" Daniel asked.

"Me and it parted company too. Sort of an accident."

"Does that make any difference throwing an inshoot?"

"Sure does, but not to me. I don't throw no more at all. Never was a pitcher, you know, but talked with plenty of 'em. Walter Johnson was my buddy. You know him? The Big Train?"

The boy shook his head.

"Don't matter. But he taught me how it was done and I ain't forgot. Put your first two fingers right on the seams, like this, and then you snap your wrist out, like this, and if you're a righty—are you a righty?"—and the boy nodded—"then the ball's gonna dance a little turnaround jig and head right inside at the batter's belly button, assumin', acourse, that he's a righty too. You followin' me?" And the boy nodded again. "Now the trick is, you got to throw the opposite of the outcurve, which is like this." And he snapped his wrist clockwise. "You got to do it like this." And he snapped his wrist counterclockwise again. Then he had the boy try it both ways and patted him on the back.

"That's how it's done," he said. "You get so's you can do it, the batter's gonna think you got a little animal inside that ball, flyin' it like an airplane."

"Let's go outside and try it," Daniel said. "I'll get another glove."

"Glove," said Francis, and he turned to Annie. "By some fluke you still got my old glove stuck away somewheres in the house? That possible, Annie?"

"There's a whole trunk of your things in the attic," she said. "It might be there."

"It is," Daniel said. "I know it is. I saw it. I'll get it."

"You will not," Annie said. "That trunk is none of your affair."

"But I've already seen it. There's a pair of spikes too, and clothes and newspapers and old pictures."

"All that," Francis said to Annie. "You saved it."

"You had no business in that trunk," Annie said.

"Billy and I looked at the pictures and the clippings one

day," Daniel said. "Billy looked just as much as I did. He's in lots of 'em." And he pointed at his grandfather.

"Maybe you'd want to have a look at what's there," Annie said to Francis.

"Could be. Might find me a new shoelace."

Annie led him up the stairs, Daniel already far ahead of them. They heard the boy saying: "Get up, Billy, Grandpa's here"; and when they reached the second floor Billy was standing in the doorway of his room, in his robe and white socks, disheveled and only half awake.

"Hey, Billy. How you gettin' on?" Francis said.

"Hey," said Billy. "You made it."

"Yep."

"I woulda bet against it happenin'."

"You'da lost. Brought a turkey too, like I said."

"A turkey, yeah?"

"We're having it for dinner," Annie said.

"I'm supposed to be downtown tonight," Billy said. "I just told Martin I'd meet him."

"Call him back," Annie said. "He'll understand."

"Red Tom Fitzsimmons and Martin both called to tell me things are all right again on Broadway. You know, I told you I had trouble with the McCalls," Billy said to his father.

"I 'member."

"I wouldn't do all they wanted and they marked me lousy. Couldn't gamble, couldn't even get a drink on Broadway."

"I read that story Martin wrote," Francis said. "He called you a magician."

"Martin's full of malarkey. I didn't do diddley. I just mentioned Newark to them and it turns out that's where they trapped some of the kidnap gang."

"You did somethin', then," Francis said. "Mentionin' Newark was somethin'. Who'd you mention it to?"

"Bindy. But I didn't know those guys were in Newark or I wouldn't of said anything. I could never rat on anybody."

"Then why'd you mention it?"

"I don't know."

"That's how come you're a magician."

"That's Martin's baloney. But he turned somebody's head around with it, 'cause I'm back in good odor with the pols, is how he put it on the phone. In other words, I don't stink to them no more."

Francis smelled himself and knew he had to wash as soon as possible. The junk wagon's stink and the bummy odor of his old suitcoat was unbearable now that he was among these people. Dirty butchers go out of business.

"You can't go out now, Billy," Annie said. "Not with your father home and staying for dinner. We're going up in the attic to look at his things."

"You like turkey?" Francis asked Billy.

"Who the hell don't like turkey, not to give you a short answer," Billy said. He looked at his father. "Listen, use my razor in the bathroom if you want to shave."

"Don't be telling people what to do," Annie said. "Get dressed and come downstairs."

And then Francis and Annie ascended the stairway to the attic.

□ □ □

When Francis opened the trunk lid the odor of lost time filled the attic air, a cloying reek of imprisoned flowers that unsettled the dust and fluttered the window shades. Francis felt drugged by the scent of the reconstituted past, and then stunned by his first look inside the trunk, for there, staring out from a photo, was his own face at age nineteen. The picture lay among rolled socks and a small American flag, a Washington Senators cap, a pile of newspaper clippings and other photos, all in a scatter on the trunk's tray. Francis stared up at himself from the bleachers in Chadwick Park on a day in 1899, his face unlined, his teeth all there, his collar open, his hair unruly in the afternoon's breeze. He lifted the picture for a closer look and saw himself among a group of men, tossing a baseball from bare right hand to gloved left hand. The flight of the ball had always made this photo mysterious to Francis, for the camera had caught the ball clutched in one hand and also in flight, arcing in a blur toward the glove. What the camera had caught was two instants in one: time separated and unified, the ball in two places at once, an eventuation as inexplicable as the Trinity itself. Francis now took the picture to be a Trinitarian talisman (a hand, a glove, a ball) for achieving the impossible: for he had always believed it impossible for him, ravaged man, failed human, to reenter history under this roof. Yet here he was in this aerie of reconstitutable time, touching untouchable artifacts of a self that did not yet know it was ruined, just as the ball, in its inanimate ignorance, did not know yet that it was going nowhere, was caught.

But the ball is really not yet caught, except by the camera, which has frozen only its situation in space.

And Francis is not yet ruined, except as an apparency in process.

The ball still flies.

Francis still lives to play another day.

Doesn't he?

The boy noticed the teeth. A man can get new teeth, store teeth. Annie got 'em.

□ □ □

Francis lifted the tray out of the trunk, revealing the spikes and the glove, which Daniel immediately grabbed, plus two suits of clothes, a pair of black oxfords and brown high-button shoes, maybe a dozen shirts and two dozen white collars, a stack of undershirts and shorts, a set of keys to long-forgotten locks, a razor strop and a hone, a shaving mug with an inch of soap in it, a shaving brush with bristles intact, seven straight razors in a case, each marked for a day of the week, socks, bow ties, suspenders, and a baseball, which Francis picked up and held out to Daniel.

"See that? See that name?"

The boy looked, shook his head. "I can't read it."

"Get it in the light, you'll read it. That's Ty Cobb. He signed that ball in 1911, the year he hit .420. A fella give it to me once and I always kept it. Mean guy, Cobb was, come in at me spikes up many a time. But you had to hand it to a man who played ball as good as he did. He was the best."

"Better than Babe Ruth?"

"Better and tougher and meaner and faster. Couldn't hit home runs like the Babe, but he did everything else better. You like to have that ball with his name on it?"

"Sure I would, sure! Yeah! Who wouldn't?"

"Then it's yours. But you better look him up, and Walter Johnson too. Find out for yourself how good they were. Still kickin', too, what I hear about Cobb. He ain't dead yet either."

"I remember that suit," Annie said, lifting the sleeve of a gray herringbone coat. "You wore it for dress-up."

"Wonder if it'd still fit me," Francis said, and stood up and held the pants to his waist and found out his legs had not grown any longer in the past twenty-two years.

"Take the suit downstairs," Annie said. "I'll sponge and press it."

"Press it?" Francis said, and he chuckled. "S'pose I could use a new outfit. Get rid of these rags."

He then singled out a full wardrobe, down to the handkerchief, and piled it all on the floor in front of the trunk.

"I'd like to look at these again," Annie said, lifting out the clippings and photos.

"Bring 'em down," Francis said, closing the lid.

"I'll carry the glove," Daniel said.

"And I'd like to borry the use of your bathroom," Francis said. "Take Billy up on that shave offer and try on some of these duds. I got me a shave last night but Billy thinks I oughta do it again."

"Don't pay any attention to Billy," Annie said. "You look fine."

She led him down the stairs and along a hallway where two rooms faced each other. She gestured at a bedroom where a single bed, a dresser, and a child's rolltop desk stood in quiet harmony.

"That's Danny's room," she said. "It's a nice big room and it gets the morning light." She took a towel down from a linen closet shelf and handed it to Francis. "Have a bath if you like."

Francis locked the bathroom door and tried on the trousers, which fit if he didn't button the top button. Wear the suspenders with 'em. The coat was twenty years out of style and offended Francis's residual sense of aptness. But he decided to wear it anyway, for its odor of time was infinitely superior to the stink of bumdom that infested the coat on his back. He stripped and let the bathwater run. He inspected the shirt he took from the trunk, but rejected it in favor of the white-on-white from the junk wagon. He tried the laceless black oxfords, all broken in, and found that even with calluses his feet had not grown in twenty-two years either.

He stepped into the bath and slid slowly beneath its vapors. He trembled with the heat, with astonishment that he was indeed here, as snug in this steaming tub as was the turkey in its roasting pan. He felt blessed. He stared at the bathroom sink, which now had an aura of sanctity about it, its faucets sacred, its drainpipe holy, and he wondered whether everything was blessed at some point in its existence, and he concluded yes. Sweat rolled down his forehead and dripped off his nose into the bath, a confluence of ancient and modern waters. And as it did, a great sunburst entered the darkening skies, a radiance so sudden that it seemed like a bolt of lightning; yet its brilliance remained, as if some angel of beatific lucidity were hovering outside the bathroom window. So enduring was the light, so intense beyond even sundown's final gloryburst, that Francis raised himself up out of the tub and went to the window.

Below, in the yard, Aldo Campione, Fiddler Quain, Harold Allen, and Rowdy Dick Doolan were erecting a wooden structure that Francis was already able to recognize as bleachers.

He stepped back into the tub, soaped the long-handled brush, raised his left foot out of the water, scrubbed it clean, raised the right foot, scrubbed that.

□ □ □

Francis, that 1916 dude, came down the stairs in bow tie, white-on-white shirt, black laceless oxfords with a spit shine on them, the gray herringbone with lapels twenty-two years too narrow, with black silk socks and white silk boxer shorts, with his skin free of dirt everywhere, his hair washed twice, his fingernails cleaned, his leftover teeth brushed and the toothbrush washed with soap and dried and rehung, with no whiskers anymore, none, and his hair combed and rubbed with a dab of Vaseline so it'd stay in place, with a spring in his gait and a smile on his face; this Francis dude came down those stairs, yes, and stunned his family with his resurrectible good looks and stylish potential, and took their stares as applause.

And dance music rose in his brain.

"Holy Christ," said Billy.

"My oh my," said Annie.

"You look different," Daniel said.

"I kinda needed a sprucin'," Francis said. "Funny duds but I guess they'll do."

They all pulled back then, even Daniel, aware they should not dwell on the transformation, for it made Francis's previous condition so lowly, so awful.

"Gotta dump these rags," he said, and he lifted his bundle, tied with the arms of his old coat.

"Danny'll take them," Annie said. "Put them in the cellar," she told the boy.

Francis sat down on a bench in the breakfast nook, across the table from Billy. Annie had spread the clips and photos on the table and he and Billy looked them over. Among the clips Francis found a yellowed envelope postmarked June 2, 1910, and addressed to Mr. Francis Phelan, c/o Toronto Baseball Club, The Palmer House, Toronto, Ont. He opened it and read the letter inside, then pocketed it. Dinner advanced as Daniel and Annie peeled the potatoes at the sink. Billy, his hair combed slick, half a dude himself with open-collared starched white shirt, creased trousers, and pointy black shoes, was drinking from a quart bottle of Dobler beer and reading a clipping.

"I read these once," Billy said. "I never really knew how good you were. I heard stories and then one night downtown I heard a guy talking about you and he was ravin' that you were top-notch and I never knew just how good. I knew this stuff was there. I seen it when we first moved here, so I went up and looked. You were really a hell of a ball player."

"Not bad," Francis said. "Coulda been worse."

"These sportswriters liked you."

"I did crazy things. I was good copy for them. And I had energy. Everybody likes energy."

Billy offered Francis a glass of beer but Francis declined

and took, instead, from Billy's pack, a Camel cigarette; and then he perused the clips that told of him stealing the show with his fielding, or going four-for-four and driving in the winning run, or getting himself in trouble: such as the day he held the runner on third by the belt, an old John McGraw trick, and when a fly ball was hit, the runner got ready to tag and head home after the catch but found he could not move and turned and screamed at Francis in protest, at which point Francis let go of the belt and the runner ran, but the throw arrived first and he was out at home.

Nifty.

But Francis was thrown out of the game.

"Would you like to go out and look at the yard?" Annie said, suddenly beside Francis.

"Sure. See the dog."

"It's too bad the flowers are gone. We had so many flowers this year. Dahlias and snapdragons and pansies and asters. The asters lasted the longest."

"You still got them geraniums right here."

Annie nodded and put on her sweater and the two of them went out onto the back porch. The air was chilly and the light fading. She closed the door behind them and patted the dog, which barked twice at Francis and then accepted his presence. Annie went down the five steps to the yard, Francis and the dog following.

"Do you have a place to stay tonight, Fran?"

"Sure. Always got a place to stay."

"Do you want to come home permanent?" she asked, not looking at him, walking a few steps ahead toward the fence. "Is that why you've come to see us?"

"Nah, not much chance of that. I'd never fit in."

"I thought you might've had that in mind."

"I thought of it, I admit that. But I see it couldn't work, not after all these years."

"It'd take some doing, I know that."

"Take more than that."

"Stranger things have happened."

"Yeah? Name one."

"You going to the cemetery and talking to Gerald. I think maybe that's the strangest thing I ever heard in all my days."

"Wasn't strange. I just went and stood there and told him a bunch of stuff. It's nice where he is. It's pretty."

"That's the family plot."

"I know."

"There's a grave there for you, right at the stone, and one for me, and two for the children next to that if they need them. Peg'll have her own plot with George and the boy, I imagine."

"When did you do all that?" Francis asked.

"Oh years ago. I don't remember."

"You bought me a grave after I run off."

"I bought it for the family. You're part of the family."

"There was long times I didn't think so."

"Peg is very bitter about you staying away. I was too, for years and years, but that's all done with. I don't know why I'm not bitter anymore. I really don't. I called Peg and told her to get the cranberries and that you were here."

"Me and the cranberries. Easin' the shock some."

"I suppose."

"I'll move along, then. I don't want no fights, rile up the family."

"Nonsense. Stop it. You just talk to her. You've got to talk to her."

"I can't say nothin' that means anything. I couldn't say a straight word to you."

"I know what you said and what you didn't say. I know it's hard what you're doing."

"It's a bunch of nothin'. I don't know why I do anything in this goddamn life."

"You did something good coming home. It's something

Danny'll always know about. And Billy. He was so glad to be able to help you, even though he'd never say it."

"He got a bum out of jail."

"You're so mean to yourself, Francis."

"Hell, I'm mean to everybody and everything."

The bleachers were all up, and men were filing silently into them and sitting down, right here in Annie's backyard, in front of God and the dog and all: Bill Corbin, who ran for sheriff in the nineties and got beat and turned Republican, and Perry Marsolais, who inherited a fortune from his mother and drank it up and ended up raking leaves for the city, and Iron Joe himself with his big mustache and big belly and big ruby stickpin, and Spiff Dwyer in his nifty pinched fedora, and young George Quinn and young Martin Daugherty, the batboys, and Martin's grandfather Emmett Daugherty, the wild Fenian who talked so fierce and splendid and put the radical light in Francis's eye with his stories of how moneymen used workers to get rich and treated the Irish like pigdog paddyniggers, and Patsy McCall, who grew up to run the city and was carrying his ball glove in his left hand, and some men Francis did not know even in 1899, for they were only hangers-on at the saloon, men who followed the doings of Iron Joe's Wheelbarrow Boys, and who came to the beer picnic this day to celebrate the Boys' winning the Albany-Troy League pennant.

They kept coming: forty-three men, four boys, and two mutts, ushered in by the Fiddler and his pals.

And there, between crazy Specky McManus in his derby and Jack Corbett in his vest and no collar, sat the runt, is it?

Is it now?

The runt with the piece out of his neck.

There's one in every crowd.

Francis closed his eyes to retch the vision out of his

head, but when he opened them the bleachers still stood, the men seated as before. Only the light had changed, brighter now, and with it grew Francis's hatred of all fantasy, all insubstantiality. I am sick of you all, was his thought. I am sick of imagining what you became, what I might have become if I'd lived among you. I am sick of your melancholy histories, your sentimental pieties, your goddamned unchanging faces. I'd rather be dyin' in the weeds than standin' here lookin' at you pinin' away, like the dyin' Jesus pinin' for an end to it when he knew every stinkin' thing that was gonna happen not only to himself but to everybody around him, and to all those that wasn't even born yet. You ain't nothin' more than a photograph, you goddamn spooks. You ain't real and I ain't gonna be at your beck and call no more.

You're all dead, and if you ain't, you oughta be.

I'm the one is livin'. I'm the one puts you on the map.

You never knew no more about how things was than I did.

You'd never even be here in the damn yard if I didn't open that old trunk.

So get your ass gone!

"Hey Ma," Billy yelled out the window. "Peg's home."

"We'll be right in," Annie said. And when Billy closed the window she turned to Francis: "You want to tell me anything, ask me anything, before we get in front of the others?"

"Annie, I got five million things to ask you, and ten million things to tell. I'd like to eat all the dirt in this yard for you, eat the weeds, eat the dog bones too, if you asked me."

"I think you probably ate all that already," she said.

And then they went up the back stoop together.

□ □ □

When Francis first saw his daughter bent over the stove, already in her flowered apron and basting the turkey, he thought: She is too dressed up to be doing that. She wore a wristwatch on one arm, a bracelet on the other, and two rings on her wedding ring finger. She wore high heels, silk stockings with the seams inside out, and a lavender dress that was never intended as a kitchen costume. Her dark-brown hair, cut short, was waved in a soft marcel, and she wore lipstick and a bit of rouge, and her nails were long and painted dark red. She was a few, maybe even more than a few, pounds overweight, and she was beautiful, and Francis was immeasurably happy at having sired her.

"How ya doin', Margaret?" Francis asked when she straightened up and looked at him.

"I'm doing fine," she said, "no thanks to you."

"Yep," said Francis, and he turned away from her and sat across from Billy in the nook.

"Give him a break," Billy said. "He just got here, for chrissake."

"What break did he ever give me? Or you? Or any of us?"

"Aaahhh, blow it out your ear," Billy said.

"I'm saying what is," Peg said.

"Are you?" Annie asked. "Are you so sure of what is?"

"I surely am. I'm not going to be a hypocrite and welcome him back with open arms after what he did. You don't just pop up one day with a turkey and all is forgiven."

"I ain't expectin' to be forgiven," Francis said. "I'm way past that."

"Oh? And just where are you now?"

"Nowhere."

"Well that's no doubt very true. And if you're nowhere, why are you here? Why've you come back like a ghost we buried years ago to force a scrawny turkey on us? Is that your idea of restitution for letting us fend for ourselves for twenty-two years?"

"That's a twelve-and-a-half-pound turkey," Annie said.

"Why leave your nowhere and come here, is what I want to know. This is somewhere. This is a home you didn't build."

"I built you. Built Billy. Helped to."

"I wish you never did."

"Shut up, Peg," Billy yelled. "Rotten tongue of yours, shut it the hell UP!"

"He came to visit, that's all he did," Annie said softly. "I already asked him if he wanted to stay over and he said no. If he wanted to he surely could."

"Oh?" said Peg. "Then it's all decided?"

"Nothin' to decide," Francis said. "Like your mother says, I ain't stayin'. I'm movin' along." He touched the salt and pepper shaker on the table in front of him, pushed the sugar bowl against the wall.

"You're moving on," Peg said.

"Positively."

"Fine."

"That's it, that's enough!" Billy yelled, standing up from the bench. "You got the feelin's of a goddamn rattlesnake."

"Pardon me for having any feelings at all," Peg said, and she left the kitchen, slamming the swinging door, which had been standing open, slamming it so hard that it swung, and swung, and swung, until it stopped.

"Tough lady," Francis said.

"She's a creampuff," Billy said. "But she knows how to get her back up."

"She'll calm down," Annie said.

"I'm used to people screamin' at me," Francis said. "I got a hide like a hippo."

"You need it in this joint," Billy said.

"Where's the boy?" Francis asked. "He hear all that?"

"He's out playin' with the ball and glove you gave him," Billy said.

"I didn't give him the glove," Francis said. "I give him the ball with the Ty Cobb signature. That glove is yours. You wanna give it to him, it's okay by me. Ain't much of a glove compared to what they got these days. Danny's glove's twice the quality my glove ever was. But I always thought to myself: I'm givin' that old glove to Billy so's he'll have a touch of the big leagues somewhere in the house. That glove caught some mighty people. Line drive from Tris Speaker, taggin' out Cobb, runnin' Eddie Collins outa the baseline. Lotta that."

Billy nodded and turned away from Francis. "Okay," he said, and then he jumped up from the bench and left the kitchen so the old man could not see (though he saw) that he was choked up.

"Grew up nice, Billy did," Francis said. "Couple of tough bozos you raised, Annie."

"I wish they were tougher," Annie said.

The yard, now ablaze with new light against a black sky, caught Francis's attention. Men and boys, and even dogs, were holding lighted candles, the dogs holding them in their mouths sideways. Specky McManus, as usual bein' different, wore his candle on top of his derby. It was a garden of acolytes setting fire to the very air, and then, while Francis watched, the acolytes erupted in song, but a song without sense, a chant to which Francis listened carefully but could make out not a word. It was an antisyllabic lyric they sang, like the sibilance of the wren's softest whistle, or the tree frog's tonsillar wheeze. It was clear to Francis as he watched this performance (watched it with awe, for it was transcending what he expected from dream, from reverie, even from Sneaky Pete hallucinations) that it was happening in an arena of his existence over which he had less control than he first imagined when Aldo Campione boarded the bus. The signals from this time lock were ominous, the spooks utterly without humor. And then, when he saw the runt (who knew he was being watched, who knew he didn't belong in this picture) putting the lighted end of the candle into the hole in the back of his neck, and when Francis recognized the chant of the acolytes at last as the "Dies Irae," he grew fearful. He closed his eyes and buried his head in his hands and he tried to remember the name of his first dog.

It was a collie.

□ □ □

Billy came back, clear-eyed, sat across from Francis, and offered him another smoke, which he took. Billy topped his own beer and drank and then said, "George."

"Oh my God," Annie said. "We forgot all about George." And she went to the living room and called upstairs to Peg: "You should call George and tell him he can come home."

"Let her alone, I'll do it," Billy called to his mother.

"What about George?" Francis asked.

"The cops were here one night lookin' for him," Billy said. "It was Patsy McCall puttin' pressure on the family because of me. George writes numbers and they were probably gonna book him for gamblin' even though he had the okay. So he laid low up in Troy, and the poor bastard's been alone for days. But if I'm clear, then so is he."

"Some power the McCalls put together in this town."

"They got it all. They ever pay you the money they owed you for registerin' all those times?"

"Paid me the fifty I told you about, owe me another fifty-five. I'll never see it."

"You got it comin'."

"Once it got in the papers they wouldn't touch it. Mixin' themselves up with bums. You heard Martin tell me that. They'd also be suspicious that I'd set them up. I wouldn't set nobody up. Nobody."

"Then you got no cash."

"I got a little."

"How much?"

"I got some change. Cigarette money."

"You blew what you had on the turkey."

"That took a bit of it."

Billy handed him a ten, folded in half. "Put it in your pocket. You can't walk around broke."

Francis took it and snorted. "I been broke twenty-two years. But I thank ye, Billy. I'll make it up."

"You already made it up." And he went to the phone in the dining room to call George in Troy.

Annie came back to the kitchen and saw Francis looking at the Chadwick Park photo and looked over his shoulder. "That's a handsome picture of you," she said.

"Yeah," said Francis. "I was a good-lookin' devil."

"Some thought so, some didn't," Annie said. "I forgot about this picture."

"Oughta get it framed," Francis said. "Lot of North Enders in there. George and Martin as kids, and Patsy McCall too. And Iron Joe. Real good shot of Joe."

"It surely is," Annie said. "How fat and healthy he looks."

Billy came back and Annie put the photo on the table so that all three of them could look at it. They sat on the same bench with Francis in the middle and studied it, each singling out the men and boys they knew. Annie even knew one of the dogs.

"Oh that's a prize picture," she said, and stood up. "A prize picture."

"Well, it's yours, so get it framed."

"Mine? No, it's yours. It's baseball."

"Nah, nah, George'd like it too."

"Well I will frame it," Annie said. "I'll take it downtown and get it done up right."

"Sure," said Francis. "Here. Here's ten dollars toward the frame."

"Hey," Billy said.

"No," Francis said. "You let me do it, Billy."

Billy chuckled.

"I will not take any money," Annie said. "You put that back in your pocket."

Billy laughed and hit the table with the palm of his hand. "Now I know why you been broke twenty-two years. I know why we're all broke. It runs in the family."

"We're not all broke," Annie said. "We pay our way. Don't be telling people we're broke. You're broke because you made some crazy horse bet. But *we're* not broke. We've had bad times but we can still pay the rent. And we've never gone hungry."

"Peg's workin'," Francis said.

"A private secretary," Annie said. "To the owner of a tool company. She's very well liked."

"She's beautiful," Francis said. "Kinda nasty when she puts her mind to it, but beautiful."

"She shoulda been a model," Billy said.

"She should not," Annie said.

"Well she shoulda, goddamn it, she shoulda," said Billy. "They wanted her to model for Pepsodent toothpaste, but Mama wouldn't hear of it. Somebody over at church told her models were, you know, loose ladies. Get your picture taken, it turns you into a floozy."

"That had nothing to do with it," Annie said.

"Her teeth," Billy said. "She's got the most gorgeous teeth in North America. Better-lookin' teeth than Joan Crawford. What a smile! You ain't seen her smile yet, but that's a fantastic smile. Like Times Square is what it is. She coulda been on billboards coast to coast. We'd be hip-deep in toothpaste, and cash too. But no." And he jerked a thumb at his mother.

"She had a job," Annie said. "She didn't need that. I never liked that fellow that wanted to sign her up."

"He was all right," Billy said. "I checked him out. He was legitimate."

"How could you know what he was?"

"How could I know anything? I'm a goddamn genius."

"Clean up your mouth, genius. She would've had to go to New York for pictures."

"And she'd of never come back, right?"

"Maybe she would, maybe she wouldn't."

"Now you got it," Billy said to his father. "Mama likes to keep all the birds in the nest."

"Can't say as I blame her," Francis said.

"No," Billy said.

"I never liked that fellow," Annie said. "That's what it really was. I didn't trust him."

Nobody spoke.

"And she brought a paycheck home every week," Annie said. "Even when the tool company closed awhile, the owner put her to work as a cashier in a trading port he owned. Trading port and indoor golf. An enormous place. They almost brought Rudy Vallee there once. Peg got wonderful experience."

Nobody spoke.

"Cigarette?" Billy asked Francis.

"Sure," Francis said.

Annie stood up and went to the refrigerator in the pantry. She came back with the butter dish and put it on the dining-room table. Peg came through the swinging door, into the silence. She poked the potatoes with a fork, looked at the turkey, which was turning deep brown, and closed the oven door without basting it. She rummaged in the utensil drawer and found a can opener and punched it through a can of peas and put them in a pan to boil.

"Turkey smells real good," Francis said to her.

"Uh-huh, I bought a plum pudding," she said to all, showing them the can. She looked at her father. "Mama said you used to like it for dessert on holidays."

"I surely did. With that white sugar sauce. Mighty sweet."

"The sauce recipe's on the label," Annie said. "Give it here and I'll make it."

"I'll make it," Peg said.

"It's nice you remembered that," Francis said.

"It's no trouble," Peg said. "The pudding's already cooked. All you do is heat it up in the can."

Francis studied her and saw the venom was gone from her eyes. This lady goes up and down like a thermometer. When she saw him studying her she smiled slightly, not a billboard smile, not a smile to make anybody rich in toothpaste, but there it was. What the hell, she's got a right. Up and down, up and down. She come by it naturally.

"I got a letter maybe you'd all like to hear while that stuff's cookin' up," he said, and he took the yellowed envelope with a canceled two-cent stamp on it out of his inside coat pocket. On the back, written in his own hand, was: *First letter from Margaret.*

"I got this a few years back, quite a few," he said, and from the envelope he took out three small trifolded sheets of yellowed lined paper. "Come to me up in Canada in nineteen-ten, when I was with Toronto." He unfolded the sheets and moved them into the best possible light at longest possible arm's length, and then he read:

" 'Dear Poppy, I suppose you never think that you have a daughter that is waiting for a letter since you went away.

I was so mad because you did not think of me that I was going to join the circus that was here last Friday. I am doing my lesson and there is an arithmetic example here that I cannot get. See if you can get it. I hope your leg is better and that you have good luck with the team. Do not run too much with your legs or you will have to be carried home. Mama and Billy are good. Mama has fourteen new little chickens out and she has two more hens sitting. There is a wild west circus coming the eighth. Won't you come home and see it? I am going to it. Billy is just going to bed and Mama is sitting on the bed watching me. Do not forget to answer this. I suppose you are having a lovely time. Do not let me find you with another girl or I will pull her hair. Yours truly, Peggy.' "

"Isn't that funny," Peg said, the fork still in her hand. "I don't remember writing that."

"Probably lots you don't remember about them days," Francis said. "You was only about eleven."

"Where did you ever find it?"

"Up in the trunk. Been saved all these years up there. Only letter I ever saved."

"Is that a fact?"

"It's a provable fact. All the papers I got in the world was in that trunk, except one other place I got a few more clips. But no letters noplace. It's a good old letter, I'd say."

"I'd say so too," Annie said. She and Billy were both staring at Peg.

"I remember Toronto in nineteen-ten," Francis said. "The game was full of crooks them days. Crooked umpire named Bates, one night it was deep dark but he wouldn't call the game. Folks was throwin' tomatoes and mudballs at him but he wouldn't call it 'cause we was winnin' and he was in with the other team. Pudge Howard was catchin' that night and he walks out and has a three-way confab on the mound with me and old Highpockets Wilson, who was pitchin'. Pudge comes back and squats behind the plate and Highpockets lets go a blazer and the ump calls it a ball, though nobody could see nothin' it was so dark. And Pudge turns to him and says: 'You call that pitch a ball?' 'I did,' says the ump. 'If that was a ball I'll eat it,' says Pudge. 'Then you better get eatin',' says the ump. And Pudge, he holds the ball up and takes a big bite out of it, 'cause it ain't no ball at all, it's a yellow apple I give Highpockets to throw. And of course that won us the game and the ump went down in history as Blindy Bates, who couldn't tell a baseball from a damn apple. Bates turned into a bookie after that. He was crooked at that too."

"That's a great story," Billy said. "Funny stuff in them old days."

"Funny stuff happenin' all the time," Francis said.

Peg was suddenly tearful. She put the fork on the sink and went to her father, whose hands were folded on the table. She sat beside him and put her right hand on top of his.

After a while George Quinn came home from Troy, Annie served the turkey, and then the entire Phelan family sat down to dinner.

# VII.

"I look like a bum, don't I?" Rudy said.

"You are a bum," Francis said. "But you're a pretty good bum if you wanna be."

"You know why people call you a bum?"

"I can't understand why."

"They feel better when they say it."

"The truth ain't gonna hurt you," Francis said. "If you're a bum, you're a bum."

"It hurt a lotta bums. Ain't many of the old ones left."

"There's new ones comin' along," Francis said.

"A lot of good men died. Good mechanics, machinists, lumberjacks."

"Some of 'em ain't dead," Francis said. "You and me, we ain't dead."

"They say there's no God," Rudy said. "But there must be a God. He protects bums. They get up out of the snow and they go up and get a drink. Look at you, brand-new clothes. But look at me. I'm only a bum. A no-good bum."

"You ain't that bad," Francis said. "You're a bum, but you ain't that bad."

They were walking down South Pearl Street toward Palombo's Hotel. It was ten-thirty, a clear night, full of stars but very cold: winter's harbinger. Francis had left the family just before ten o'clock and taken a bus downtown. He went straight to the mission before they locked it for the night, and found Pee Wee alone in the kitchen, drinking leftover coffee. Pee Wee said he hadn't seen, or heard from, Helen all day.

"But Rudy was in lookin' for you," Pee Wee told Francis. "He's either up at the railroad station gettin' warm or holed up in some old house down on Broadway. He says you'd know which one. But look, Francis, from what I hear, the cops been raidin' them old pots just about every night. Lotta guys usually eat here ain't been around and I figure they're all in jail. They must be repaintin' the place out there and need extra help."

"I don't know why the hell they gotta do that," Francis said. "Bums don't hurt nobody."

"Maybe it's just cops don't like bums no more."

Francis checked out the old house first, for it was close to the mission. He stepped through its doorless entrance into a damp, deep-black stairwell. He waited until his eyes adjusted to the darkness and then he carefully climbed the stairs, stepping over bunches of crumpled newspaper and fallen plaster and a Negro who was curled up on the first landing. He stepped through broken glass, empty wine and soda bottles, cardboard boxes, human droppings. Streetlights illuminated stalagmites of pigeon leavings on a windowsill. Francis saw a second sleeping man curled up near the hole he heard a fellow named Michigan Mac fell through last week. Francis sidestepped the man and the hole and then found Rudy in a room by himself, lying on a slab of board away from the broken window, with a newspaper on his shoulder for a blanket.

"Hey bum," Francis said, "you lookin' for me?"

Rudy blinked and looked up from his slab.

"Who the hell you talkin' to?" Rudy said. "What are you, some kinda G-man?"

"Get your ass up off the floor, you dizzy kraut."

"Hey, is that you, Francis?"

"No, it's Buffalo Bill. I come up here lookin' for Indians."

Rudy sat up and threw the newspaper off himself.

"Pee Wee says you was lookin' for me," Francis said.

"I didn't have noplace to flop, no money, no jug, nobody around. I had a jug but it ran out." Rudy fell back on the slab and wept instant tears over his condition. "I'll kill myself, I got the tendency," he said. "I'm last."

"Hey," Francis said. "Get up. You ain't bright enough to kill yourself. You gotta fight. you gotta be tough. I can't even find Helen. You seen Helen anyplace? Think about that woman on the bum somewheres on a night like this. Jesus I feel sorry for her."

"Where the wind don't blow," Rudy said.

"Yeah. No wind. Let's go."

"Go where?"

"Outa here. You stay here, you wind up in jail tonight. Pee Wee says they're cleanin' out all these joints."

"Go to jail, at least it's warm. Get six months and be out in time for the flowers."

"No jail for Francis. Francis is free and he's gonna stay free."

They walked down the stairs and back to Madison because Francis decided Helen must have found money somewhere or else she'd have come looking for him. Maybe she called her brother and got a chunk. Or maybe she was holding out even more than she said. Canny old dame. And sooner or later, with dough, she'd hit Palombo's because of the suitcase.

"Where we goin'?"

"What the hell's the difference? Little walk'll keep your blood flowin'."

"Where'd you get them clothes?"

"Found 'em."

"Found 'em? Where'd you find 'em?"

"Up a tree."

"A tree?"

"Yeah. A tree. Grew everything. Suits, shoes, bow ties."

"You never tell me nothin' that's true."

"Hell, it's all true," Francis said. "Every stinkin' damn thing you can think of is true."

□ □ □

At Palombo's they met old man Donovan just getting ready to go off duty, making way for the night clerk. It was a little before eleven and he was putting the desk in order. Yes, he told Francis, Helen was here. Checked in late this morning. Yeah, sure she's all right. Looked right perky. Walked up them stairs lookin' the same as always. Took the room you always take.

"All right," said Francis, and he took out the ten-dollar bill Billy gave him. "You got change of this?" Donovan made change and then Francis handed him two dollars.

"You give her this in the mornin'," he said, "and make sure she gets somethin' to eat. If I hear she didn't get it, I'll come back here and pull out all your teeth."

"She'll get it," Donovan said. "I like Helen."

"Check her out now," Francis said. "Don't tell her I'm here. Just see is she okay and does she need anything. Don't say I sent you or nothin' like that. Just check her out."

So Donovan knocked on Helen's door at eleven o'clock and found out she needed nothing at all, and he came back and told Francis.

"You tell her in the mornin' I'll be around sometime during the day," Francis said. "And if she don't see me and she wants me, you tell her to leave me a message where she'll be. Leave it with Pee Wee down at the mission. You know Pee Wee?"

"I know the mission," Donovan said.

"She claim the suitcase?" Francis asked.

"Claimed it and paid for two nights in the room."

"She got money from home, all right," Francis said. "But you give her that deuce anyway."

Francis and Rudy walked north on Pearl Street then, Francis keeping the pace brisk. In a shopwindow Francis saw three mannequins in formal dresses beckoning to him. He waved at them.

"Now where we goin'?" Rudy asked.

"The all-night bootlegger's," Francis said. "Get us a couple of jugs and then go get a flop and get some shuteye."

"Hey," Rudy said. "Now you're sayin' somethin' I wanna hear. Where'd you find all this money?"

"Up in a tree."

"Same tree that grows bow ties?"

"Yep," said Francis. "Same tree."

Francis bought two quarts of muscatel at the upstairs bootlegger's on Beaver Street and two pints of Green River whiskey.

"Rotgut," he said when the bootlegger handed him the whiskey, "but it does what it's supposed to do."

Francis paid the bootlegger and pocketed the change: two dollars and thirty cents left. He gave a quart of the musky and a pint of the whiskey to Rudy and when they stepped outside the bootlegger's they both tipped up their wine.

And so Francis began to drink for the first time in a week.

□ □ □

The flop was run by a bottom-heavy old woman with piano legs, the widow of somebody named Fennessey, who had died so long ago nobody remembered his first name.

"Hey Ma," Rudy said when she opened the door for them.

"My name's Mrs. Fennessey," she said. "That's what I go by."

"I knew that," Rudy said.

"Then call me that. Only the niggers call me Ma."

"All right, sweetheart," Francis said. "Anybody call you sweetheart? We want a couple of flops."

She let them in and took their money, a dollar for two flops, and then led them upstairs to a large room that used to be two or three rooms but now, with the interior walls gone, was a dormitory with a dozen filthy cots, only one occupied by a sleeping form. The room was lit by what Francis judged to be a three-watt bulb.

"Hey," he said, "too much light in here. It'll blind us all."

"Your friend don't like it here, he can go somewhere else," Mrs. Fennessey told Rudy.

"Who wouldn't like this joint?" Francis said, and he bounced on the cot next to the sleeping man.

"Hey bum," he said, reaching over and shaking the sleeper. "You want a drink?"

A man with enormous week-old scabs on his nose and forehead turned to face Francis.

"Hey," said Francis. "It's the Moose."

"Yeah, it's me," Moose said.

"Moose who?" asked Rudy.

"Moose what's the difference," Francis said.

"Moose Backer," Moose said.

"That there's Rudy," Francis said. "He's crazier than a cross-eyed bedbug, but he's all right."

"You sharped up some since I seen you last," Moose said to Francis. "Even wearin' a tie. You bump into prosperity?"

"He found a tree that grows ten-dollar bills," Rudy said.

Francis walked around the cot and handed Moose his wine. Moose took a swallow and nodded his thanks.

"Why'd you wake me up?" Moose asked.

"Woke you up to give you a drink."

"It was dark when I went to sleep. Dark and cold."

"Jesus Christ, I know. Fingers cold, toes cold. Cold in here right now. Here, have another drink and warm up. You want some whiskey? I got some of that too."

"I'm all right. I got an edge. You got enough for yourself?"

"Have a drink, goddamn it. Don't be afraid to live." And Moose took one glug of the Green River.

"I thought you was gonna trade pants with me," Moose said.

"I was. Pair I had was practically new, but too small."

"Where are they? You said they were thirty-eight, thirty-one, and that's just right."

"You want these?"

"Sure," said Moose.

"If I give 'em to you, then I ain't got no pants," Francis said.

"I'll give you mine," Moose said.

"Why you tradin' your new pants?" Rudy asked.

"That's right," said Francis, standing up and looking at his own legs. "Why am I? No, you ain't gonna get these. Fuck you, I need these pants. Don't tell me what I need. Go get your own pants."

"I'll buy 'em," Moose said. "How much you want? I got another week's work sandin' floors."

"Well shine 'em," Francis said. "They ain't for sale."

"Sandin', not shinin'. I sand 'em. I don't shine 'em."

"Don't holler at me," Francis said. "I'll crack your goddamn head and step on your brains. You're a tough man, is that it?"

"No," said Moose. "I ain't tough."

"Well I'm tough," Francis said. "Screw around with me, you'll die younger'n I will."

"Oh I'll die all right. I'm just as busted as that ceiling. I got TB."

"Oh God bless you," Francis said, sitting down. "I'm sorry."

"It's in the knee."

"I didn't know you had it. I'm sorry. I'm sorry anybody's got TB."

"It's in the knee."

"Well cut your leg off."

"That's what they wanted to do."

"So cut it off."

"No, I wouldn't let them do that."

"I got a stomach cancer," Rudy said.

"Yeah," said Moose. "Everybody's got one of them."

"Anybody gonna come to my funeral?" Rudy asked.

"Probably ain't nothin' wrong with you work won't cure," Moose said.

"That's right," Francis said to Rudy. "Why don't you go get a job?" He pointed out the window at the street. "Look at 'em out there. Everybody out there's workin'."

"You're crazier than he is," Moose said. "Ain't no jobs anyplace. Where you been?"

"There's taxis. There goes a taxi."

"Yeah, there's taxis," Moose said. "So what?"

"Can you drive?" Francis asked Rudy.

"I drove my ex-wife crazy," Rudy said.

"Good. What you're supposed to do. Drive 'em nuts is right."

In the corner of the room Francis saw three long-skirted women who became four who became three and then four again. Their faces were familiar but he could call none of them by name. Their ages changed when their number changed: now twenty, now sixty, now thirty, now fifty, never childish, never aged. At the house Annie would now be trying to sleep, but probably no more prepared for it than Francis was, no more capable of closing the day than Francis was. Helen would be out of it, whipped all to hell by fatigue and worry. Damn worrywart is what she is. But not Annie. Annie, she don't worry. Annie knows how to live. Peg, she'll be awake too, why not? Why should she sleep when nobody else can? They'll all be up, you bet. Francis give 'em a show they ain't gonna forget in a hurry.

He showed 'em what a man can do.

A man ain't afraid of goin' back.

Goddamn spooks, they follow you everywheres but they don't matter. You stand up to 'em is all. And you do what you gotta do.

Sandra joined the women of three, the women of four, in the far corner. Francis gave me soup, she told them. He carried me out of the wind and put my shoe on me. They became the women of five.

"Where the wind don't blow," Rudy sang. "I wanna go where the wind don't blow, where there ain't no snow."

Francis saw Katrina's face among the five that became four that became three.

□ □ □

Finny and Little Red came into the flop, and just behind them a third figure Francis did not recognize immediately. Then he saw it was Old Shoes.

"Hey, we got company, Moose," Francis said.

"Is that Finny?" Moose asked. "Looks like him."

"That's the man," Francis said. Finny stood by the foot of Francis's cot, very drunk and wobbling, trying to see who was talking about him.

"You son of a bitch," Moose said, leaning on one elbow.

"Which son of a bitch you talkin' to?" Francis asked.

"Finny. He used to work for Spanish George. Liked to use the blackjack on drunks when they got noisy."

"Is that true, Finny?" Francis asked. "You liked to sap the boys?"

"Arrrggghhh," said Finny, and he lurched off toward a cot down the row from Francis.

"He was one mean bastard," Moose said. "He hit me once."

"Hurt you?"

"Hurt like hell. I had a headache three weeks."

"Somebody burned up Finny's car," Little Red announced. "He went out for somethin' to eat, and he came back, it was on fire. He thinks the cops did it."

"Why are the cops burnin' up cars?" Rudy asked.

"Cops're goin' crazy," Little Red said. "They're pickin' up everybody. American Legion's behind it, that's what I heard."

"Them lard-ass bastards," Francis said. "They been after my ass all my life."

"Legionnaires and cops," said Little Red. "That's why we come in here."

"You think you're safe here?" Francis asked.

"Safer than on the street."

"Cops'd never come up here if they wanted to get you, right?" Francis said.

"They wouldn't know I was here," Little Red said.

"Whataya think this is, the Waldorf-Astoria? You think that old bitch downstairs don't tell the cops who's here and who ain't when they want to know?"

"Maybe it wasn't the cops burned up the car," Moose said. "Finny's got plenty of enemies. If I knew he owned one, I'da burned it up myself. The son of a bitch beat up on us all, but now he's on the street. Now we got him in the alley."

"You hear that, Finny?" Francis called out. "They gonna get your ass good. They got you in the alley with all the other bums."

"Ngggghhhh," said Finny.

"Finny's all right," Little Red said. "Leave him alone."

"You givin' orders here at the Waldorf-Astoria, is that it?" Francis asked.

"Who the hell are you?" Little Red asked.

"I'm a fella ready to stomp all over your head and squish it like a grape, you try to tell me what to do."

"Yeah," said Little Red, and he moved toward the cot beside Finny.

"I knew it was you soon as I come in," Old Shoes said, coming over to the foot of Francis's cot. "I could tell that foghorn voice of yours anyplace."

"Old Shoes," Francis said. "Old Shoes Gilligan."

"That's right. You got a pretty good memory. The wine ain't got you yet."

"Old Shoes Gilligan, a grand old soul, got a cast-iron belly and a brass asshole."

"Not cast-iron anymore," Old Shoes said. "I got an ulcer. I quit drinkin' two years ago."

"Then what the hell you doin' here?"

"Just came by to see the boys, see what was happenin'."

"You hangin' out with Finny and that redheaded wiseass?"

"Who you callin' a wiseass?" Little Red said.

"I'm callin' you wiseass, wiseass," Francis said.

"You got a big mouth," Little Red said.

"I got a foot's even bigger and I'm gonna shove it right up your nose, you keep bein' nasty to me when I'm tryna be polite."

"Cool off, Francis," Old Shoes said. "What's your story? You're lookin' pretty good."

"I'm gettin' rich," Francis said. "Got me a gang of new clothes, couple of jugs, money in the pocket."

"You're gettin' up in the world," Old Shoes said.

"Yeah, but what the hell you doin' here if you ain't drinkin' is what I don't figure."

"I just told you. I'm passin' through and got curious about the old joints."

"You workin'?"

"Got a steady job down in Jersey. Even got an apartment and a car. A car, Francis. You believe that? Me with a car? Not a new car, but a good car. A Hudson two-door. You want a ride?"

"A ride? Me?"

"Sure, why not?"

"Now?"

"Don't matter to me. I'm just sightseein'. I'm not sleepin' up here. Wouldn't sleep here anyway. Bedbugs'd follow me all the way back to Jersey."

"This bum here," Francis explained to Rudy, "I saved from dyin' in the street. Used to fall down drunk three, four times a night, like he was top-heavy."

"That's right," Old Shoes said. "Broke my face five or six times, just like his." And he gestured at Moose. "But I don't do that no more. I hit three nuthouses and then I quit. I been off the bum three years and dry for two. You wanna go for that ride, Francis? Only thing is, no bottle. The wife'd smell it and I'd catch hell."

"You got a wife too?" Francis said.

"You got a car and a wife and a house and a job?" Rudy asked. He sat up on his cot and studied this interloper.

"That's Rudy," Francis said. "Rudy Tooty. He's thinkin' about killin' himself."

"I know the feelin'," Old Shoes said. "Me and Francis we needed a drink somethin' awful one mornin'. We walked all over town but we couldn't score, snow comin' through our shoes, and it's four below zero. Finally we sold our blood and drank the money. I passed out and woke up still needin' a drink awful bad, and not a penny and no chance for one, couldn't even sell any more blood, and I wanted to die and I mean die. Die."

"Where there ain't no snow," Rudy sang. "Where the handouts grow on bushes and you sleep out every night."

"You wanna go for a ride?" Old Shoes asked Rudy.

"Oh the buzzin' of the bees in the cigarette trees, by the soda water fountains," Rudy sang. Then he smiled at Old Shoes, took a swallow of wine, and fell back on his cot.

"Man wants to go for a ride and can't get no takers," Francis said. "Might as well call it a day, Shoes, stretch out and rest them bones."

"Naaah, I guess I'll be movin' on."

"One evenin' as the sun went down, and the jungle fires were burnin'," Rudy sang, "Down the track came a hobo hikin', and said, Boys, I am not turnin'."

"Shut up that singin'," Little Red said. "I'm tryna sleep."

"I'm gonna mess up his face," Francis said and stood up.

"No fights," Moose said. "She'll kick us the hell out or call the cops on us."

"That'll be the day I get kicked out of a joint like this," Francis said. "This is pigswill. I lived in better pigswill than this goddamn pigswill."

"Where I come from–" Old Shoes began.

"I don't give a goddamn where you come from," Francis said.

"Goddamn you, I come from Texas."

"Name a city, then."

"Galveston."

"Behave yourself," Francis said, "or I'll knock you down. I'm a tough son of a bitch. Tougher than that bum Finny. Licked twelve men at once."

"You're drunk," Old Shoes said.

"Yeah," said Francis. "My mind's goin'."

"It went there. Rattlesnake got you."

"Rattlesnake, my ass. Rattlesnake is nothin'."

"Cottonmouth?"

"Oh, cottonmouth rattler. Yeah. That's somethin'. Jesus, this is a nice subject. Who wants to talk about snakes? Talk about bums is more like it. A bum is a bum. Helen's got me on the bum. Son of a bitch, she won't go home, won't straighten up."

"Helen did the hula down in Hon-oh-loo-loo," Rudy sang.

"Shut your stupid mouth," Francis said to Rudy.

"People don't like me," Rudy said.

"Singin' there, wavin' your arms, talkin' about Helen."

"I can't escape myself."

"That's what I'm talkin' about," Francis said.

"I tried it before."

"I know, but you can't do it, so you might as well live with it."

"I like to be condemned," Rudy said.

"No, don't be condemned," Francis told him.

"I like to be condemned."

"Never be condemned."

"I like to be condemned because I know I done wrong in my life."

"You never done wrong," Francis said.

"All you screwballs down there, shut up," yelled Little Red, sitting up on his cot. Francis instantly stood up and ran down the aisle. He was running when he lunged and grazed Little Red's lips with his knuckles.

"I'm gonna mess you up," Francis said.

Little Red rolled with the blow and fell off the cot. Francis ran around the cot and kicked him in the stomach. Little Red groaned and rolled and Francis kicked him in the side. Little Red rolled under Finny's cot, away from Francis's feet. Francis followed him and was ready to drive a black laceless oxford deep into his face, but then he stopped. Rudy, Moose, and Old Shoes were all standing up, watching.

"When I knew Francis he was strong as a bull," Old Shoes said.

"Knocked a house down by myself," Francis said, walking back to his cot. "Didn't need no wreckin' ball." He picked up the quart of wine and gestured with it. Moose lay back down on his cot and Rudy on his. Old Shoes sat on the cot next to Francis. Little Red licked his bleeding lip and lay quietly on the floor under the cot where Finny was supine and snoring. The faces of all the women Francis had ever known changed with kaleidoscopic swiftness from one to the other to the other on the three female figures in the far corner. The trio sat on straight-backed chairs, witnesses all to the whole fabric of Francis's life. His mother was crocheting a Home Sweet Home sampler while Katrina measured off a bolt of new cloth and Helen snipped the ragged threads. Then they all became Annie.

"When they throw dirt in my face, nobody can walk up and sell me short, that's what I worry about," Francis said. "I'll suffer in hell, if they ever got such a place, but I still got muscles and blood and I'm gonna live it out. I never saw a bum yet said anything against Francis. They better not, goddamn 'em. All them sufferin' bastards, all them poor souls waitin' for heaven, walkin' around with the snow flyin', stayin' in empty houses, pants fallin' off 'em. When I leave this earth I wanna leave it with a blessing to everybody. Francis never hurt nobody."

"The mockin'birds'll sing when you die," Old Shoes said.

"Let 'em. Let 'em sing. People tell me: Get off the bum. And I had a chance. I had a good mind but now it's all flaked out, like a heavin' line on a canal boat, back and forth, back and forth. You get whipped around so much, everything comes to a standstill, even a nail. You drive it so far and it comes to a stop. Keep hittin' it and the head'll break off."

"That's a true thing," Moose said.

"On the Big Rock Candy Mountain," Rudy sang, "the cops got wooden legs." He stood up and waved his wine in a gesture imitative of Francis; then he rocked back and forth as he sang, strongly and on key: "The bulldogs all got rubber teeth, and the hens lay soft-boiled eggs. The boxcars all are empty and the sun shines every day. I wanna go where there ain't no snow, where the sleet don't fall and the wind don't blow, on the Big Rock Candy Mountain."

Old Shoes stood up and made ready to leave. "Nobody wants a ride?" he said.

"All right, goddamn it," Francis said. "Whataya say, Rudy? Let's get outa this pigswill. Get outa this stink and go where I can breathe. The weeds is better than this pigswill."

"So long, friend," Moose said. "Thanks for the wine."

"You bet, pal, and God bless your knee. Tough as nails, that's what Francis is."

"I believe that," Moose said.

"Where we goin'?" Rudy asked.

"Go up to the jungle and see a friend of mine. You wanna give us a lift to the jungle?" Francis asked Old Shoes. "Up in the North End. You know where that is?"

"No, but you do."

"Gonna be cold," Rudy said.

"They got a fire," Francis said. "Cold's better than this bughouse."

"By the lemonade springs, where the bluebird sings," Rudy sang.

"That's the place," Francis said.

□ □ □

As Old Shoes' car moved north on Erie Boulevard, where the Erie Canal used to flow, Francis remembered Emmett Daugherty's face: rugged and flushed beneath wavy gray hair, a strong, pointed nose truly giving him the look of the Divine Warrior, which is how Francis would always remember him, an Irishman who never drank more than enough, a serious and witty man of control and high purpose, and with an unkillable faith in God and the laboring man. Francis had sat with him on the slate step in front of Iron Joe's Wheelbarrow and listened to his endless talk of the days when he and the country were young, when the riverboats brought the greenhorns up the Hudson from the Irish ships. When the cholera was in the air, the greenhorns would be taken off the steamboats at Albany and sent west on canal boats, for the city's elders had charged the government with keeping the pestilential foreigners out of the city.

Emmett rode up from New York after he got off the death ship from Cork, and at the Albany basin he saw his brother Owen waving frantically to him. Owen followed the boat to the North Albany lock, ran along the towpath yelling advice to Emmett, giving him family news, telling him to get off the boat as soon as they'd let him, then to write saying where he was so Owen could send him money to come back to Albany by stagecoach. But it was days before Emmett got off that particular packet boat, got off in a place whose name he never learned, and the authorities there too kept the newcomers westering, under duress.

By the time Emmett reached Buffalo he had decided not to return to such an inhospitable city as Albany, and he moved on to Ohio, where he found work building streets, and then with the railroads, and in time went all the way west on the rails and became a labor organizer, and eventually a leader of the Clann na Gael, and lived to see the Irish in control of Albany, and to tell his stories and inspire Francis Phelan to throw the stone that changed the course of life, even for people not yet born.

That vision of the packet moving up the canal and Owen running alongside it telling Emmett about his children was as real to Francis, though it happened four decades before he was born, as was Old Shoes' car, in which he was now bouncing ever northward toward the precise place where the separation took place. He all but cried at the way the Daugherty brothers were being separated by the goddamned government, just as he was now being separated from Billy and the others. And by what? What and who were again separating Francis from those people after he'd found them? It was a force whose name did not matter, if it had a name, but whose effect was devastating. Emmett Daugherty had placed blame on no man, not on the cholera inspectors or even the city's elders. He knew a larger fate had moved him westward and shaped in him all that he was to become; and that moving and shaping was what Francis now understood, for he perceived the fugitive thrust that had come to be so much a part of his own spirit. And so he found it entirely reasonable that he and Emmett should be fused in a single person: the character of the hero of the play written by Emmett's son, Edward Daugherty the playwright: Edward (husband of Katrina, father of Martin), who wrote *The Car Barns*, the tale of how Emmett radicalized Francis by telling his own story of separation and growth, by inspiring Francis to identify the enemy and target him with a stone. And just as Emmett truly did return home from the west as a labor hero, so also did the playright conjure an image of Francis returning home as underground hero for what that stone of his had done.

For a time Francis believed everything Edward Daugherty had written about him: liberator of the strikers from the capitalist beggars who owned the trolleys, just as Emmett had helped Paddy-with-a-shovel straighten his back and climb up out of his ditch in another age. The playwright saw them both as Divine Warriors, sparked by the socialistic gods who understood the historical Irish need for aid from on high, for without it (so spoke Emmett, the golden-tongued organizer of the play), "how else would we rid ourselves of those Tory swine, the true and unconquerable devils of all history?"

The stone had (had it not?) precipitated the firing by the soldiers and the killing of the pair of bystanders. And without that, without the death of Harold Allen, the strike might have continued, for the scabs were being imported in great numbers from Brooklyn, greenhorn Irish the likes of Emmett on the packet boat, some of them defecting instantly from the strike when they saw what it was, others bewildered and lost, lied to by men who hired them for railroad work in Philadelphia, then duped them into scabbery, terror, even death. There were even strikers from other cities working as scabs, soulless men who rode the strike trains here and took these Albany men's jobs, as other scabs were taking theirs. And all of that might have continued had not Francis thrown the first stone. He was the principal hero in a strike that created heroes by the dozen. And because he was, he lived all his life with guilt over the deaths of the three men, unable to see any other force at work in the world that day beyond his own right hand. He could not accept, though he knew it to be true, that other significant stones had flown that day, that the soldiers' fusillade at the bystanders had less to do with Harold Allen's death than it did with the possibility of the soldiers' own, for their firing had followed not upon the release of the stone by Francis but only after the mob's full barrage had flown at the trolley. And then Francis, having seen nothing but his own act and what appeared to be its instant consequences, had fled into heroism and been suffused further, through the written word of Edward Daugherty, with the hero's most splendid guilt.

But now, with those events so deeply dead and buried, with his own guilt having so little really to do with it, he saw the strike as simply the insanity of the Irish, poor against poor, a race, a class divided against itself. He saw Harold Allen trying to survive the day and the night at a moment when the frenzied mob had turned against him, just as Francis himself had often had to survive hostility in his flight through strange cities, just as he had always had to survive his own worst instincts. For Francis knew now that he was at war with himself, his private factions mutually bellicose, and if he was ever to survive, it would be with the help not of any socialistic god but with a clear head and a steady eye for the truth; for the guilt he felt was not worth the dying. It served nothing except nature's insatiable craving for blood. The trick was to live, to beat the bastards, survive the mob and that fateful chaos, and show them all what a man can do to set things right, once he sets his mind to it.

Poor Harold Allen.

"I forgive the son of a bitch," Francis said.

"Who's that?" Old Shoes asked. Rudy lay all but blotto across the backseat, holding the whiskey and wine bottles upright on his chest with both tops open in violation of Old Shoes' dictum that they stay closed, and not spilling a drop of either.

"Guy I killed. Guy named Allen."

"You killed a guy?"

"More'n one."

"Accidental, was it?"

"No. I tried to get that one guy, Allen. He was takin' my job."

"That's a good reason."

"Maybe, maybe not. Maybe he was just doin' what he had to do."

"Baloney," Old Shoes said. "That's what everybody does, good, bad, and lousy. Burglars, murderers."

And Francis fell quiet, sinking into yet another truth requiring handling.

□ □ □

The jungle was maybe seven years old, three years old, a month old, days old. It was an ashpit, a graveyard, and a fugitive city. It stood among wild sumac bushes and river foliage, all fallen dead now from the early frost. It was a haphazard upthrust of tarpaper shacks, lean-tos, and impromptu constructions describable by no known nomenclature. It was a city of essential transiency and would-be permanency, a resort of those for whom motion was either anathema or pointless or impossible. Cripples lived here, and natives of this town who had lost their homes, and people who had come here at journey's end to accept whatever disaster was going to happen next. The jungle, a visual manifestation of the malaise of the age and the nation, covered the equivalent of two or more square city blocks between the tracks and the river, just east of the old carbarns and the empty building that once housed Iron Joe's saloon.

Francis's friend in the jungle was a man in his sixties named Andy, who had admitted to Francis in the boxcar in which they both traveled to Albany that people used to call him Andy Which One, a name that derived from his inability, until he was nearly twenty, to tell his left hand from his right, a challenge he still faced in certain stressful moments. Francis found Andy Which One instantly sympathetic, shared the wealth of cigarettes and food he was carrying, and thought instantly of him again when Annie handed him two turkey sandwiches and Peg slipped him a hefty slice of plum pudding, all three items wrapped in waxed paper and intact now in the pockets of his 1916 suitcoat.

But Francis had not seriously thought of sharing the food with Andy until Rudy had begun singing of the jungle. On top of that, Francis almost suffocated seeing his own early venom and self-destructive arrogance reembodied in Little Red, and the conjunction of events impelled him to quit the flop and seek out something he could value; for above all now, Francis needed to believe in simple solutions. And Andy Which One, a man confused by the names of his own hands, but who survived to dwell in the city of useless penitence and be grateful for it, seemed to Francis a creature worthy of scrutiny. Francis found him easily when Old Shoes parked the car on the dirt road that bordered the jungle. He roused Andy from shallow sleep in front of a fading fire, and handed him the whiskey bottle.

"Have a drink, pal. Lubricate your soul."

"Hey, old Francis. How you makin' out there, buddy?"

"Puttin' one foot in front of the other and hopin' they go somewheres," Francis said. "The hotel open here? I brought a couple of bums along with me. Old Shoes here, he says he ain't a bum no more, but that's just what he says. And Rudy the Cootie, a good ol' fella."

"Hey," said Andy, "just settle in. Musta known you was comin'. Fire's still goin', and the stars are out. Little chilly in this joint. Lemme turn up the heat."

They all sat down around the fire while Andy stoked it with twigs and scraps of lumber, and soon the flames were trying to climb to those reaches of the sky that are the domain of all fire. The flames gave vivid life to the cold night, and the men warmed their hands by them.

A figure hovered behind Andy and when he felt its presence he turned and welcomed Michigan Mac to the primal scene.

"Glad to meet ya," Francis said to Mac. "I heard you fell through a hole the other night."

"Coulda broke my neck," Mac said.

"Did you break it?" Francis asked.

"If I'da broke my neck I'd be dead."

"Oh, so you're livin', is that it? You ain't dead?"

"Who's this guy?" Mac asked Andy.

"He's an all-right guy I met on the train," Andy said.

"We're all all right," Francis said. "I never met a bum I didn't like."

"Will Rogers said that," Rudy said.

"He did like hell," Francis said. "I said it."

"All I know. That's what he said. All I know is what I read in the newspapers," Rudy said.

"I didn't know you could read," said Francis.

"James Watt invented the steam engine," Rudy said. "And he was only twenty-nine years old."

"He was a wizard," Francis said.

"Right. Charles Darwin was a very great man, master of botany. Died in nineteen-thirty-six."

"What's he talkin' about?" Mac asked.

"He ain't talkin' about nothin'," Francis said. "He's just talkin'."

"Sir Isaac Newton. You know what he did with the apple?"

"I know that one," Old Shoes said. "He discovered gravity."

"Right. You know when that was? Nineteen-thirty-six. He was born of two midwives."

"You got a pretty good background on these wizards," Francis said.

"God loves a thief," Rudy said. "I'm a thief."

"We're all thieves," Francis said. "What'd you steal?"

"I stole my wife's heart," Rudy said.

"What'd you do with it?"

"I gave it back. Wasn't worth keepin'. You know where the Milky Way is?"

"Up there somewheres," Francis said, looking up at the sky, which was as full of stars as he'd ever seen it.

"Damn, I'm hungry," Michigan Mac said.

"Here," said Andy. "Have a bite." And from a coat pocket he took a large raw onion.

"That's an onion," Mac said.

"Another wizard," Francis said.

Mac took the onion and looked at it, then handed it back to Andy, who took a bite out of it and put it back in his pocket.

"Got it at a grocery," Andy said. "Mister, I told the guy, I'm starvin', I gotta have somethin'. And he gave me two onions."

"You had money," Mac said. "I told ya, get a loaf of bread, but you got a pint of wine."

"Can't have wine and bread too," Andy said. "What are you, a Frenchman?"

"You wanna buy food and drink," said Francis, "you oughta get a job."

"I caddied all last week," Mac said, "but that don't pay, that shit. You slide down them hills. Them golf guys got spikes on their shoes. Then they tell ya: Go to work, ya bum. I like to, but I can't. Get five, six bucks and get on the next train. I'm no bum, I'm a hobo."

"You movin' around too much," Francis said. "That's why you fell through that hole."

"Yeah," said Mac, "but I ain't goin' back to that joint. I hear the cops are pickin' the boys outa there every night. That pot is hot. Travel on, Avalon."

"Cops were here tonight earlier, shinin' their lights," Andy said. "But they didn't pick up anybody."

Rudy raised up his head and looked over all the faces in front of the fire. Then he looked skyward and talked to the stars. "On the outskirts," he said, "I'm a restless person, a traveler."

□ □ □

They passed the wine among them and Andy restoked the fire with wood he had stored in his lean-to. Francis thought of Billy getting dressed up in his suit, topcoat, and hat, and standing before Francis for inspection. You like the hat? he asked. I like it, Francis said. It's got style. Lost the other one, Billy said. First time I ever wore this one. It look all right? It looks mighty stylish, Francis said. All right, gotta get downtown, Billy said. Sure, said Francis. We'll see you again, Billy said. No doubt about it, Francis said. You hangin' around Albany or movin' on? Billy asked. Couldn't say for sure, said Francis. Lotta things that need figurin' out. Always is, said Billy, and then they shook hands and said no more words to each other.

When he himself left an hour and a little bit later, Francis shook hands also with George Quinn, a quirky little guy as dapper as always, who told bad jokes (Let's all eat tomatoes and catch up) that made everybody laugh, and Peg threw her arms around her father and kissed him on the cheek, which was a million-dollar kiss, all right, all right, and then Annie said when she took his hand in both of hers: You must come again. Sure, said Francis. No, said Annie, I mean that you must come so that we can talk about the things you ought to know, things about the children and about the family. There's a cot we could set up in Danny's room if you wanted to stay over next time. And then she kissed him ever so lightly on the lips.

"Hey Mac," Francis said, "you really hungry or you just mouthin' off for somethin' to say?"

"I'm hungry," Mac said. "I ain't et since noon. Goin' on thirteen, fourteen hours, whatever it is."

"Here," Francis said, unwrapping one of his turkey

sandwiches and handing Mac a half, "take a bite, take a couple of bites, but don't eat it all."

"Hey all right," Mac said.

"I told you he was a good fella," Andy said.

"You want a bite of sandwich?" Francis asked Andy.

"I got enough with the onion," Andy said. "But the guy in the piano box over there, he was askin' around for something awhile back. He's got a baby there."

"A baby?"

"Baby and a wife."

Francis snatched the remnants of the sandwich away from Michigan Mac and groped his way in the firelight night to the piano box. A small fire was burning in front of it and a man was sitting cross-legged, warming himself.

"I hear you got a kid here," Francis said to the man, who looked up at Francis suspiciously, then nodded and gestured at the box. Francis could see the shadow of a woman curled around what looked to be the shadow of a swaddled infant.

"Got some stuff here I can't use," Francis said, and he handed the man the full sandwich and the remnant of the second one. "Sweet stuff too," he said and gave the man the plum pudding. The man accepted the gifts with an upturned face that revealed the incredulity of a man struck by lightning in the rainless desert; and his benefactor was gone before he could even acknowledge the gift. Francis rejoined the circle at Andy's fire, entering into silence. He saw that all but Rudy, whose head was on his chest, were staring at him.

"Give him some food, did ya?" Andy asked.

"Yeah. Nice fella. I ate me a bellyful tonight. How old's the kid?"

"Twelve weeks, the guy said."

Francis nodded. "I had a kid. Name of Gerald. He was only thirteen days old when he fell and broke his neck and died."

"Jeez, that's tough," Andy said.

"You never talked about that," Old Shoes said.

"No, because it was me that dropped him. Picked him up with the diaper and he slid out of it."

"Goddamn," said Old Shoes.

"I couldn't handle it. That's why I run off and left the family. Then I bumped into one of my other kids last week and he tells me the wife never told nobody I did that. Guy drops a kid and it dies and the mother don't tell a damn soul what happened. I can't figure that out. Woman keeps a secret like that for twenty-two years, protectin' a bum like me."

"You can't figure women," Michigan Mac said. "My old lady used to peddle her tail all day long and then come home and tell me I was the only man ever touched her. I come in the house one day and found her bangin' two guys at once, first I knew what was happenin'."

"I ain't talkin' about that," Francis said. "I'm talkin' about a woman who's a real woman. I ain't talkin' about no trashbarrel whore."

"My wife was very good-lookin', though," Mac said. "And she had a terrific personality."

"Yeah," said Francis. "And it was all in her ass."

Rudy raised up his head and looked at the wine bottle in his hand. He held it up to the light.

"What makes a man a drunk?" he asked.

"Wine," Old Shoes said. "What you got in your hand."

"You ever hear about the bears and the mulberry juice?" Rudy asked. "Mulberries fermented inside their stomachs."

"That so?" said Old Shoes. "I thought they fermented before they got inside."

"Nope. Not with bears," Rudy said.

"What happened to the bears and the juice?" Mac asked.

"They all got stiff and wound up with hangovers," Rudy said, and he laughed and laughed. Then he turned the wine bottle upside down and licked the drops that flowed onto his tongue. He tossed the bottle alongside the other two empties, his own whiskey bottle and Francis's wine that had been passed around.

"Jeez," Rudy said. "We got nothin' to drink. We on the bum."

In the distance the men could hear the faint hum of automobile engines, and then the closing of car doors.

□ □ □

Francis's confession seemed wasted. Mentioning Gerald to strangers for the first time was a mistake because nobody took it seriously. And it did not diminish his own guilt but merely cheapened the utterance, made it as commonplace as Rudy's brainless chatter about bears and wizards. Francis concluded he had made yet another wrong decision, another in a long line. He concluded that he was not capable of making a right decision, that he was as wrongheaded a man as ever lived. He felt certain now that he would never attain the balance that allowed so many other men to live peaceful, nonviolent, nonfugitive lives, lives that spawned at least a modicum of happiness in old age.

He had no insights into how he differed in this from other men. He knew he was somehow stronger, more given to violence, more in love with the fugitive dance, but this was all so for reasons that had nothing to do with intent. All right, he had wanted to hurt Harold Allen, but that was so very long ago. Could anyone in possession of Francis's perspective on himself believe that he was responsible for Rowdy Dick, or the hole in the runt's neck, or the bruises on Little Red, or the scars on other men long forgotten or long buried?

Francis was now certain only that he could never arrive at any conclusions about himself that had their origin in reason. But neither did he believe himself incapable of thought. He believed he was a creature of unknown and unknowable qualities, a man in whom there would never be an equanimity of both impulsive and premeditated action. Yet after every admission that he was a lost and distorted soul, Francis asserted his own private wisdom and purpose: he had fled the folks because he was too profane a being to live among them; he had humbled himself willfully through the years to counter a fearful pride in his own ability to manufacture the glory from which grace would flow. What he was was, yes, a warrior, protecting a belief that no man could ever articulate, especially himself; but somehow it involved protecting saints from sinners, protecting the living from the dead. And a warrior, he was certain, was not a victim. Never a victim.

In the deepest part of himself that could draw an unutterable conclusion, he told himself: My guilt is all that I have left. If I lose it, I have stood for nothing, done nothing, been nothing.

And he raised his head to see the phalanx of men in Legionnaires' caps advancing into the firelight with baseball bats in their hands.

□ □ □

The men in caps entered the jungle with a fervid purpose, knocking down everything that stood, without a word. They caved in empty shacks and toppled lean-tos that the weight of weather and time had already all but collapsed. One man who saw them coming left his lean-to and ran, calling out one word: "Raiders!" and rousing some jungle people, who picked up their belongings and fled behind the leader of the pack. The first collapsed shacks were already burning when the men around Andy's fire became aware that raiders were approaching.

"What the hell's doin'?" Rudy asked. "Why's everybody gettin' up? Where you goin', Francis?"

"Get on your feet, stupid," Francis said, and Rudy got up.

"What the hell did I get myself into?" Old Shoes said, and he backed away from the fire, keeping the advancing raiders in sight. They were half a football field away but Michigan Mac was already in heavy retreat, bent double like a scythe as he ran for the river.

The raiders moved forward with their devastation clubs and one of them flattened a lean-to with two blows. A man following them poured gasoline on the ruins and then threw a match on top of it all. The raiders were twenty yards from Andy's lean-to by then, with Andy, Rudy, and Francis still immobilized, watching the spectacle with disbelieving eyes.

"We better move it," Andy said.

"You got anything in that lean-to worth savin'?" Francis asked.

"Only thing I own that's worth anything's my skin, and I got that with me."

The three men moved slowly back from the raiders, who were clearly intent on destroying everything that stood. Francis looked at the piano box as he moved past it and saw it was empty.

"Who are they?" Rudy asked Francis. "Why they doin' this?"

But no one answered.

Half a dozen lean-tos and shacks were ablaze, and one had ignited a tall, leafless tree, whose flames were reaching high into the heavens, far above the level of the burning shacks. In the wild firelight Francis saw one raider smashing a shack, from which a groggy man emerged on hands and knees. The raider hit the crawling man across the buttocks with a half swing of the bat until the man stood up. The raider poked him yet again and the man broke into a limping run. The fire that rose from the running man's shack illuminated the raider's smile.

Francis, Rudy, and Andy turned to run then too, convinced at last that demons were abroad in the night. But as they turned they confronted a pair of raiders moving toward them from their left flank.

"Filthy bums," one raider said, and swung his bat at Andy, who stepped deftly out of range, ran off, and was swallowed up by the night. The raider reversed his swing and caught the wobbling Rudy just above neck level, and Rudy yelped and went down. Francis leaped on the man and tore the bat from him, then scrambled away and turned to face both raiders, who were advancing toward him with a hatred on their faces as anonymous and deadly as the exposed fangs of rabid dogs. The raider with the bat raised it above his own head and struck a vertical blow at Francis, which Francis sidestepped as easily as he once went to his left for a fast grounder. Simultaneously he stepped forward, as into a wide pitch, and swung his own bat at the man who had struck Rudy. Francis connected with a stroke that would have sent any pitch over any center-field fence in any ball park anywhere, and he clearly heard and truly felt bones crack in the man's back. He watched with all but orgasmic pleasure as the breathless man twisted grotesquely and fell without a sound.

The second attacker charged Francis and knocked him down, not with his bat but with the weight and force of his moving body. The two rolled over and over, Francis finally separating himself from the man by a glancing blow to the throat. But the man was tough and very agile, fully on his feet when Francis was still on his knees, and he was raising his arms for a horizontal swing when Francis brought his own bat full circle and smashed the man's left leg at knee level. The knee collapsed inward, a hinge reversed, and the raider toppled crookedly with a long howl of pain.

Francis lifted Rudy, who was mumbling incoherent sounds, and threw him over his shoulder. He ran, as best he could, toward the dark woods along the river, and then moved south along the shore toward the city. He stopped in tall weeds, all brown and dead, and lay prone, with Rudy beside him, to catch his breath. No one was following. He looked back at the jungle through the barren trees and saw it aflame in widening measure. The moon and the stars shone on the river, a placid sea of glass beside the sprawling, angry fire.

Francis found he was bleeding from the cheek and he went to the river and soaked his handkerchief and rinsed off the blood. He drank deeply of the river, which was icy and shocking and sweet. He blotted the wound, found it still bleeding, and pressed it with the handkerchief to stanch it.

"Who were they?" Rudy asked when he returned.

"They're the guys on the other team," Francis said. "They don't like us filthy bums."

"You ain't filthy," Rudy said hoarsely. "You got a new suit."

"Never mind my suit, how's your head?"

"I don't know. Like nothin' I ever felt before." Francis touched the back of Rudy's skull. It wasn't bleeding but there was one hell of a lump there.

"Can you walk?"

"I don't know. Where's Old Shoes and his car?"

"Gone, I guess. I think that car is hot. I think he stole it. He used to do that for a livin'. That and peddle his ass."

Francis helped Rudy to his feet, but Rudy could not stand alone, nor could he put one foot in front of the other. Francis lifted him back on his shoulder and headed south. He had Memorial Hospital in mind, the old Homeopathic Hospital on North Pearl Street, downtown. It was a long way, but there wasn't no other place in the middle of the damn night. And walking was the only way.

You wait for a damn bus or a trolley at this hour, Rudy'd be dead in the gutter.

Francis carried him first on one shoulder, then on the other, and finally piggyback when he found Rudy had some use of both arms and could hold on. He carried him along the river road to stay away from cruising police cars, and then down along the tracks and up to Broadway and then Pearl. He carried him up the hospital steps and into the emergency room, which was small and bright and clean and empty of patients. A nurse wheeled a stretcher away from one wall when she saw him coming, and helped Rudy to slide off Francis's back and stretch out.

"He got hit in the head," Francis said. "He can't walk."

"What happened?" the nurse asked, inspecting Rudy's eyes.

"Some guy down on Madison Avenue went nuts and hit him with a brick. You got a doctor can help him?"

"We'll get a doctor. He's been drinking."

"That ain't his problem. He's got a stomach cancer too, but what ails him right now is his head. He got rocked all to hell, I'm tellin' you, and it wasn't none of his fault."

The nurse went to the phone and dialed and talked softly.

"How you makin' it, pal?" Francis asked.

Rudy smiled and gave Francis a glazed look and said nothing. Francis patted him on the shoulder and sat down on a chair beside him to rest. He saw his own image in the mirror door of a cabinet against the wall. His bow tie was all cockeyed and his shirt and coat were spattered with blood where he had dripped before he knew he was cut. His face was smudged and his clothes were covered with dirt. He straightened the tie and brushed off a bit of the dirt.

After a second phone call and a conversation that Francis was about to interrupt to tell her to get goddamn busy with Rudy, the nurse came back. She took Rudy's pulse, went for a stethoscope, and listened to his heart. Then she told Francis Rudy was dead. Francis stood up and looked at his friend's face and saw the smile still there. Where the wind don't blow.

"What was his name?" the nurse asked. She picked up a pencil and a hospital form on a clipboard.

Francis could only stare into Rudy's glassy-eyed smile. Isaac Newton of the apple was born of two midwives.

"Sir, what was his name?" the nurse said.

"Name was Rudy."

"Rudy what?"

"Rudy Newton," Francis said. "He knew where the Milky Way was."

□ □ □

It would be three-fifteen by the clock on the First Church when Francis headed south toward Palombo's Hotel to get out of the cold, to stretch out with Helen and try to think about what had happened and what he should do about it. He would walk past Palombo's night man on the landing, salute him, and climb the stairs to the room he and Helen always shared in this dump. Looking at the hallway dirt and the ratty carpet as he walked down the hall, he would remind himself that this was luxury for him and Helen. He would see the light coming out from under the door, but he would knock anyway to make sure he had Helen's room. When he got no answer he would open the door and discover Helen on the floor in her kimono.

He would enter the room and close the door and stand looking at her for a long time. Her hair would be loose, and fanned out, and pretty.

He would, after a while, think of lifting her onto the bed, but decide there was no point in that, for she looked right and comfortable just as she was. She looked as if she were sleeping.

He would sit in the chair looking at her for an amount

of time he later would not be able to calculate, and he would decide that he had made a right decision in not moving her.

For she was not crooked.

He would look in the open suitcase and would find his old clippings and put them in his inside coat pocket. He would find his razor and his penknife and Helen's rhinestone butterfly, and he would put these in his coat pockets also. In her coat hanging in the closet he would find her three dollars and thirty-five cents and he would put that in his pants pocket, still wondering where she got it. He would remember the two dollars he left for her and that she would never get now, nor would he, and he would think of it as a tip for old Donovan. Helen says thank you.

He would then sit on the bed and look at Helen from a different angle. He would be able to see her eyes were closed and he would remember how vividly green they were in life, those gorgeous emeralds. He would hear the women talking together behind him as he tried to peer beyond Helen's sheltered eyes.

Too late now, the women would say. Too late now to see any deeper into Helen's soul. But he would continue to stare, mindful of the phonograph record propped against the pillow; and he would know the song she'd bought, or stole. It would be "Bye Bye Blackbird," which she loved so much, and he would hear the women singing it softly as he stared at the fiercely glistening scars on Helen's soul, fresh and livid scars whitening among the old, the soul already purging itself of all wounds of the world, flaming with the green fires of hope, but keeping their integrity too as welts of insight into the deepest secrets of Satan.

Francis, this twofold creature, now an old man in a mortal slouch, now again a fledgling bird of uncertain wing, would sing along softly with the women: Here I go, singin' low, the song revealing to him that he was not looking into Helen's soul at all but only into his own repetitive and fallible memory. He knew that right now both Rudy and Helen had far more insight into his being than he himself ever had, or would have, into either of theirs.

The dead, they got all the eyes.

He would follow the thread of his life backward to a point well in advance of the dying of Helen and would come to a vision of her in this same Japanese kimono, lying beside him after they had made sweet love, and she saying to him: All I want in the world is to have my name put back among the family.

And Francis would then stand up and vow that he would one day hunt up Helen's grave, no matter where they put her, and would place a stone on top of it with her name carved deeply in its face. The stone would say: *Helen Marie Archer, a great soul.*

Francis would remember then that when great souls were being extinguished, the forces of darkness walked abroad in the world, filling it with lightning and strife and fire. And he would realize that he should pray for the safety of Helen's soul, since that was the only way he could now help her. But because his vision of the next world was not of the court of heaven where the legion of souls in grace venerate the Holy Worm, but rather of a foul mist above a hole in the ground where the earth itself purges away the stench of life's rot, Francis saw a question burning brightly in the air: How should this man pray?

He would think about this for another incalculably long moment and decide finally there was no way for him to pray: not for Helen, not even for himself.

He would then reach down and touch Helen on the top of the head and stroke her skull the way a father strokes the soft fontanel of his newborn child, stroke her gently so as not to disturb the flowing fall of her hair.

Because it was so pretty.

Then he would walk out of Helen's room, leaving the light burning. He would walk down the hall to the landing, salute the night clerk, who would be dozing in his chair, and then he would reenter the cold and living darkness of the night.

□ □ □

By dawn he would be on a Delaware & Hudson freight heading south toward the lemonade springs. He would be squatting in the middle of the empty car with the door partway open, sitting a little out of the wind. He would be watching the stars, whose fire seemed so unquenchable only a few hours before, now vanishing from an awakening sky that was between a rose and a violet in its early hue.

It would be impossible for him to close his eyes, and so he would think of all the things he might now do. He would then decide that he could not choose among all the possibilities that were his. By now he was sure only that he lived in a world where events decided themselves, and that all a man could do was to stay one jump into their mystery.

He had a vision of Gerald swaddled in the silvery web of his grave, and then the vision faded like the stars and he could not even remember the color of the child's hair. He saw all the women who became three, and then their impossible coherence also faded and he saw only the glorious mouth of Katrina speaking words that were little more than silent shapes; and he knew then that he was leaving behind more than a city and a lifetime of corpses. He was also leaving behind even his vivid memory of the scars on Helen's soul.

Strawberry Bill climbed into the car when the train slowed to take on water, and he looked pretty good for a bum that died coughin'. He was all duded up in a blue seersucker suit, straw hat, and shoes the color of a new baseball.

"You never looked that good while you was livin'," Francis said to him. "You done well for yourself over there."

Everybody gets an Italian tailor when he checks in, Bill said. But say, pal, what're you runnin' from this time?

"Same old crowd," Francis said. "The cops."

Ain't no such things as cops, said Bill.

"Maybe they ain't none of 'em got to heaven yet, but they been pesterin' hell outa me down here."

No cops chasin' you, pal.

"You got the poop?"

Would I kid a fella like you?

Francis smiled and began to hum Rudy's song about the place where the bluebird sings. He took the final swallow of Green River whiskey, which tasted sweet and cold to him now. And he thought of Annie's attic.

That's the place, Bill told him. They got a cot over in the corner, near your old trunk.

"I saw it," said Francis.

Francis walked to the doorway of the freight car and threw the empty whiskey bottle at the moon, an outshoot fading away into the rising sun. The bottle and the moon made music like a soulful banjo when they moved through the heavens, divine harmonies that impelled Francis to leap off the train and seek sanctuary under the holy Phelan eaves.

"You hear that music?" Francis said.

Music? said Bill. Can't say as I do.

"Banjo music. Mighty sweet banjo. That empty whiskey bottle's what's makin' it. The whiskey bottle and the moon."

If you say so, said Bill.

Francis listened again to the moon and his bottle and

heard it clearer than ever. When you heard that music you didn't have to lay there no more. You could get right up offn that old cot and walk over to the back window of the attic and watch Jake Becker lettin' his pigeons loose. They flew up and around the whole damn neighborhood, round and round, flew in a big circle and got themselves all worked up, and then old Jake, he'd give 'em the whistle and they'd come back to the cages. Damnedest thing.

"What can I make you for lunch?" Annie asked him.

"I ain't fussy. Turkey sandwich'd do me fine."

"You want tea again?"

"I always want that tea," said Francis.

He was careful not to sit by the window, where he could be seen when he watched the pigeons or when, at the other end of the attic, he looked out at the children playing football in the school athletic field.

"You'll be all right if they don't see you," Annie said to him. She changed the sheets on the cot twice a week and made tan curtains for the windows and bought a pair of black drapes so he could close them at night and read the paper.

It was no longer necessary for him to read. His mind was devoid of ideas. If an idea entered, it would rest in the mind like the morning dew on an open field of stone. The morning sun would obliterate the dew and only its effect on the stone would remain. The stone needs no such effect.

The point was, would they ever know it was Francis who had broken that fellow's back with the bat? For the blow, indeed, had killed the murdering bastard. Were they looking for him? Were they pretending not to look for him? In his trunk he found his old warm-up sweater and he wore that with the collar turned up to shield his face. He also found George Quinn's overseas cap, which gave him a military air. He would have earned stripes, medals in the military. Regimentation always held great fascination for him. No one would ever think of looking for him wearing George's overseas cap. It was unlikely.

"Do you like Jell-O, Fran?" Annie asked him. "I can't remember ever making Jell-O for you. I don't remember if they had Jell-O back then."

If they were on to him, well that's all she wrote. Katie bar the door. Too wet to plow. He'd head where it was warm, where he would never again have to run from men or weather.

The empyrean, which is not spatial at all, does not move and has no poles. It girds, with light and love, the primum mobile, the utmost and swiftest of the material heavens. Angels are manifested in the primum mobile.

But if they weren't on to him, then he'd mention it to Annie someday (she already had the thought, he could tell that) about setting up the cot down in Danny's room, when things got to be absolutely right, and straight.

That room of Danny's had some space to it.

And it got the morning light too.

It was a mighty nice little room.